THE POLISH POPCORN COMPANY

HAROLD MYERS

ISBN
978-1-962868-09-9 (Paperback)
978-1-962868-10-5 (eBook)
978-1-962868-08-2 (Hardcover)

The POLISH
POPCORN
COMPANY

CHAPTER 1

Jack and Debra were skilled CIA operatives and had worked together in exposing a number or illegal arms merchants throughout Europe and the Middle East. Between them they spoke seven different languages and were proficient in using firearms. Additionally, Jack was also a very skilled computer investigator and sometimes a successful hacker.

They worked separately in various countries and soon after they retired, they met again at a party and eventually married and made their home in Virginia. They had been married almost two years and Jack was determined to surprise his wife with a special birthday gift.

Although Debra's birthday was a couple of weeks away, Jack had run out of gift ideas. He knew Debra loved Maui and decided he would surprise her by celebrating her birthday in style.

He booked an ocean view suite at the Grand Wailea on Maui for ten days along with first class flights from Washington D.C. They would enjoy the time to relax and the amenities of a four-star resort. "We will make it a post-honeymoon vacation to remember forever," he thought.

The next day, Jack booked all the reservations, and their Maui trip would soon be started. Jack had not informed Debbie of the plans he made for either their flights or hotel. He wanted to surprise her and all he would tell her that he booked a nice place in Maui, for her birthday, and they would leave in two days. They had little to do except to begin packing their suitcases for the trip.

The time for departure arrived and Jack had arranged a private car to take them to the airport. After arriving, he led her to the first-class reception area, and there, they obtained their boarding passes, checked their luggage and then they were led through the security section to the first-class lounge to relax, enjoy drinks, and appetizers before boarding their flight.

Once their flight was announced, they leisurely walked to the gate, showed their boarding passes, and entered the plane into the comfort of first class.

"Jack, is this always going to be the way we travel?"

"It is until we get the private jet."

"She gave him her bright smile and snuggled next to him knowing he had done all of this for her.

The flight took almost ten hours, but they had enjoyed a good meal, some wine and a few hours of dozing. They landed almost on time and quickly went to the luggage retrieval area to claim their suitcases. A driver had been waiting for them in the luggage area and he handled their suitcases while they casually followed him to the car.

The drive to Wailea took about twenty minutes and Debra was surprised when the car pulled up to the main entrance framed by palm trees. Her smile lit up the lobby when she walked into the reception area, and they were greeted by the staff with leis to put around their neck. Then, they were escorted to their suite by a staff member who described all the amenities available to them.

The room had a clear ocean view plus an expansive view of the lush property along with two luxury rooms of fine furniture and décor. Debbie checked the linens and oohed and aahed as she inspected the whole suite. After the staff member left, she rolled on to the bed and invited Jack to her side.

"You have a wonderful way of showing your love for me. Please don't ever stop and I will try my best to meet your wishes. They embraced and passionately kissed and soon were naked and making love.

They had dozed off in each other's arms and awoke later in the afternoon.

Jack suggested they take a walk around the property to see the restaurants, pools, and other amenities of the hotel. They stopped at one restaurant and read the menu and made reservations to have dinner there later in the week.

They stopped at an outdoor bar overlooking the ocean and Debbie ordered wine and Jack a scotch on the rocks. They sat there for about thirty minutes enjoying the sights, the soft ocean breezes, and the people walking by.

After completing their walk around the property, they went back to their suite and watched the TV news until dinner time.

They had been told the nearby Four Seasons Hotel had a very nice restaurant and they planned to have dinner there tonight. It was not far from their hotel and it didn't take more than ten minutes to walk the short distance.

CHAPTER 2

The Four Seasons Hotel appeared to be as opulent as the Grand Wailea. They asked for directions to the restaurant and soon were eating their meal. The dinner they enjoyed was elegant and costly, but they didn't care as the food tasted wonderful along with excellent service.

After dinner, they decided to go to a bar with music and found one not far from the restaurant. They chose to sit at the bar, just to enjoy the music and ordered their usual drinks of wine for her and scotch for him.

One stool away from Debbie sat two darker skinned men speaking a foreign language and they appeared to be semi-drunk. Debbie listened for a moment and her ears perked up as she listened to their conversation in Arabic. She nudged Jack and snuggled a little closer to him.

"Do as I say and don't ask questions" and she kissed him on the cheek.

"Honey, let's take a selfie." She pulled him close and raised the camera. When she could see the two guys near her on her screen, she snapped the picture.

"Jack, I am going to the lady's room. She picked up her purse and headed to the restrooms."

She went into an empty stall and immediately dialed an FBI executive's number, who had also worked with Debra and Jack in the past.

"Jeff, it's me Debbie. Just listen please. Jack and I are in a bar at the Four Seasons in Maui. Two guys sitting at the bar next to me were speaking Arabic and talked of blowing up a hotel in Oahu. Get an FBI agent to join us at the bar ASAP. Jack and I are sitting on the left side of the bar when you walk into the place. I will text pictures of these guys now."

She then texted Jack what she had just done and why and walked back to her seat and the two Arabs were staring straight ahead at the bar and still talking.

"Hi again sweetie and she hugged Jack."

She listened as the Arabs continued to talk and she heard Sheraton in Oahu and something about a rental truck. She hoped an FBI agent would soon join them and she could translate for him.

To Debbie, she had the feeling whatever is to happen, it will be in one or two days and maybe it can be stopped before any damage or deaths occur.

About twenty minutes later a guy in casual clothes walked up to them. "Damn, don't you people ever stay home? I've been trying to get you for two days and no answer. Debbie, you look great and Jack, when are we going to play golf again?"

"Ken, we have been busy laying on the beach and getting massages. No time for golf."

"C'mon, sit over here at this table and I will buy the drinks."

They all sat at a round table not too far from where they had sat at the bar. Debbie had her back close to the Arabs and could hear them very well. She started to make notes on her phone as they talked and sent her notes to Jack. Ken sent Jack a message with his phone number and Jack sent it to Debbie.

Soon they were texting back and forth, and Debbie made it very clear these guys were serious and knew about what had been planned to take place at the Sheraton.

Ken texted Debbie the following," in a few minutes, we will arrest these guys and confiscate their phones and determine where they are staying or living locally and will quickly raid those premises."

"When things begin to happen, stay with me because we will go to headquarters and interrogate these guys but we don't speak Arabic and so we need Debbie's assistance and maybe yours too Jack."

Debbie continued to listen as the Arabs began boasting to each other how smart they were and how they outfoxed the local cops. "They are in for a big surprise on Thursday."

The Arabs had just made that statement when two men and a woman suddenly walked up to the bar, and as they got close, each man grabbed one of the Arabs and told them they were under arrest. They quickly and skillfully handcuffed them and led them out of the bar. The woman told the bartender who they were and showed her FBI ID and then left. She did not give any recognition to Jack, Debbie or Ken.

Less than a minute after this had happened, Jack went to the bar and put forty dollars down to cover their bill and they also left. They walked with Ken to his car and went with him to their headquarters in Maui.

Entering the building, the supervisor of the detail in Maui greeted them. "My name is Rodney and thanks for your help guys. You two are well known at the US headquarters and what a break for us that you just happened to be there to overhear the Arabs and to understand what they were saying."

"Where are you staying?"

"We are at the Grand Wailea for the next six days."

"Well, we could use both of you to help us quickly figure out the total plan. Debbie, do you also read Arabic?"

"Yes, I do and if you have their phones or computers, I can interpret for you very fast."

"We have just got into their house and should have computer equipment or documents here real soon."

"That is good, because Jack is also a skilled computer expert and is well known for his hacking abilities and he will find things you might think are not there."

"Jack, I guess our vacation is on hold for a couple of days."

"I was just getting relaxed, but we are needed, and we know what to do"

"Rodney, is there a way I can listen to the interrogation without being seen? These guys may speak some Arabic of importance and I could translate for you."

"Debbie, come with me and sit here. You can watch and hear but they cannot see you or hear you but, all of this is being recorded and I think you could be more useful looking at their phones for text messages in my office with Jack."

"Jack, come sit in my office and Debbie is also coming here. Can I get the both of you a cup of coffee and then we can talk while we wait for the computers to arrive? I do have their phones and you and Debra could also look at them as they may be in Arabic."

"Thanks, we would like a cup of coffee and Rodney, Debbie overheard them speak of a truck. You may want to check all the truck rental places in Oahu for rentals over the last three days."

"Good idea Jack and I'll get you both some coffee."

Debbie came into the office and picked up one of the phones and looked at text messages. They where in Arabic but easy to understand. "Jack, the truck rental occurred today in Oahu. The contacts name is Omar and he is in Oahu and probably will drive the truck."

Rodney returned with Jack's coffee and Debbie gave him the truck information. "I am sure you can find the rental place, name of the renter and driver's license number very easy."

"You guys are making this too easy for me, but I can't believe how lucky Hawaii is that you two were visiting at this time. I heard you were the top two CIA agents on a recent case, and I have been instructed to listen to you."

"Rodney, we recently retired for the second time and came here to relax. Not to chase spies or extremists but to get a tan, sleep late and drink wine. Jack, they are testing us."

Rodney, we are happy to help, and we are fortunate to have been at the right place and at the right time. We don't need a hotel with innocent tourists and families to experience death. We can always extend our stay."

"Thanks to you both, let's hope we can make this go away for all of us in a day or two."

They had just finished the conversation when three agents walked into Rodney's office with a number of large boxes containing documents and computers. "There is interesting stuff in these boxes if we can interpret it, said one of the agents."

"Well Debbie, there is about a full day of work here. We are trying to get another knowledgeable Arabic reading agent, but they are all in the states and it will take a day or so to get them here."

"It's ok, I can pick out the important stuff pretty fast and the rest can wait. Stopping the truck is he number one priority."

"It is a U-Haul rental and we have the address of the driver and hopefully, he will be in custody shorty. We hope he is at the place where the potential explosives are stored and that would bring a quick end to at least the disaster part."

Debra began reading the scores of documents retrieved from the home of the two arrested suspects. Many of them were in Arabic but she had enough experience to easily read them and isolate the important information. About halfway through the second box of papers, she discovered a layout of the Sheraton Hotel and where the truck would be parked to cause maximum damage to the building and perhaps death to many. She immediately gave this document to Rodney and continued the search for additional incriminating evidence.

Meanwhile, Jack and another agent began analyzing two computers found at the home of the suspects and the hoped to determine if this had been an international conspiracy, A large number of the emails and messages were in Arabic which Debbie would eventually interpret for the FBI.

Jack noted the two men had been in contact with other foreigners in Russia, Saudi Arabia and Iran. He knew this from the email address coding used by all countries to show origin of the senders. The Arabic messages would have to be translated at a later date.

Rodney's phone rang and he quickly answered it and all Debbie and Jack could hear him saying yes, yes, very good and then he said get him into the second street holding facility and make sure he is isolated and watched. We don't need him to commit suicide and then he hung up the phone.

"Interesting and good information for us. Omar is in custody; his residence is being searched and the truck has been quarantined by the Oahu bomb squad and it had enough explosive to bring down a large building. The agents also found a number of weapons at Omar's house and we have his computer and cell phone.

This maybe the end of the destruction threat but only the beginning of a long investigation not only domestically but also internationally. Isn't that both of your specialties?"

"Are we being offered a job?" Jack laughed as he said it.

"Not really, but we certainly could use some local guidance to avoid contacting headquarters every five minutes to answer questions, when you and Debbie already know the answers.

"Rodney, we will be happy to help in any way we can. Jack told me a number of the emails were from places we don't necessarily like. He doesn't read Arabic, but the address suffixes give away the country of origin." I can begin reading the emails ASAP."

"Here is a suggestion, we will give you and Jack one of the confiscated computers to take to your hotel to analyze and after you finish the first one, you can have the second one. This will allow you to work and enjoy some leisure at the same time. Will this work for you?"

'Yes, it would be okay, but we would like to limit it to two days. After that, you should be able to get one of your currently employed agents to do the job."

"That sounds good and reasonable. Now, I assume you need a ride back to your hotel?"

"Yes, we do need one and it is now late, and we will probably grab some sleep and work tomorrow."

"Let me get you a ride."

A local agent helped them load the computer and some document boxes into the car and drove them back to the Grand Wailea. The ride took about forty minutes and when they arrived, Jack got a staff member with a luggage rack to unload the boxes and computer and bring them to the suite.

They thanked the agent who drove them to the hotel and then proceeded to their suite to get some sleep. The investigation can wait until tomorrow.

CHAPTER 3

Jack and Debbie woke early when, Jeff the FBI executive, called them from the mainland and inquired how everything turned out. He happily heard it went well and all suspects were behind bars. They told him they would work today on both retrieved documents and a confiscated computer.

After the conversation ended, Jack ordered al large breakfast to be delivered to the suite. When it had been delivered and the table set, Jack asked the staff member to let maid service know it would not be necessary to clean the suite today as they would be working all day long.

They sat and ate their breakfast, had their coffee and put all the dishes and utensils on a cart and put it outside their door. They could use the table for their work and Jack felt reading computer emails should be their priority because it would more than likely be of about recent interest.

Jack started up the computer and when it had completed booting up, he clicked on emails.

"Debbie, you read the emails and I will keep notes for each relevant one. I think it is best to read the latest ones first."

"Agreed and I will feed you the info as I translate it, but only if I find it relevant to the case."

"Jack, here is one sent today from Saudi Arabia wishing them luck. We are now on an international case. Make a note of the date with a comment about a possible Saudi accessary."

She continued to read slowly each message and as she read the sixth message, it talked about the possibility of a second target but this one, on the mainland of the United States. It had no further description as to when or where.

"Jack, get on the phone to Rodney or another agent as this is very serious.

There is mention in this email of a second target within the mainland US. Get us the other computer over here fast and we can probably find the target mentioned within the past two weeks. I will continue reading these and maybe something will pop up soon."

Jack immediately made the call and Rodney answered the phone.

"Rodney, Jack here, there is a possible second target but not here, it is on the mainland. If you can get me the second computer here fast, I can isolate all emails within a two-week window and hopefully, a clue will arise. Also, send me an email address and contact name and I will forward all the emails from both computers to the USA for analysis.

Debbie is working her way through the last two to three weeks to see if additional info can be found. As an aside, she did find a best wishes note from a potential Saudi accomplice."

"Wow, you guys are good, and I will get you the computer and info you requested ASAP. This is scary Jack because the second site could possibly be scheduled for tomorrow."

"We will do our best to quickly try to identify the where and when."

Jack relayed to Debra the gist of the conversation as she continued to read each message for additional clues.

She had now began reading messages older than one week ago when a reference to Philadelphia showed up in a conversation between Omar and someone named Babu Hasson with AOL.com address.

Jack, get Rodney back on the phone and Jack immediately pressed his last call and Rodney answered fast. Debbie needs to speak to you now.

"Rodney the target maybe Philly and I have an AOL email address from Babu Hasson to Omar talking about this with no further specifics. I will continue looking but it could be on the other computers."

"Debbie, get all the stuff repacked and I have an agent who is on his way to you, and he was told to get you back here fast. We will have a conference room set up for the three computers and you and Jack can do your magic from here while we relay info to the USA mainland. This is a life and death situation and the guys in custody will not help us."

"Okay, we will see you in probably forty-five minutes."

"Maybe faster, I have asked for you and Jack to get a police escort with sirens blaring."

"Jack pack everything back in the boxes. We are going back to the offices to work on all three computers and will have a police escort to get us there fast."

"When we are ready, it will be faster for us to carry this stuff to the lobby and be at the front door when the agent arrives."

The left the suite in less than two minutes after the call with Rodney and were in the lobby just as the FBI car arrived. The loaded boxes were put in the trunk and suddenly and quickly the car was following a police vehicle with flashing lights and sirens, leading the way.

This time the trip took just over twenty minutes and a few minutes later, they began looking at all three computers simultaneously.

Debra would glance at an email on one computer and then at the second or third computer to verify the sender or receiver of the email. She found the Philly reference on all three computers and sensed she was getting close to solving the puzzle.

"Jack, this is it. Get Rodney in here fast as he must immediately contact the right people to start looking for accomplices. The target is the Liberty Bell at the Liberty Bell Center on Market Street in Philly."

"You are not only beautiful, but you are also an American hero and I love you."

Rodney came to room immediately and Debra explained what she had uncovered to Rodney.

"Debbie, great job and the FBI has already begun to search for Hasson who they had been previously watching. Unless, you find additional leads, I believe we have concluded this part of the investigation. We have an Arabic translator arriving later today and he can study all the rest of the stuff. In the meantime, you can keep looking at all the emails sent or received over the past three weeks and see if anything else suspicious appears. If not, we will send you back to paradise."

Debra worked for another hour and there had not been any mention of anything beyond what they already knew. Rodney informed them of the arrest of Babu Hassan and the discovery of another truck loaded with explosives at his residence outside of Philadelphia.

"Well, again our thanks and now you and Jack can go back to the swaying palm trees and warm ocean while we slave away. I promise, we will keep you informed of our findings and hopefully more arrests. You and Jack have saved us and this nation a lot of sadness and you should be honored for your acts of bravery.

We have contacted the security personnel of the Grand Wailea, and they have extended your stay for three additional days compliments of the hotel. I will now get an agent to take you back to the hotel. Again, our heartfelt thanks."

They got into the car to return them to the hotel and along the way, Jack said to Debbie, "So what do you want to do for the rest of today?"

"I am going to start with an El Grande Margarita and maybe followed by a second one."

CHAPTER 4

Jack and Debra slept well that night and again were awakened early by their FBI friend Jeff calling from Washington.

"Good morning people. I'm sorry to disturb your day but something interesting happened with the bomb case in Hawaii and Philly. We were able to trace the manufacturer of the explosives and in both cases, we found the explosives had been solen from construction company warehouses.

We then contacted Interpol to see if they had any recent experiences of a similar nature and they did not know of any. However, it seems they have had at least three or four recent cases within Europe of untraceable explosives used to assassinate people who have been using unkind words against certain dictators.

These actions are serious, and Interpol asked if we might be able to help them. I told them we might consider it if we could get the right personnel. Well, I know you two have relationships in the European and Middle Eastern arms world and once more we need your help."

"Jeff, we are on vacation. Can you start to gather more information and we can discuss it with you in five or six days."

"That seems reasonable. I will get a team together to start trying to determine if this is a coincidence or part of an ongoing dangerous trend that could eventually spread to our country. Call me when we can meet back here in Washington."

"Thanks Jeff. We'll inform you about our travel plans. Now, it's a vacation day." Jack slowly placed the phone back on the cradle.

"Jack did I hear right? We must go back to work, again?"

"Honey, you know work is not all the bad. We are together and we travel the world and maybe get shot at occasionally. Exciting huh?" Jack was laughing as he said this.

"You know Jack, sitting around watching television all day isn't as exciting and once more, we get to see our old friends and along the way, help our government and Interpol solve a problem. Let's do it but not today as we have spa reservations for a soothing message."

'Sounds good to me but first, let's order breakfast."

CHAPTER 5

While Jack and Debra continued their luxurious vacation of massages, fine dining and love making, the CIA had selected a team of skilled investigators to gather the facts of each explosive incident in Europe.

After identifying each location to find a common area or target, no links stood out. The Hawaii incident along with the Liberty Bell threat were the only closely related attempts and the explosives were traceable. The FBI had already identified the involvement of Middle Eastern terrorists.

Interpol were able to determine the main explosive element used in all the assassination cases was a common explosive and manufactured by multiple manufacturers, globally. However, in each case, the trace chemical, used by all manufacturers to identify the source of manufacture was nonexistent.

The CIA now needed skilled operators in the global arena of terrorists, spies, and rogue arms dealers. Jack and Debra were at the top of the list, based on their experience and knowledge.

Five days after his conversation with Jeff, Debra and Jack were on their return trip back to Virginia and more than likely returning to another harrowing challenge.

They landed safely at Reagan Washington National Airport, gathered their luggage, and started the final lap of their journey to their home and after ten hours of travel, they went to bed minutes after their arrival home.

There awoke shortly after nine the following morning and after a cup of coffee, Jack called Jeff to arrange a meeting to discuss their next challenge.

He was told the meeting would be held in two days at Jeff's office in D.C.

Jeff and Debra had discussed all their options and had decided they would accept an offer if included their being based in Paris and the opportunity to return to the United States for thirty consecutive days yearly. They knew they would have a suitable expense account and they expected an abundance of travel within Europe.

Because of morning traffic into D.C., they left their home about an hour before the scheduled meeting and were surprised, when they arrived about fifteen minutes early.

Jeff's office was in a nondescript building close to the Ellipse, with a view of the White House. Jeff met them in the lobby and escorted them to a meeting room where four other agents were already seated. Jack and Debra took seats near the front of a large oval table.

After introductions, Jeff opened the meeting stressing the importance and challenges facing both Interpol and FBI agents seeking this deadly trend emerging as an assassination tool.

The FBI knew it was only a matter of time before this plague began to be used on high level government personnel and it had to be stopped in the next three to six months. In a classified meeting, congress had been warned of the threat and had agreed to initiate safety measures among their members.

Jeff then addressed the group regarding their potential roles in the investigation. "Jack, Debra, the FBI views you two as the key to unlocking this mystery and helping to bring an end to this pending disaster as quickly as possible. I value your skills, but you will be threatened once the criminals learn of your presence in Europe. Interpol and the FBI will do all it can to protect you but for the most part you will be on your own."

"Are you both willing to take this risk?"

Jack quickly answered, "Jeff, Debra and I discussed both the challenge and

the potential consequences of failure for ourselves and our country. We have been there before, and we have no doubts of the strength of our foes and their ability to kill us. We will rely on our experiences and our multiple skills to overcome whatever threatens us and hopefully we will succeed."

"Lastly, for us to agree to continue, we are requesting the following: an apartment in Paris along with a suitable expense allowance plus the possibility of having up to 30 days back in the USA once per year dependent on the current situation."

"We can agree to all of that as we recognize your abilities and relationships will require much travel and we suggest you don't go there as American citizens. We will arrange the proper identifications for you and Debra, and we will inform our contacts at our embassy and Interpol of your presence.

Hopefully we solidify our planning quickly and if you accept this project, you can plan on starting within the next three weeks."

"I'll push Jack and we will be ready" said Debra laughing.

"Thank you both and I will be providing complete details as the planning moves towards completion and we wish you both success and safe travel."

The meeting ended and Jack and Debra made their way back to their car.

"Jack are we sure we want to do this?"

"I'm sure and let's look at it as an exciting extension of our honeymoon. Lots of luxury, love making and sightseeing." They both laughed as he started the car to drive them home.

CHAPTER 6

"Well, we have about three weeks to do little except to pack," Jack casually said. "But seriously, we should contact our friends and put them on alert about our presence and let them know we will meet once we arrive in France."

"That will give us a good start Jack and fortunately our friends deal in a lot of dangerous stuff and maybe explosives are on their lists."

Possibly, but we should be able to get some introductions to others who might have the information we are seeking."

Minutes later the phone and it was Jeff. "Folks, we have a slight change of plans. We are sending you to Paris within three or four days as we continue our planning, and it will give you some free time to relax and meet up with some of your old contacts."

"Jeff, is our phone tapped as we were just discussing that matter when you called?"

"No, your phone is clean, but we know you and Debra have quite a few friends because I met some of them at your wedding and I am sure you want to renew old acquaintances."

"Your right and once we get situated, we can do our own planning, talk to our friends, and overcome jet lag. Beside we will have a learning curve while taking time to develop our cover. We can let you know tomorrow about our departure."

"Great, talk to you then."

"Well honey, you probably heard a portion of that conversation and basically says we're free to go at our leisure."

"Jack, we like Paris so let's start planning about our identities and decide about our starting point. We can notify our friends once we

get settled."

"You want a glass of Zin as I am buying and treating myself to my 15-year-old Scotch."

"Sure, let's get comfy in the den and gather your thoughts. I'll get a pad and pen and we can select our nationality, our names and think about a cover story. Besides Jeff must get us some ID cards and passports ASAP."

"True. Here's your wine and let's begin. Certainly, we are travelling as a married couple, so let's pick a country we can be comfortable with and go from there."

"Jack, you're from Russia and I'm from Belgium. We've been married twenty years and no kids. You select our educations and occupations."

"I'll need two scotches to work on those issues" he said laughing and then took a big gulp of his drink. "I can pass for a computer programmer, and you teach middle Eastern languages. How's that sound?"

"Not good. Remember there are Arabs involved in this convoluted case and we don't have to tip them off telling them I speak Arabic. I would like a new career. How about a buyer of artistic jewelry. You know, odd stuff done by local artisans."

"Debra, you are right about the Arabic part, and you do have a fine eye for art. Let's go with that as our cover story. Now, who are we going to be?"

"How is Marie and Ivan Sokolov. Easy to remember and although your parents grew up in Russia, you were born and raised in Belgium and your father was a baker."

"It is good, and I'll text Jeff to get us our identity papers in two days. Now, I'm tired and I'm ready to sleep."

Me too. Once we get our ID's, it should be easy to get a flight to Paris. I also need some sleep because I feel we may be running ragged for the next two days."

CHAPTER 7

The phone rang just after eight am and Jack reached to get the phone and once more it was Jeff.

"Jack, sorry to disturb you but we learned overnight of two new assassinations and one of them was a police chief in Poland and the other unlucky soul was a car dealer in the UK. I told Interpol we would have people in Europe in two or three days."

"Jeff, we are about ready to leave but we will need ID's, Passports, etcetera asap and we could leave hours after receipt of the documents. Tell Interpol,

we will be based in Paris but can meet them anywhere they choose within a day after arriving. Send me the Interpol contact name and we'll advise them of our flight and hotel arrangements."

"Thanks Jack. I'll text you details in a few minutes. Please have Debra call Lance on my line and he will expedite whatever documents you need. Travel safe."

"Honey, no sleeping late today as things are getting worse in Europe and we must move fast. Jeff asked for you to call Lance on his line and give him the details for the passports and other papers we may need. I am going to start packing including a couple of weapons for each of us. Once Lance gives you a completion date, I'll book our flight and hotel."

"And I thought I would sleep in this morning. Oh well, duty calls so After I get myself together, I'll call Lance and get him started and I will also start to pack my stuff. I'm only taking one bag and if we need more things, we'll buy them as we go."

He kissed her on the cheek and then told her, "I'll get the coffee ready and some toast and see you downstairs."

Within a few minutes, Debra and Jack were enjoying their morning coffee.

"Jack, Lance will have all our ID needs finalized later today and will have a courier deliver them to us by early evening today. I'm about finished packing and if you can be ready, we can leave tomorrow for Paris. We can stay in a hotel until we can arrange an apartment rental."

"I'm fine with that honey and after I finish my coffee, I'll start arranging our travel plans."

Jack took care of the travel arrangements and their flights had been booked for a late afternoon departure tomorrow on Air France, scheduled to arrive in Paris about eight am the next day due to time differences between DC and Paris.

Jack had also arranged for hotel transportation from the airport in Paris and notified an Interpol contact of their arrival time and hotel booking under the names of Mr. and Mrs. Ivan Sokolov.

The documents requested by Debra arrived as the couple were preparing dinner. They reviewed them while they ate and then created back-up stories for each identity.

Their preparation was a good beginning, but they knew the real and dangerous work would begin in Paris.

CHAPTER 8

As the couple began finalizing their travel plans, another scenario was taking place in the city of Kolobrzeg located in Poland on the Bearing Sea coast. It is a relatively small city of about 50,000 people and is know for its spas and tourism.

It is also home to Pauli Zukowski, the popular owner of the Zukowski Candy Store and a newer business called the Polish Pop Corn Company.

Pauli had been born and raised in Poland and his father owned a successful candy store facing the beach, usually crowded in the summertime and during the holidays.

He was the last of six children and for most of his young life he was the smallest and sickliest child in the family. Because he was small, he was often bullied in school and at times wished he was dead. It seems no one, including his siblings and parents gave much support to him. His father had a business to run, and his mother had five other kids who also needed attention along with all the other chores required of a homemaker.

Despite the obstacles he often faced, he managed to do well in school, and after reading a story about Marie Curie, he fell in love with chemistry and decided he would work hard to achieve his dream of attending the university to study his favorite subject. His dream also included him winning a Nobel prize, just as Marie Curie had accomplished in 1903.

He graduated the university achieving good grades and without any major issues. However, within one month of graduation, his father died suddenly and since none of his brothers or sisters had any interest in the candy business, Pauli assumed ownership.

Thus, he began his adult life as a business owner and soon realized he could be his own boss and earn good money along the way. Many years ago, his father had purchased the two-story building housing the candy store. Pauli furnished the second floor as his living quarters and with his strong interest in chemistry, he assembled equipment for a small laboratory where he could run experiments to test the random ideas he thought up about chemical compositions.

His understanding of chemistry and experimentation in his lab allowed him to create some unique candy assortments and the candy business grew due to his ingenuity. The word quickly spread, and his candy shop became the place to stop whenever people went to the beach or needed a specific treat for a special occasion.

In a short period of time, he was able to purchase another shop, not far from the candy store where he intended to create a business, he named the Polish Popcorn Company.

Once again, his chemistry knowledge came in handy as he developed unique flavors of popcorn and he received similar responses he had heard at the candy shop, the public raved about his new business.

Time quickly passed and at the age of thirty-five, he now owned two successful businesses and enjoyed having a decent bank account balance. As a bachelor, mothers were always interested in introducing him to their daughters. He had accepted a dinner offer from one of his customers and was introduced to Marie. He quickly learned she was a graduate chemical engineer and they immediately bonded when they both discovered their common interests.

They began to see each other regularly and soon they were engaged to be married. They married and over a three-year period, they had two children. They purchased a large house in Kolobrzeg and spent time together in the lab Pauli, had started, creating unusual concoctions of candy and popcorn.

They were a happy family, but Pauli still dreamed of creating something that would make him famous while his wife was content with their children and wealth and did not desire much more.

At the age of forty-seven, he was reading a chemistry newsletter when he came across an article describing how explosive companies globally were required to add a specific trace chemical into their products. By being able to identify the trace chemical, it allowed law enforcement investigating any explosive incident to quickly identify the manufacturer of the explosive material.

Pauli was fascinated by this discovery, and he wondered if he could develop a way of eliminating the trace material. Initially, his thoughts were just a challenge to his chemical skills. But the more he thought about it, he wondered if he could make money selling his knowledge and he did this with no awareness of the legality of his actions.

He remembered an incident where he over-cooked a batch of candy, and it ruined the taste of one of the main ingredients. Maybe I could have similar results using the same process?

His business kept him busy the entire summer and his thoughts were stored away. He never discussed them with his wife as she would only encourage him not to waste his time but to pay attention to the two businesses, he successfully owned and managed.

As the summer passed and he had more time to experiment, he learned about the various trace elements and their specific chemical characteristics. He also studied the ways enforcement agencies detected trace elements such as the methods used by security at airports and points of entry and other venues where large crowds would be in attendance.

He began to realize by eliminating the trace detection, he would be supporting the evil portions of society who might use this technique to harm others. However, this did not faze him as his objective was to achieve notoriety regardless of the human cost to society.

He continued his efforts undeterred and after about six weeks of trial and error he discovered a way to eliminate trace detection by vaporization. He now channeled all his efforts on testing his discovery in the real world.

Interpol would never know that the killing of an outspoken critic of Putin, took place in Finland and was the first test sample supplied by Pauli to Russian secret agents.

CHAPTER 9

Jack and Debra left their home via a private car and soon arrived at the airport. They easily passed through security and boarded the flight to Paris. Minutes later the plane the plane was airborne, and both wondered what awaited them on this new journey, because they knew, they would be playing against sophisticated foreign agents and known killers.

About six hours later they deplaned at Orly, cleared customs, and met their driver to take them to their hotel. In less than 30 minutes, they checked into the hotel and were sitting in the suite Jack had previously booked.

"Debra, I am going to contact Interpol and arrange an appointment for ourselves, and I believe we should request French identifications and passports before we seek an apartment rental. I don't feel right having a Russian name in France as it could raise suspicions about us. I also will not contact our friends and other contacts until we have a better understanding from Interpol about the current situation and challenges."

"I fully agree, especially considering a Putin adversary was the first person killed and more than likely by Russian agents. I would also suggest keeping our mission between ourselves when we first contact our friends. We can be more open if we meet them here in France and seek their assistance."

"Your right, once we have a meeting with Interpol, I will contact Boris and Franz and you can contact Anna and Ethan and we'll all meet here at the hotel hopefully early next week. We should both be careful about revealing our new names. Although we trust our friends, phones get tapped, emails are hacked, etcetera. Let's try our best to remain silent and vigilant."

"Got It. We've been away from the game for a while, and we need to quickly climb back up the learning curve."

Jack then made a call to the Interpol contact. He only knew his first name, Perry. They spoke for a few minutes and agreed to meet at the hotel tomorrow morning at ten AM.

"Let's, go get a quick lunch and then try to catch up on our sleep" Jack suggested.

"Both sound good to me".

They ate at an outdoor café a short distance from the hotel and then returned to take a nap before jetlag set in.

They awoke as the sun was setting and decided to order room service which would allow them time to rehearse their stories and avoid any mistakes when they eventually would meet their friends.

After dinner, they watched the news on CNN for a short while and around nine PM went back to bed and quickly fell asleep. They woke early and again ordered room service and while eating discussed the meeting with the Interpol agent in about one hour.

Perry arrived on time, and they met in their suite to avoid any shady persons looking or listening to the conversations. After introductions, Perry suggested he start by updating them with the latest news.

"First, thank you both for joining with us on this crazy event. We know you both are retired and have extensive experience, knowledge of the area, and your overall expertise is welcomed by everyone working on this challenging problem.

We can now confirm at least five murders using untraceable explosives. The latest one occurred two days ago in Spain where a government police agent was murdered by an explosive blowing his car apart. This agent was investigating known Mafia individuals and may have been close to identifying the ring master."

"Is there any correlation between these incidents." Asked Jack.

"No, it is very puzzling as we have looked at every aspect and there is no relation between any of the killings that we could find. The only common feature is that the person killed was a potential enemy of someone in a position of power. In fact, in the case of the car dealer, it might have been some kind of revenge. Honestly, we just don't know."

"Thanks Perry. Jack and I know we have a tough and possibly long duration assignment to help you find answers to the many unanswered questions.

Here is how we are going to start. Jack and I will rent an apartment here in Paris and it will serve as our base for now. To do this, we would need papers as French citizens with a little bit of history. We came here with Russian sounding names, but we would stand out less being French citizens.

Once we have an apartment, we will contact a short list of friends, located in Belgium, Germany, and Russia whom we trust to aid us. We have worked with these people for many years on very serious investigations. In fact, they all attended our wedding."

"Debra, we need all the support we can gather, and your contacts will remain unknown to us. I can arrange papers for you and Jack, and they will be delivered tomorrow. The quicker we can solve this problem; we will avoid a lot of future killings. You have my number, and as you Americans would say, I am available 24/7. Again, we are glad to have you onboard and once more I thank you but now, I must leave for another meeting."

It was close to noontime when the meeting ended, and Jack suggested they take a stroll and have lunch nearby their hotel. We should start practicing speaking French since we are soon to be French citizens.

"Mon cheri, je t'aime" Debra quickly stated.

"Moi aussi, je t'aime" replied Jack laughing as he said it. "Well, that sums up our French lesson for today.

They took seats at a different café, ordered their food in French, and after being served, discussed the meeting they had had with Perry.

"Jack, we are starting an investigation from ground zero. We have no clues except five murders. No suspects, almost no information on the method of the killings, and no idea of when and where the next assassination will happen and to who. We must dig deep to find the roots of this mystery."

"Debra: I once had a similar situation in Russia, and it took months to be resolved. We must realize there will be more deaths, in many different locations involving different relationships. It will take time and a lot of thought to solve this, but sooner or later, a mistake will be made, there always is at least one, and suspects will be identified. We will have to be both patient and vigilant at the same time and hope the clues begin to make sense to us."

"I understand that, but I would prefer to know where to start so we can find an ending."

"We are going to start tomorrow by renting an apartment, meeting with our friends and together piece together each clue and see where it leads us.

This will not be a quick and easy assignment and we will have a lot of disappointing days. We must stay on a proven course working towards a successful ending. The accumulation of clues will steer our course and until we see light at the end of the tunnel we will be working in a dark and mirky situation."

"Let us hope tomorrow is better than today."

Chapter 10

The telephone rang early in the morning and awoke Jack. "Hello, who is this?"

"Sorry Jack for the rude awaking but this is Perry and we have had another murder and it happened here in Paris. Can you and Debra be ready for a pick-up in 15 minutes, and we can bring you to the scene?"

"We'll be waiting outside for the car." as he hung up the phone.

"Debra, wake up honey. It's seven am and we are about to begin our investigation the hard way. Viewing another dead body. A car will pick us up in 15 minutes."

"Yikes, not much time to even brush my teeth or put on make-up."

"The incident is here in Paris."

"Well, we said there would be a lot more deaths before we have a solution."

"I'm ready: let's head for the lobby and wait the car."

In a few minutes they were speeding through Paris and soon arrived at what appeared to be an up-scale neighborhood. Perry was waiting for them as they approached, he told them what was known about the victim.

"He was a middle-aged man from Iran and an outspoken critic of the leading clerics of Iran. Obviously, they don't like any criticism and take drastic steps to eliminate the source.

The body is over here, and it appears the explosive material was contained in a package addressed to him. The moment he attempted to open the package it exploded, and the force was sufficient to kill him.

We are reviewing footage from the security cameras to try and identify the delivery source."

"Was he carrying the package as he left the building? asked Debra."

"He probably picked it up in the lobby and then tried to open it once he got outside. We'll learn a lot more after seeing the security video."

Jack had walked over to wear the body laid and slowly removed the cover from the top so he could see the face of the man. He initially saw extensive wounds to the face and body of the victim but upon closer examination he noted several small round wounds.

"Perry, it appears the culprits are using ball bearings mixed into the explosive as the victim has a large number of round holes in his body, almost like he has been shot by an assault rifle."

"Yes, we noticed, it is very clear to us and troubling to know, we are dealing with professional killers. This will not make the job easier for any of us."

"It's certainly a wake-up call for Debra and myself. We have dealt with these types before but not on the scale you have already experienced.

The killers seem to be in many locations and have several unrelated targets. It is already both challenging and dangerous. I would also guess, whoever is supplying the material has a large customer base."

"I have been notified your French identities are waiting for you at your hotel. You have my direct number and later today, I will provide you the name and number of an additional contact. Do not hesitate to call us at any hour and particularly if you sense you are being threatened or realize either of you or both of you have been unmasked. We take all threats seriously and can respond rapidly when needed."

"Thanks Perry, Jack and I have weapons and based upon what we have heard and now experienced, we will not be walking around unarmed.

With our new identities, we will begin searching for an apartment today and will try to have something firm in a few days. Now, we will take a taxi back to our hotel and from now onward, we are also available 24/7. Adieu."

Jack and Debra walked about a block from the crime scene and found a taxi to return them to the hotel. Once there, they picked up their documents at the front desk and went to their room.

Jack ordered breakfast from room service and they began to search the internet for rental companies. A few minutes search provided Jack all the information he needed and after calling a couple of companies, he was able to make an appointment for later in the day for a rental in a newer apartment complex located a few miles from the city center.

Debra was eating her breakfast when Jack joined her at the small table.

"Honey, this morning's episode remined me why I retired and yet here I am once more exposing not only myself to danger but also you. This will not be an open and shut case but continue until the mastermind who created this evil method of murder is exposed. I promise you I will be at your side whenever I sense danger and together, we will be a strong team against all enemies'."

"Interesting, after the show today, I also wondered why we are we doing this? Haven't we had enough excitement to last a lifetime? We are treading on dangerous ground and although we have experience, we better stay sharp and alert with our weapons always unlocked."

"My only answer, we're patriotic."

"Okay, when do we get to look at a rental?"

"A rental agent will pick us around one pm and we'll be looking at furnished units in a nice setting."

"Well, let's hope we get settled fast and meet our friends and start searching for the source of misery."

"Oh yes, but it will be nice to see Franz, Boris, Ethan, and Anna once more and put our collective skills together working towards a solution. They have provided us a lot of help in the past and I hope they are available when we need them."

"If I had a glass of wine, I would drink to that wish."

CHAPTER 11

The rental agent picked them up at their hotel and along the way described the area where they would possibly be living. To Jack and Debra, it was interesting, it was only a mile or so from the Place de la Concorde close to where the American embassy was located. To them, the embassy always served as a haven for operatives in need.

Since Debra and Jack were speaking to the agent in French, he would never realize they would enjoy being close to the embassy.

The apartment, the agent had selected to show them, was on the fourth floor of a six-story building and included an indoor pool and workout room. It was furnished nicely and had a sufficient area for them to work plus, they learned, it was near a series of outdoor cafes and a large farmers market which opened daily. It also provided high speed internet service and free cable TV.

After some back-and-forth comments and questions, they agreed on a price and signed a one-year lease with an option for additional years and they could relocate to the apartment in a couple of days.

After they had signed an agreement, the agent returned them to their hotel and once in their room, they began to organize their move and would begin to contact the people who could help them solve the mystery.

It was getting late in the day and Jack suggested they once again go out for dinner, and they talk later about their plans and making contacts.

They returned to a small café they had chosen earlier in the week and decided to sit inside the restaurant. They sat at a table for two, ordered drinks and then selected their food for the evening meal. A TV was close to where they sat and reported news on the murder of an Iranian critic using an explosive with ball bearings. The news included comments from Interpol seeking information from the public. The news reported nothing else of the murder which Jack and Debra did not already know.

Suddenly, the station France 24, announced they had just been advised of addition murders in Europe involving similar deadly devices, as the Iranian had experienced. Interpol would only say they cannot discuss ongoing investigations.

Their meal was served and after hearing the leaked news, they quickly ate and returned to the hotel.

"Jack, releasing the news of additional murders only lets the bad guys know that Interpol doesn't have a clue about who did what to whom."

"Fortunately, they don't know about the American involvement."

"That's true, but we better start moving asap. I'm going to call Anna now and see if she and Ethan can meet us in Paris next week. You can call Franz and Boris with a similar request."

"When you call your friends, see if they can be here quickly and then I will call my buddies with a similar approach. Keep the details to yourself and just say it's an urgent request. We can provide a meeting place once we confirm they can be here on our time schedule. If we can only get three of the four people, we will still hold the meeting."

Moments later, Debra was speaking to Anna and after they shared greetings, Debra asked her, "Anna, are we on a secure phone?"

Anna assured her the line was clean. "Anna, we need you to come to Paris early next week. It is urgent. We want you to also ask Ethan if he can attend as well. If you and Ethan are available, text me and we will advise the meeting location. If you can, check on your schedules and let me know tonight. We will fully advise you the details after you meet with us. Nice talking to you again. Au revoir."

"Jack, knowing Anna and our friendship, I would guess we hear from her in the next thirty minutes."

"I am assuming she will attend and I'm not sure about Ethan. Hence, I am going to make a similar call to Boris and Franz and hopefully they will also be available to quickly meet with us,"

Jack called Franz first and greeted his old friend warmly as they had not seen each other for a couple of years. "Franz, I am in Paris and have an urgent project and I would appreciate your help. If possible, I would appreciate if you could meet me early next week and then I will explain the full details to you. The meeting may last two days maximum and please text if you can be available and I will provide the location of the meeting. I am also asking Boris to join us at that time. Again, warm wishes to you and your family. Hope to see you soon."

He next tried to call Boris, but he was advised the line had been discontinued. He then sent a text to him on another number asking him to provide a number so they could talk.

Within a few minutes, he received a text from Boris saying he was hospitalized and expected to be released in three to four days. He promised to call Jack after he was released.

"Honey, Boris is in the hospital until early next week and I don't know why but he promised to contact me after he is released. Franz will soon text me his availability. Have you heard from Anna?"

"Yes, she is available and expects Ethan will also be available. Where and when are we going to meet? I think a conference room here at the hotel would be acceptable and will be a good time saver for us. If you agree, I will check out the rooms and make the reservation."

"Great idea. Today is Saturday, so let's shoot for Tuesday and we may need the room for two days plus three additional guest rooms for the same time. I have doubts If Boris can make it."

"I am going to the lobby now to see what I can arrange. All expenses on our account, right?"

"It's the cost of doing business, honey."

Just as Debra was leaving, Jack received the text from Franz, and he would be available to arrive on Monday afternoon. Jack replied thanking him and provided the hotel information where they would be staying.

Debra returned after 30 minutes and advised Jack she had booked a nice room close to the lobby for the meeting plus three guest rooms. "We get seriously involved starting Tuesday."

CHAPTER 12

Pauli Zukowski was also busy carefully lining up hitmen to peddle his explosive kits to those needing a new way to murder.

His wife's nephew had a history of being in and out of prison for various felonies. In prison, the other inmates named him the Cool Poloch. He wasn't a murderer, but he had the right contacts and Pauli used him as his main sales agent.

The nephew relished the danger and swore to Pauli, he would never reveal the source of the illicit goods, nor would any family member be aware of his actions. He shared with Pauli the names of his contacts and what they were capable of doing.

Cool Poloch was selling the units from $5000 to $8000 and custom configurations, maybe double the normal price. Pauli trusted him and paid him twenty-five percent of all sales.

Pauli manufactured his goods in a lab he had built inside the popcorn factory. He acquired his raw materials through Russian and Iranian middlemen, who were always ready to earn a quick buck or two.

He had singlehandedly developed a process to treat the explosive materials, making them untraceable, using a combination of chemicals and steam. Basically, he would sterilize the material and then package it along with detonators triggered by a pressure switch. Once the package was opened and the pressure relieved on the switch, the device would explode in ten seconds.

His invention was remarkable and well thought out, but it was a device developed only to kill humans.

Based upon his discovery, Pauli considered himself a genius and he had figured out a revengeful way to get even with all the people who bullied and made fun of him in his early life. I will get revenge and slap them much harder than they ever slapped me.

The murdered car dealer was one of his bullies and there were others on Pauli's list.

CHAPTER 13

Shortly after Debra had returned to the room, Jack received a call from Boris.

"Jack old buddy, how are you?"

"I'm fine but I was concerned about hearing you were in the hospital. What is wrong?"

"I am fine now but my doctor decided I needed a stent to undue a blockage and while they were at it, they gave a pacemaker to regulate a heart issue called A fib. You learn so many medical terms as you age.

I spent an extra day in the hospital so they could observe any issues relating to the procedures but, I am fine now and can resume my normal life."

"I am glad to hear you are well but are you allowed to travel?"

"Absolutely. In fact, my wife and I are leaving for Vienna tomorrow just to relax and do the tourist stuff. Why, do you have a job for me?"

"Boris, you know me too well and the answer is yes. Would you and your wife wish to spend a couple of days in Paris, all expenses paid?"

"Jack my wife loves Paris and if we get to see you and Debra, that would be great. What kind of job do you have in mind?"

"If you can be here by Tuesday morning, you'll learn everything at that time. If your answer is yes, I will text your hotel information in a few minutes."

"It sounds interesting, and I am sure we can arrange to arrive Monday evening. Will any of our other friends be there or is it just you and I?"

"Sorry, no further details until we meet on Tuesday morning, and I am damn happy you sound well and are available to help. We'll talk more then."

Within a minute, a text had been sent to Boris with the hotel name.

"Debra, we need another guest room."

"I overheard your conversation and booked the additional room before you disconnected."

He thanked her and gave her a loving hug.

"Jack, let's go out for a great meal, have a drink or two and come back to our suite where we can cuddle for a while. Starting tomorrow, we will be busy, and our romantic lust times will be put on hold."

"Okay but I want to be back here early, Europe's Got Talent has their final show tonight but your alternative sounds more exciting. I'll skip the show."

Both laughed and held hands as they made their way to the elevator and would look for a cozy restaurant nearby. They found one with a decent menu and music in the bar area. The food was very good combined with excellent wine and soft music.

After about two hours, they returned to the hotel and quickly rushed to their room. It didn't take long before they were naked and engaged in a passionate love session and then fell asleep in each other's arms.

The awoke about nine on Sunday morning it would probably be a long day of planning for their Tuesday meeting with their contacts.

Jack took a shower and dressed casually since they had no reason to leave the hotel today. He ordered breakfast and a large pot of coffee to last them a few hours. When they finished their meal and a second cup of coffee, they knew it was time to get to work.

As always, the first question is "Where do we start?"

Jack started, "We need to first let our contacts know why we are in Paris and the urgent threat of potential global killings by hitmen using an explosive device, which up to now is untraceable.

We are supported by our government and Interpol in this effort to find the source of the device and as quickly as possible, bring a stop to the killings. We should also have a list of those killed to date and the motivation for the killing if it is known. What have I left out?"

"I think we also need to detail the locations of each killing and then try to determine, what persons have similar views may also become a target. For example, the guy killed yesterday was not the only critic of the Iranian clergy, there could be hundreds of people who have stated their public views about this subject. Then again, maybe the clerics are messaging the others to shut up or die. So, after we provide all this information, where do we start?"

"I wish I could answer that question, honey, but the killings are so dispersed, and every person was a critic. an election foe or an enemy. I think we need more information from Interpol about each person and their social media friends and contacts. Did they have wives, and do they know who their husband had thoughts about who would want to kill him?

Now that I am raising questions, I'm going to call Perry and see what he thinks."

Jack immediately used his cell phone to contact the only source who could have the answers to his questions.

"Perry, Jack here, I want to update you on our activity and hope that you can answer some questions I have regarding the victims. First, tomorrow we will meet with four of our key contacts from Europe and Russia who individually possess a lot of skill and knowledge about the illegal activities in this part of the world. Debra and I have known all these people for ten to fifteen years and previously relied on them to assist us. They have never disappointed us.

We will advise them as to what we know but it would be beneficial if more information could be had about the victims."

"Jack, before you continue, let me update you about Interpol's activities. We have approximately 30 personnel assigned to these cases and their instructions are to leave no stone unturned. Here is an example of what we are finding.

Every person killed except the car dealer, had an extensive record on social media. In three of the cases, they had stated their lives were in danger and they expected to be killed. They also identified the group that would probably kill them.

We have tried to connect a lot of dots but there are no connections. We can identify potential victims, but they are scattered across Europe, Russia, and Asia. Up until now, there are few similarities, but they are not enough to get anyone excited.

I will arrange to send you basic information on each victim along with where and when they died. Beyond that there is not much more to speak about.

I am glad to hear you are adding more personnel to the task force and maybe they will see things unnoticed by our people. All we both can do is to try and support each other and hope one of us finds the path to success.

I wish I could tell you more Jack, but as we uncover meaningful information, we will share with you immediately. Thanks for the call."

Thank you, Perry, we are both in the same boat and I promise you we will also share our findings as they arise and hope for the best, Au revoir."

"Well Debra, our contacts will know almost as much as we do about this case which is very little. This maybe the most we have been challenged in all the years we spent chasing spies. The problem is the limited amount of information, and it is no fault of Interpol or us. It's just a mystery without clues."

"I know, but we will have six of us to think about it very soon and we may be able to start walking in the right direction.

Chapter 14

Jack and Debra worked most of Sunday to summarize what they would discuss with their contacts. They had a short list of known facts and a long list of the unknow. It was not the ideal way to start a meeting, but they had to accept what they had until more relevant data could be received from Interpol.

Their contacts began arriving shortly after noon on Monday. Anna and Ethan were first to arrive, and they were happily greeted in the lobby by Jack and Debra. Franz arrived next and in the early evening, Boris and his wife arrived.

They all gathered around eight pm to go to dinner and renew their long friendships. After dinner and a round of drinks they went back to the hotel and agreed to meet in the lobby at nine am to begin the anticipated meeting when Jack and Debra would reveal the details and known facts of the project.

The meeting started promptly at nine am and Jack thanked all of them for attending and then he started to explain the purpose of this meeting.

"My friends, you have known Debra and myself for many years and we have cooperated on several prior projects successfully together. I will now tell you about a new project where the information is scarce, and what we do know, smells of danger.

My government selected Debra and I for this special and urgent project and to cooperate and work alongside with Interpol. Here is what we know.

Five people have already been killed and one of them was here in Paris last week. We saw the results of a person killed a by an explosive device which has yet to be identified and the explosive residue material collected is untraceable. The other four people were killed in a similar fashion in different areas of Europe.

We do know of a killing in Finland could possibly be tied to Russian agents because the victim was a very vocal critic of Putin. The killing here in Paris involved an Iranian citizen who criticized the Iranian clerics, and he may have been killed by Iranian agents aligned with the government.

In these two cases and others, they all have one thing in common. They were killed by an untraceable explosive device very likely detonated by a cell phone or perhaps a pressure switch. At this point, the detonation mechanism is unknown.

Although tiny parts were collected at the scene of each incident, nobody has any idea as to the make-up of this device, no clues as to where it is being manufactured, the source of the materials used and how the hitmen can acquire the finished product.

Both Interpol and my government are fearful, continued success by the killers could result in government officials in many countries becoming victims along with others who challenge dictators and even challengers to elected officials, would become potential targets.

This is not any easy assignment and as I stated earlier, it will be dangerous. I would hope we can all work as a team, but I also understand if you don't have the time or do not wish to participate. Lastly, we want to assure you that your identities will be hidden from Interpol.

Now, Debra and I are open to questions."

Franz was the first to reply, "how long do you expect this might take to be solved?"

"Franz, Jack, and I wish we could answer the question, but in all honesty, we don't know. However, we have signed a one-year apartment lease here in Paris and we would be very happy to be able to cancel it after a couple of months.

Jack didn't say it, but we were hoping to openly discuss the challenge and hear your opinions and options as a starting point for our investigation. All of you are very talented and have been tested many times. We need the variety of talents, all of you have shown us in the past.

We really do need your help."

"Well, you can count on me to help in any way I can. Jack has been my close friend for a long time, and together as a team, we have been fortunate to have some very rewarding successes. I'm ready Jack."

"Thanks Boris. Maybe it's a good time to ask each of you if you intend to help us on this mysterious and difficult project. Please raise your hand if you intend to assist us."

All four people raised their hands together.

"Thank you again for your support. Based upon the limited information we have provided, in front of you is a pad and pen. I am asking each of you to describe how you would approach this problem. I am doing it this way so not to influence your ideas and opinions based upon what others have stated. Please take about ten minutes to write down your thoughts and then I will put your questions on this white board so we can discuss the merits of each response."

After ten minutes, Debra collected the written sheets and handed them to Jack who began to list question on the board.

1. Does Interpol have a documented summary of each victim's current relatives, contacts, and social media activity.
2. Were all the victim's male?
3. How large was the explosive, i.e., was it limited to a small area, or did it extend beyond the victim?
4. Did the victims have any forewarning signs of danger such as victims receiving messages warning them to cease their rhetoric?
5. How were the explosives delivered to the victims and are there any surveillance videos from the area?
6. If the explosives were detonated by a cell phone, the killer had to be within a short distance from the victim.
7. Has Interpol checked on any individual buying cell phone parts or multiple phones from one supplier?

"Thanks people, each of these questions are relevant to our investigation and Debra and I will now try to answer each question listed which we known will probably lead to additional questions. That is fine because we want to zero in on what may be the most logical place to start.

I will answer questions 1, 4 and 5. Interpol is still gathering the detailed information we all are seeking, and they have promised to forward their summarized results to us in a few days. They have previously stated it is a lot of information, but what has been analyzed thus far, they feel very little of it leads to any meaningful conclusions.

Question 2; they were all males.

Question 3; The killing we studied, the explosive area was very limited and not extending very far from the victim. Debra will answer the balance of the questions."

"Thanks Jack. gave his answers to numbers 1,4 and 5. I am also confident that Interpol data will probably be available soon based upon their summary investigation. I can also add that Interpol is interviewing close relatives and contacts of the deceased.

In response to question 6, and 7, we will know more when we see the Interpol report. We can also ask those questions the next time we talk with them."

"We have provided you every bit of information we have received and both Debra and I understand it doesn't even get us near to a solution.

Prior to our meeting, had any of you heard about these incidents?"

No one responded.

"Interesting; probably because each event was in a different country, and it did not involve any well-known personality. Hopefully the little knowledge we have will grow quickly, so we can begin heading in the winning direction.

I now suggest we break for lunch here at the hotel and when we return from lunch, we will suggest some areas each of you can investigate.

Lastly, during all phases of our investigating, we would appreciate if everyone kept all our efforts under wraps for the safety of all."

CHAPTER 15

The group reconvened to the conference meeting room after lunch.

Jack again opened the meeting. "I am beginning to wonder if we arranged this meeting too early without having any evidence and analyzed data from Interpol. We have so little information making it difficult to make decisions. Since it is clear, what we only know is five people have been murdered in a similar fashion. So, this is where we start.

"May I say something?"

"Sure Anna."

"To all of us here today, I wish to remind everyone that not all cases are open and shut. In some cases, they sit for years before we learn who did what to whom.

It is never too early to start looking at a situation like one facing us now. Yes, we don't know much but maybe in the coming days, clues may become available and any one of us may find the proverbial needle in a haystack.

The skills gathered here today would put fear into the hearts of the villains if they got wind of our meeting. It is the reason you invited us.

"I know Boris has something to add to my comments and I'll let him speak now."

"Jack, Debra, Anna said the right things. We do have the skill set to solve this mystery. Once we start using our individual skills, something will occur to lead us to where we want to go.

Give us our assignments so we can start the research and if we are lucky, you and Debra can get another gold star."

The other contacts laughed and applauded Boris's comments.

"Thanks, guys, for your truthful and pointed comments and your trust in everyone's abilities. Here is how I envision we will start.

Anna, Ethan, and Franz. I would like you to see what you can learn from your contacts without raising suspicions. Maybe a story line: like I heard some guy got blown up in Paris. What's going on in this world?

Boris, you have the computer skills to search places most people would not be aware existed and if you find the hidden secrets, we can move onto more normal investigating.

Franz, now spoke. "Because of what we know now, there will be nothing normal about this investigation. You have multiple killers roaming in a vast territory using weapons yet to be identified and there are only exponential clues. Nothing meaningful yet, but we will find something to investigate.

Please, let's stay in touch with each other so we don't duplicate our efforts. When you hit a wall let everyone know and when you hit upon something interest, also let us know because we can then divide the work and look at multiple possibilities."

"Thanks Anna, Boris, and Franz for your words. and thanks to all of you for coming to help us.

Some good did come out of our meeting. We got to see each other once more after being apart for a couple of years. We have a mystery to solve but tonight let's dine in style, raise a few glasses to our friendship and just enjoy being together for the evening. You can all plan on leaving tomorrow except Boris and his wife are going to do the tourist bit while Debra and I get back to work.

Please send me a note regarding your expenses and we will ensure they are remitted promptly along with a suitable consultant's fee. Let's meet here in the lobby at eight and I'm buying the drinks and Debra is covering the dining. Let's have some fun."

The group spent the evening having fun and remembering the good times and tough times they spend together. They also remembered the number of successes they experienced working with Debra and Jack long before the couple really knew each other.

The friends all agreed the duo of Jack and Debra is the best team capable of solving almost any problem in the spy world.

They all went to bed happy knowing together, this team would be hard to beat.

CHAPTER 16

Early the next morning, everyone met in the hotel lobby to say goodbye to

Franz, Anna, and Ethan who arranged a car to the airport. Boris and his wife planned on doing some sightseeing during the day.

Jack and Debra would spend their time arranging their possessions and would move into their new apartment tomorrow to begin a new life as a successful French couple from the wine area of Bordeaux.

It would have been an unexciting day except for the call from Interpol.

"Jack, Perry here, we have another murder and this time it's in Portugal. At this moment, I'm not sure of who got killed but it was by an explosive, detonated at his business. We should have more complete details in the next hour, and I will forward them to you.

How did your meeting go?"

"It went well even though we were short of details, our contacts understand the situation and will begin their research starting tomorrow. They are all long established in their respective areas and know the ins and outs of the underworld. I would except some responses in a few days."

"I don't want to rush our investigators who will provide a lot of data on the previous killings, but I do expect it will be available very soon. They all know how hot this situation is and it seems to be getting worse."

"Thanks Perry, Debra and I will move into our apartment tomorrow and we could use some help getting decent computers and someone to install software to link us with your team. We could then quickly share all our findings and try to compare them to what your guys are finding."

"Send me the address and we will provide the equipment and set-up for you. I'll try to talk to you later."

"Okay, we'll stay in touch."

Debra had walked into the room and overheard part of the conversation.

"Another killing. Where was it?"

"Portugal, but not details are available yet. Perry said he would inform us as soon as he feels he has a complete picture. He also will send a technician to our apartment to set up a computer network so we can work closer to the Interpol team."

"I hope this killing trend does not become a daily event. We must get our program working quickly and let all our contacts know we are all on a fast track."

"I'll inform them of the latest killing, and they will get the message. No fun times until this mystery is solved."

"It's okay, you will probably forget about that thought within two days."

Jack laughed and they both returned to the job of preparing for their move.

They were almost finished packing when Perry called again.

"Here is the latest on the Portugal killing and it is rather interesting but no help whatsoever in painting a complete picture. The guy was just a salesperson for a paper company. He had lived there almost twenty years, Married with two kids, no political ties, no legal issues, or any other questionable behavior. Just an average guy. Jack, we are at a loss because we keep thinking the next victim will provide clues, we need to solve this case. Unfortunately, no such luck."

"Sorry Perry, I wish we could contribute something to help you, but

nothing fits together. It's a puzzle with too many pieces. I sense there is something we are missing, but I can't put my finger on it yet. More than likely, there will be more killings and eventually a mistake will be made by the killer and the true story will begin to unfold.

Let's hope my contacts will be able to provide some useful information soon."

Jack's hope was based upon the varied backgrounds and specialties of each contact. Although they were all friends, they were raised in different countries, they could all speak multiple languages and the each had extensive experience working with illegal arms dealers.

Ethan was born and raised in Russia and was college educated and had been trained in an elite section of the KGB, now called the GRU. He spoke perfect English along with three other European languages. He maintained strong relationships in Russia and elsewhere.

Anna was raised in the Netherlands and had resided in Belgium for many years. She was known for her knowledge of military alliances between dictators normally kept secret from outsiders. Her knowledge of many countries' activities put her life in danger, and she has maintained a security force for personal protection,

Franz raised in Germany had been an active illegal arms trader until he met Jack who convinced there was more earning power being a spy. They have been friends for many years and Jack has used his knowledge several times to capture illegal dealers.

Boris was Jack's closest Russian friend while he was a CIA agent in Russia and Jack learned his computer hacking skills from Boris and used many programs Boris had developed to gather information or in some cases to remove cash from selected bank accounts.

All the contacts had previous partnerships with either Jack or Debra when they both were active CIA agents. They maintained their relationships after Jack and Debra retired and they all attended their wedding two years ago in the United States.

Together as a team, led by Jack and Debra, they would eventually help gather enough information and clues to bring justice for those that died and prison time for the suspects.

CHAPTER 17

The couple woke early on their move day, ordered room service for breakfast, and continued to finish their packing. They had arranged a car to transport them to their rental unit and would leave the hotel by noon.

The leasing agent was there to greet them and to ensure everything went smoothly during the move.

After the agent left, Jack and Debra rearranged some of the furnishings to make space for the computers and accessories where they would spend a lot of time during the investigation of the numerous explosive murders.

The Interpol technician arrived later in the afternoon, and it took him less than one hour to connect the hardware and install new software. Jack was familiar with the setup and would have no difficulties operating the system. He would also install additional software Boris had created to assist Jack's possible hacking attempts.

By dinner time, they had unpacked, arranged furniture, tested the computers and were ready to eat.

"Tomorrow, I will go to the market and try to get us essentials, so we can start eating at home. It might take two trips."

"While you are doing that, I will prepare an email with all the latest news to share with the contacts. It also strikes me that two of the dead men were not politically active and just average businesspeople. In fact, they were in totally unrelated businesses. We'll talk more about this when you return from the market."

"Bye honey."

After Debra left, Jack continued to dwell on this one thought but, then decided it could be just a killer getting even with an old foe. There were more important things to learn about the people who had died because of their political beliefs. He continued his thought process but still without more data from Interpol, he had hit a roadblock like Perry was experiencing.

Debra returned from her shopping and Jack helped putting the items where he felt they belonged. Soon, the chores were complete, and they could now begin to discuss what they had learned and what they need to know to proceed with a meaningful investigation.

"Honey, here is what we now know. Multiple killings in different countries mainly against political opponents of dictators and those in powerful positions. There have been two murders where there is no known connection about the deaths because of opposing political oppression.

All were murdered using a similar explosive device of unknown manufacture and untraceable materials. This is where we are today."

"I agree, so what we need is some Interpol input regarding everyone.

and any conclusions about possible interconnections between each of the murdered victims. There will be something which may spark a thought and maybe an exploratory avenue for us to follow."

As Debra finished saying her thoughts, her phone rang, and it was Ethan from Belgium.

"Hi Ethan, what's new?"

"Debra, I just spoke to a Russian friend, and he told me he had heard from another source that the explosive devices can be purchased from a European country. He did not say which country, but it rules out the Middle East, Russia and China and other Far Eastern countries. It is still a lot of countries to search but it might make our search a little easier."

"Thanks Ethan. We will pass the info to Interpol and the rest of the team. Stay safe and keep up the good work."

After disconnecting from Ethan, she immediately provided the news to Jack. He then posted emails containing the new information to Interpol and the other team members.

"Ethan is right when he says our job may have gotten a lot easier since we can now contain our search boundaries within Europe. It's still a lot of territory but at least we have made one positive step forward."

Jack and Debra continued to discuss the many unknown factors that still required answers before they could proceed further. They went to bed that night with a pile of thoughts without answers.

The next day did not bring them a new news and Interpol had not received calls of additional murders relating to explosives. It would remain quiet for a few more days.

Suddonly, Interpol advised them a report was being delivered to their apartment along with significant data collected by their agents. They were requested to read the report, study the data, and advise Interpol of their conclusions.

Interpol would then compare their findings with there own analysis and hopefully some solid clues would emerge.

Jack would read the report and Debra would take notes and ask questions. It took them just over three hours to read the report and conclusions by Interpol. It took another two hours to interpret all the data collected about each victim.

An initial summary by Interpol concluded three of the six victims were active political spokespersons against a regime or a political opponent. Their criticism was directed at different leaders of different countries, and they were most likely killed by order of the regime being criticized.

Three other victims were unrelated to the other killings. They were not active on any social media site nor were they noteworthy within their respective communities. They did have one thing in common. They all were born and schooled in Poland before two of them moved to their new homes and careers in the UK and Spain.

"Debra, here is a very interesting connection. A police chief gets killed in Poland. A car dealer gets killed in the UK and a paper salesman gets killed in Portugal. All three were born and raised in Poland. Someone in Poland doesn't like his former country men and we are going to find out why, and who their friend is who wanted them dead."

CHAPTER 18

It was morning in Kolobrzeg and Pauli had just opened the popcorn company for business. He had a store manager to take care of business while he stayed in his private lab manufacturing devices totally unrelated to the popcorn business.

Cool Poloch came to see him and told him it was urgent they speak in private.

"Pauli, the last killing of the guy in Portugal may have opened a can of worms. This is the third guy to get hit and I am sure Interpol will learn they are all from Poland. They will start asking questions of family and friends to determine a connection. They will determine their past and your relationship to them when you were classmates.

I believe you have less than one week to get out of Poland and set up somewhere new with a new identity and some money. We can then continue selling your product and because of its success, we can raise the price. Staying here is dangerous for you."

"Those three bastards deserved what they got. They beat on me daily and stole my lunch money all the time. They may have forgot but I didn't and now they are dead, and I got even with them.

You know I have a wife and kids here. What am I to do?

"Would you prefer prison for the rest of your life or a new life? Your wife can always sell the business and have enough to live on forever. You can only rot in prison."

"Oh my god. I never thought I would get caught."

"You haven't been caught yet, but time is not on your side.

Every bad guy makes a mistake, and it only takes one to get caught. If you had killed just one of your tormentors maybe you would have been okay, but you chose three and their history will incriminate you. You have very little time to make your choice."

"Where will I go and how much money do I need?"

"I am not sure where we will go at this point and where we will end up. But I can quickly get you and myself new identities for about 4000 Zlolys for each of us. My guess is we will need between two to three million Zlolys to get ourselves settled and have enough for equipment, housing, and other stuff to continue the business."

"The bank will question my withdrawal of so much money. It will be hard to keep it from my wife."

"Tell, the bank, you're buying another business and it must be finalized rapidly or the owner may change his mind about selling. Tell them it's another candy store and a confidential sale and they are not to tell anyone including your wife.

Start the process today and you will arrange a money transfer in three days to the seller. I can get you a new account in a European Bank using your new identity and that is where the money will be sent."

"I have about six million in the bank, and I will withdraw two to three million which leaves my wife enough to live on for quite a while plus she can run the business or sell both stores because they sit on prime land across from the beach. I will begin the money process after you leave."

"Let me take a quick picture of you to start the new identity process. Trust me, the guy doing the work will make us both look different. I will also find a temporary place for us to go until we can select a more permanent location.

You should also begin to pack the equipment and materials needed to continue our operation and I will rent a vehicle to transport all of it."

Pauli didn't really want to move and especially leave his wife and kids but, he also did not want to spend the rest of his life in prison for being an instigator to murder. He told the store manager he had a meeting at the bank and would return later in the day.

He wasn't sure where he was going but he trusted his nephew and he had successfully created untraceable explosives and now, like the explosives, he would make himself untraceable.

Chapter 19

Jack had called Perry at Interpol and advised him of Ethan's comment, that the explosive devices were being manufactured in a European country.

Now, we have a direct killing link of three people from Poland with no political agenda. There must be another reason as this is not normal nor a coincidence. This is the first obvious connection we have, and I strongly feel, the investigation must start in Poland.

Perry agreed and he would gather a team familiar with Poland and immediately assign them to find the truth and search for the manufacturer of the deadly devices. He suggested that a daily briefing would be appropriate, and Jack agreed.

Neither Jack nor Debra spoke Polish and there was no time to begin learning a new language. They knew Interpol will help us with the language barrier and our team probably doesn't need to know the language because many of their contacts speak many languages.

Jack composed a lengthy email to the team regarding Interpol results and specifically about the Polish connection of three of the victims. He relied on his intuition suggesting the explosive devices were being made in Poland and he asked them to start looking immediately using their contacts and try to determine if his intuition was valid.

He received confirmation from the entire team of their initiating an investigation to find the source making and selling the deadly devices, Jack was confident that between the Interpol team and his team, things would happen rapidly.

"Debra, I am wondering, what relationship the dead men had with the killer or maybe the device maker? It certainly raises a lot of questions which are not answered with the data we received.

Are they related and this is a family thing, or did they treat the killer badly either physically or financially, or is it something else?"

"All logical questions but I think logic doesn't work well when you're dealing with a madman. He maybe getting revenge, or he realized he had invented something he finally could be doing successfully. Maybe, he doesn't care who gets killed if he makes a lot of money.

No sense in guessing and hopefully we'll eventually get logical answers."

"We have some sharp people working on this case and I expect answers to all our questions will be to flow. First as a drizzle and then a downpour and we will get the answers to all our questions."

There was not much left to do and so all they could do was wait three or four days for results.

Chapter 20

Pauli being a long-time banking customer with a substantial balance was able to convince the bank of his immediate need of 2.5 million Zlotys or approximately, 500,000 American dollars. He told the bank he would arrange an international transfer in two days.

Meanwhile, his nephew had already completed the fake identity process, arranged a vehicle to transport the equipment and he obtained travel documentation for them to leave on a ferry from Kolobrzeg to Rostock, Germany in two days.

From Rostock they would then travel using their vehicle, to Schwerin Germany where they would remain until more permanent housing could be arranged.

Once Pauli had his new documentation, he arranged a money transfer to a Mr. Adelbert Schmidt at the German Bank of Rostock. He also had completed packing his equipment for transfer to their new location.

The nephew picked up the equipment the next morning and told Pauli to meet him at the Rostock ferry tomorrow at 8 am and they would board the ferry and depart to a new life.

Pauli had written a final letter to his wife admitting he was in trouble and leaving for his own protection. She assumed ownership of the two businesses and there were sufficient funds in the bank to last her for years. He was sorry it had to end this way and not to try and find him.

He had already boarded the ferry and was on his way with his wife's nephew headed for Rostock, approximately 100 miles from Kolobrzeg.

There, they would drive to Schwerin where the nephew, through ex-con friends, had arranged a small house for them to stay for up to three months while looking for a safe final residence.

Two days later, they once again changed identities and Pauli Zukowski alias Adelbert Schmidt became Otto Weber. Cool Polack became Hans Fischer as an attempt to erase their paper trail from Poland to Germany.

CHAPTER 21

On the third day of the Jack's team investigation, Franz called Jack with a possible clue. A person selling the devices was an unnamed felon who had served at least a few years in a Polish prison for robbery and other crimes. He was only known as Cool Poloch, and it will take awhile to figure out his real name.

Franz had no information as to what company or person was manufacturing the devices.

For Jack, it was a start and perhaps Interpol can determine the real identity of Cool Poloch. It was a good start but without more details, it wasn't very useful.

Nothing else emerged over the next week. Then to everyone's surprise, another murder took place in Sweden at the home of a Russian exile and known to be fervently against Putin as a dictator. The explosive provided the same result as the prior explosive murders, and it will be another statistic for Interpol and others to study.

Neither Jack and Debra nor Interpol were any closer than they were six weeks ago, and frustration set in among the many people working to solve the case.

Debra suddenly had an instinct to maybe turn the investigation in another direction.

"Let's think about this Jack. We've run out of luck doing the normal investigation stuff. So why not steer the ship in a new direction? The guy is making big money on his sales but, where is the money going? Maybe you and Boris aught to practice your magic bank tricks and see what you can find.

Remember the old saying darling, follow the money."

"My beautiful wife did it again. Brilliant idea. I'm calling Boris now.

Hey Boris, it's me your favorite hacking partner. How did you and Natasha enjoy Paris?"

"We had a great time but that is not why you called. I bet You need help finding something."

"You are right Boris. Debra suggested we try to follow or find the money because she senses whoever it is, must be bringing in some big bucks. More than likely, it's in Poland. So, she wants us to do our magic bank tricks. Are you ready to go or do you need some time?"

"If money is involved, I am ready to go. I can do from here or we can meet at your place in Paris so the wife can help the economy."

"Paris sounds great, and you can stay at our place."

"Give me two days to get my equipment ready and I'll text our plans.

Start picking out banks we want to target, and we'll figure out what approach will work. See you in two days."

Jack hung up the phone and he and Debra decided they better get the second bedroom ready for their guests. When that was done, they went to the dining area where the computers were located.

"We can work here honey. We won't be using this room for anything else.

I will start looking at the various bank organizations in Poland. Maybe Interpol can provide some guidance. I'll give Perry a call tomorrow.

Let's quit for today and go out for a casual dinner at one of the local cafes."

"That's fine with me. I'll be ready in about five minutes."

They found a small café and enjoyed dinner and wine. It was late when they strolled back to the apartment. They set the alarm for eight am knowing they would be researching Polish banks most of the day.

When Boris arrives, they would have very long stressful days trying to find some clues about the dark money.

CHAPTER 22

Prior to Boris's arrival, Jack, with some input from Interpol, began to search. for the major banking organizations in Poland. The major banks totaled twenty and when he added in foreign international banks the number exceeded forty.

This would be a difficult search because Jack realized the major banks alone had facilities in every major city and town and the number could exceed more than two hundred. Hopefully the major banks identify the accounts of large depositors.

It is even more difficult since the person they would be trying to identify is nameless. Then I would have to investigate every large depositor without knowing even where they reside.

Boris arrived later in the day with Natasha and when the four went to dinner, they began to assess the challenge they would have without any knowledge of a person's name, a city or town where they might reside and which of the forty banks do they use to wash their funds?

Debra had thought of this and asked Boris a question.

"What do we think one of the devices used in the killings may cost? My guess would be ten thousand or more. So why not look for a depositor who deposits that amount weekly or every two weeks?"

"The difficulty Debra is there are thousands of small businesses who deposit funds in the amounts you suggested weekly. Without an account name or a business name, we are nowhere. My guess would be this person or persons own a small business to hide their illicit cash flows.

Maybe we only look for small businesses. In fact, since this is a technical device, then it is being made by a techie. Just maybe, it might be a business in the tech sales or repair business. Maybe we start there and as more information is gathered, we begin a search specifically targeted towards those types of businesses. What do you think Jack?"

"First, I believe your thoughts and Debra's mesh very well and you hit the nail on the head when you said a tech business. The maker is not a stupid guy, because this is a dangerous assembly, and you better know what you are doing or have your ass blown away.

Secondly, I don't think we can proceed without knowing a city or town or even an area. Poland has a population of 37 million people living in almost 900 cities and towns. Even knowing a name isn't a big help because more than likely there are 100 people with that same name living in 100 different cities or towns. Once more, I may be premature in trying to chase the money, this is an extremely complex case, but this discussion just jolted by brain. We know the people from Poland who were killed probably knew the killer before they were killed.

I'm calling Perry now."

"Perry, I am trying to determine the name of the killer. The people who died knew him. So how did they know him is currently a mystery but should be easy to find.

Did they all go to school together? Did they go to church together? Are they related? Where did they all live in their youth? There is a solution buried in those questions. How fast can we get an answer?"

"We are working on those very issues now. The only thing we have proven, is they all lived in Kolobrzeg."

"Perry, you're my hero. When you get more let me know. We're going to start chasing money. Again, thanks."

"You're welcome and good luck to you and your team."

"Boris, we are going to work."

They all left the café smiling and quickly walked back to the apartment where Boris and Jack would begin their computer magic to find answers.

CHAPTER 23

The four of them returned to the recently rented apartment and Jack and Boris immediately headed for the computers. Boris had brought his own equipment and software to accommodate a search.

"Jack, you look at the population of Kolobrzeg and then the number of banks, and I will find small businesses involved in technical work. Those chores shouldn't take more than five minutes. Ready set go."

"Boris this is easy. The population is 47 thousand and there are at least ten banks. What did you find?"

"I found two TV repair shops and four computer sales and repair shops."

"Well let's get started and try to get into Bank of Kolobrzeg. Use your computer Boris as I am sure it's more suited to hacking then Interpol's computers."

Boris typed in the bank name in Polish and then tried to sign-in as a guest. At the beginning it appeared to be easy, but when he attempted other sign-ins leading to a look at their account listings, up popped a warning notification; "Entry Denied".

He opened a different software package he had created, and he had named, Walk Around. It was designed to avoid firewalls and other malware blockages. His first attempt almost got to where he wanted to go, and another notification appeared as a warning.

Well, he thought, if at first you don't succeed, try, try, try again. This time he used another software tool and suddenly his screen lit up with a menu of choices including daily account activity. He clicked on the icon and typed in the name of the first tv repair shop.

Invalid Account was the only reply. He then typed in the second name and again, he saw the same answer. He repeated this process for the four computer shops and only one had an open account.

He returned to the main menu and typed in account activity for Hans Computer sales and repair.

The screen changed and he was able to see the daily deposits and withdrawals of the account. The largest deposit over a four-week span was equivalent to one thousand six hundred American dollars.

"Jack, no good news from this Bank, Give me another name."

"BNP Parabas. See if that works."

After Boris was able to investigate just four of the ten banks, he could find no large deposits by any businesses. He concluded this was a waste of time.

"Well Jack, that didn't work but maybe I should return to each of the banks and see if I can seek depositors of more than ten thousand per month. If I find some, I can then look at their weekly amounts."

"Can I help in any way?"

"Sure, tomorrow have Debra take Natasha shopping. We've got a lot of hacking to do."

Jack could only laugh and assured Boris, "Debra will be happy to get away for some shopping time."

They ended their searches and shut down all the computers. They went to their respective bedrooms and promised they would begin again tomorrow.

Chapter 24

They all woke up early and decided to go out for breakfast and later return to their search efforts. After breakfast Debra and Natasha left for their shopping tour and Boris and Jack walked back to the apartment to again try to find a connection between a business and large cash deposit.

Boris started his computers and began a relook at each of the banks in the area and soon he was finding many accounts which consistently deposited large sums of cash.

One by one, he began to rule out grocery, furniture, department, automotive and other related stores. He concentrated on smaller businesses involved in selling niche items.

Hour by hour he continued his search and had already looked at seven banks without anything to attract his attention. It was the eighth bank where he found an account with large deposits, about the size of the estimated cost of a device as suggested by Debra. After further looking at the numbers and dates, he learned, it was a candy store.

The funds deposited were a few hundred Polish Slotys every third or fourth day and then a forty or fifty thousand Slotys would show up.

This was equivalent to about ten or more thousand American dollars. Very suspicious for a candy store.

This pattern repeated itself periodically over the past few months and grabbed Boris's attention.

"Jack, in what months did each murder occur for each victim. I need to know that now."

"I'll call Perry and get the information for you."

Jack immediately called his contact at Interpol who provided the information."

"Here is what I got Boris, starting with the first murder. All of these occurred in the later part of last year. First one in August, next one in October, two in November and then one in January and one in February. I hope that helps you."

"Thanks Jack and now I will shock you. Large deposit in July, another one in September and two large ones in October and another two in in early January. All from a candy store in Kolobrzeg."

"Give the name of the store Boris as I will call Perry back and have his agents contact the Bank."

"It is the Kolobrzeg Candy Shop."

"Perry. I think we have a solid clue and t would require your agents to interview the bank to get more complete information. The store name is Kolobrzeg Candy Shop and we have been able to confirm large, unusual deposits for last year in July, September, October, and January of this year.

They correspond to the dates you gave me about the explosive victims. Obviously, the circumstantial evidence maybe just a coincidence but your agents can determine whether this is fact or fiction. I'll send you dates and amounts in a few minutes."

"Jack, great work and how you got this info would be interesting, but I don't have a need to know. I'll get the right people to investigate starting tomorrow. By the end of the day, we will know all about the owner and his current location information.

If it is factual, we have a lot of people to start working on a much narrower investigation thanks to your team. I'll be in touch with you tomorrow."

"Boris let's quit for the day. The ladies will be home soon with all their assorted purchases, and we can all go out and have a good dinner. We deserve it based upon what you accomplished today."

"That's wonderful Jack and I will be anxious to hear the news from Interpol tomorrow. We can do an ownership search ourselves tomorrow as a separate piece of evidence we can then compare to Interpol's findings."

"It should be easy to do and what we learn we can provide to the rest of the team to keep our investigation moving towards a solution.

CHAPTER 25

Pauli and Cool Poloch or known now as Otto Weber and Hans Fischer had settled into their temporary home in Schwerin Germany and continued the manufacture and sales of explosive devices to just about anyone who could pay the high price and needed an untraceable weapon.

Hans suggested to Otto since business was good, they should rent a house in a rural part of Germany, and it should be well isolated from nosey neighbors. He also told Otto; they should never reveal their correct names nor where they intended to live. Hans knew from experience how loose lips can result in long prison terms.

Otto was smart enough to realize that sooner or later, one of his customers will get caught with a device in his possession. Interpol will offer a short sentence to the felon for information to track down Pauli. Hence, he okayed the suggestion to rent a house and asked Hans to start looking immediately.

It took about five weeks to find a house in an ideal location. They had agreed to rent a deserted farmhouse west of Bremen and close to the border of the Netherlands. Additionally, it would be less then a couple of hours from Belgium and France. They knew they would always need an escape route.

They moved one week after signing rental agreements for the farmhouse without telling anybody where they were going. I fact, they packed and loaded all their equipment and possessions into a rented truck and disappeared into the night. Two days later they moved into the farmhouse.

Hans drove the empty truck to the Netherlands where he returned it to the rental agency and then bought a used car to drive back to his new home.

Otto and Hans knew nothing about conversations between the Kolobrzeg bank and Interpol. Nor did they suspect they were being sought by Jack's team and several European federal agencies.

Being on a most wanted list never entered their mind nor was it their goal.

Chapter 26

The day after discovering the candy shop and its varied deposits matching the month prior to the murders, Jack and Boris set out to determine who were the owners of the shop.

Searching government records of established businesses took little time and they began to gather historical information about the shop ownership.

The shop was more than forty years old and had been established by Jakub Zukowski and after he died the business was transferred to his son Pauli Zukowski. The business thrived under the ownership of Pauli, but his dream was to do something great in the field of chemistry. The discovering how to make explosive trace material become untraceable was his great accomplishment.

It led to his developing bombs for the purpose of killing people including those that had harmed him as a youth. And finally, it led to his leaving his business and his family only to make bombs.

About two months ago, ownership was transferred to Pauli's wife, Marie Zukowski.

Now Boris and Jack had a name and because of the recent transfer, they assumed Pauli Zukowski was their man. Later discussions with Interpol validated the team's guess.

Bank discussions and further work by Interpol investigators revealed Pauli along with his wife's nephew had left Kolobrzeg around two months ago. Pauli had withdrawn a large sum of money on the pretext of buying another candy store. The money was retrieved all in cash by Adelbert Schmidt at a bank branch in Rostock Germany. The bank had a video of the transaction, but it did not resemble Pauli or the nephew. From there, the trail ended.

"Well Boris, we did a good job, but the trail has gotten cold. We have names which probably have been changed and maybe even their looks may be very different. I will let the others know of our little success and from all appearances we again have the whole of Europe to search. Poland was only the starting point."

"Jack, now I doubt if I can contribute any more to this case but if you need some additional computer search, you have my number. Natasha and I will return to Russia in the next day or so."

"Thanks Boris, you helped quite a bit but now we need to get more active on the street. I am sure they have set up a lab to manufacture the devices, but where is anybody's guess. I'll keep you updated on our progress and findings and if you feel you can contribute, your welcome to try."

Jack contacted the other team members and Debra and Jack said their goodbyes to Natasha and Boris as they left to return to Russia.

Jack and Debra returned to the planning mode and started to plot what would be their future actions. They speculated it was now their brains against those of a madman intent on killing anybody without remorse.

"Jack, maybe we can become big time buyers and trap the seller into meeting us. How about an order for ten devices going to the Iranian hitmen or the Russian mafia doing good deeds for Putin."

"Good idea. I was thinking something similar but maybe using our contacts to find a serious buyer and dupe him into buying for us and at least try to learn where their main operation is located. Searching all of Europe requires a lot of eyes and we don't even know what Pauli looks like now."

They went back and forth with additional scenario's without concluding anything. Success sometimes shows up using the wildest of thoughts.

They finally tired themselves out and decided to try to sleep with some of the thoughts still on their mind and perhaps wake up with a new and brazen plan.

They woke up rather late the following morning and soon were sitting in the kitchen area having their breakfast,

"How did you sleep honey?" Jack asked.

""It feels like I tossed and turned all night, and I ran out of ideas and today I'm not sure what direction to take. How about you?"

"Just about the same. We got so close and yet we are no closer to solving this case then we were when we started. Damn, I hate it when I hit a wall without a clue. Maybe we take a step back and let our contacts try to find a new avenue for us to travel."

"It's a good idea Jack. Any information from our contacts at least will give us something new to investigate. Two months have slipped by, and we are back to step one again. The bomb maker is still doing his evil trade, but the day will come when he trips and maybe we will be there to catch him."

CHAPTER 27

Approximately 250 miles from Paris in the small town of Halsdorf Germany, southeast of Dusseldorf, a man entered the only post office in town to mail a package. When the man approached the clerk, she had an eerie feeling about him.

Halsdorf is town of about 85 people and the clerk, who had been born there, new almost every family by their first name. She immediately knew this man did not live there.

"Can I help you sir", she asked in German.

The man hesitated to answer her as if he was trying to remember the proper German words. "Thank you, I want to send this package to a friend."

The clerk had recently read a Post office alert from Interpol regarding small packages containing bombs. Two things troubled the clerk. One her instinctive feeling about him and the alert. She then stepped on a switch below the counter to activate a hidden camera and audio system.

"Per postal regulations, I have to ask you, what is in the package sir?"

"That is ok. It is a small gift to a friend. Just a cigarette box."

Based upon his broken German phases, the clerk suspected otherwise but accepted his explanation.

"That will be forty-two Euros sir."

The man paid the amount requested and handed the package to the clerk. She gave him a receipt and he casually left the post Office.

There was another customer waiting who the clerk knew and she quickly said to him, "See if you can get the license number of the man's car who just left. It may be important."

The man stepped outside and looked in the direction the man had taken when he left the post office. He entered an older model Opel, and the man could only read the first three numbers on the license plate as the car sped away.

The man returned into the post office. "Frieda, the man is driving an old Opel and he had a Belgium plate with the first three numbers of 128. I am sorry, that is all I could see."

"It's okay Rolf, it may be nothing. Just a woman's instinct, let me get your mail for you."

She handed the mail to the man, and after he left, she reviewed the alert again and called the number on the Interpol alert.

"Hello, I wish to speak to someone with knowledge of the bomb alert recently distributed to the post office."

"Can I have your name please and then I will switch you to a person who can help you."

"My name is Frieda Steinmann, and I am a clerk in the post office in Halsdorf."

"One moment please."

"Hello, I am inspector Wolfson, I understand you are calling about the alert recently transmitted to all German and European post offices. So, how may I assist you?"

"Less than twenty minutes ago, a man walked into my post office, and I just didn't feel right about him. Halsdorf is a small town and I know most of the people here, but I knew he was not from here.

He wanted to mail a small package to a friend he said but his German was broken and not to understandable. I turned on our hidden camera and recorded our transaction.

After the man left, I had another customer go out and see he they could identify his car and get a license number. He got the car model and the first three digits of the number of a car registered in Belgium."

"Frieda, put that package safely away and far from yourself and customers. I am sending a couple of agents to your post office, and they should arrive in about thirty minutes. They will identify themselves to you and they will want the package and video plus the car information.

You have been very helpful, but we do not know if this is what we are looking for, but you have done a good deed today; regardless. Lastly, please do not mention anything about this incident to anybody except the agents."

"Thank you, inspector, I will ask someone to handle my duties while I meet with the agents, and I understand the need of secrecy."

As Inspector Wolfson had told Frieda, the agents arrived in just over thirty minutes and identified themselves to her.

"Freida, start from the beginning and tell us the story you told Inspector Wolfson."

Frieda repeated what she had told the inspector over the phone and added the time the man entered the post office and when he left. She also provided the car description and the first three digits of the Belgium license plate, 128.

The agent then asked to see the package and Frieda retrieved it from where she had placed it. The agents noted the send to address and the sender's address.

"Freida, do you recognize the senders address?"

"Strange, it is an address of a town close by, but I do not recognize the street address and I know that town."

"It's probably another sign of a felon trying to hide." One of the agents suggested.

Let's look at the video on a computer and you can send us a copy to my phone while we are here to ensure we receive it."

The video clearly showed the man and the clerk during the entire transaction. The agents made no comments concerning the man.

The task took about ten minutes and the agents thanked Frieda and informed her they would let her know what they find in the package. The agents had been assigned to this inspection from the very beginning and believed they recognized the man in the video.

They left the post office knowing the postal clerk may have supplied the agents a very significant lead.

CHAPTER 28

Immediately after leaving the Halsdorf post office, one of the agents placed a call to their supervisor at the Interpol facility in Luxembourg to report their findings and request assistance.

"Lucas, James, and I believe we are in possession of a significant clues to the untraceable bomber case. Please arrange to have a bomb squad expert available when we return in about forty-five minutes. We have a package for him to check out.

We also have a clear video of the suspect sending the package to a potential killer. I believe we will be able to identify him as Fillip Curie, the nephew of Pauli Zukowski's wife Marie.

The post office clerk supplied us part of a license number to the suspect's car. It was an older model Opel with a Belgium plate starting with the numbers 128. We should get that run through the ownership, sales, or registration records to try and find a match.

Based upon the identity of the suspect, we believe we could be on a path towards a solution to this case."

"Great job guys. I'll get the bomb experts here immediately to investigate what is in the package and I will assign someone to begin search the auto records.

I will also call Senior Leader Perry in Paris to let him know of our discovery."

After the call from the two agents, Lucas placed a call to Perry, the Senior Leader for this case.

"Perry, Lucas from the Luxembourg office. I want to report a significant step in the bomber case. A post office clerk in Germany became suspicious of a customer who wanted to send a gift to his friend. She had previously read the Interpol alert sent to all post offices. She wisely turned on her hidden video and audio setup and recorded the entire transaction. After the customer left, she called our office to report the matter and we sent two agents to her facility to further investigate.

I have arranged for the bomb squad to be here when the agents return, and I have also assigned an agent to research the automobile he was driving. Lastly, one of the agents investigating believes the man in the video is Fillip Curie, a convicted felon and nephew of Pauli Zukowski's wife.

What else would you suggest we do?"

Lucas, this is exciting news. Here is what I suggest you do.

Take some good pictures of the unopened package. Copy the senders address and the same for the intended recipient and forward both to me.

If the package contains a bomb, the bomb squad will know what steps to take towards analyzing the components of the bomb.

We may reproduce the packaging including the post office identity and send it to the original recipient and see if we can capture a suspected killer.

I want you to notify me for every step you take and immediately report all findings. Remember, we are not only trying to catch a maniac, but we are also trying to save lives.

I await your future calls, and what a fantastic stroke of luck as we were running out of clues."

CHAPTER 29

The bomb squad carefully dissected the package and quickly learned about the materials contained within the bomb housing and what would trigger the detonator.

They determined the bomb could be detonated by a simple pressure switch and activated in ten seconds after the box is opened.

Although the components of the bomb materials fit nicely into a five by six-inch package almost three inches thick, it contained enough explosive and metal ball bearings to kill the average person. There was now seven dead people to prove their findings.

The auto was eventually traced to a used car dealer in the Netherlands who had sold the car to a Hans Fischer, a German Resident living in Schwerin Germany.

All the information regarding the bomb and the vehicle was transmitted to Senior Leader Perry at the Interpol headquarters.

Perry requested photographs of the sender and receiver information from the package along with the exact dimensions of the package and color of the package wrapping.

After receiving the important information, he sent an urgent message to his assistant, Special Agent Bascal and to Jack and Debra to attend an urgent meeting tomorrow at ten am in the Paris office. He requested everyone to respond if they could attend the meeting. He did not specify the details of the meeting.

He arrived at his office at his usual eight am time and started to prepare for the important meeting. His plan was to present what they now knew and in conjunction with his assistant and the assistance of Jack and Debra, together plan a broad approach to capturing the wanted felons.

At ten O'clock all the members invited to this meeting were present and Inspector Perry began his presentation.

"Ladies and Gentlemen, what am about to tell you, now we have some meaningful evidence concerning the bomb manufacturer, his product, his automobile, and his mode of delivering his evil goods to the killers.

We do not know his whereabouts, nor do we know where he gets his materials but what we do know is that he is still making and selling his weapons.

I have prepared a listing of the evidence we obtained yesterday. This evidence came to us via a German postal clerk who had read the alert message we had prepared for wide distribution. We are happy it had been read by this clerk and she acted per our directions.

You will note on the list I gave you; we were able to identify Pauli Zukowski's nephew along with enough auto details to learn when and where he purchased it. We now also have solid knowledge of all the materials used to make the bombs and how they are detonated.

The question now is how do we proceed?

We have already put out feelers for the auto and we suspect it is in Germany. We also have duplicated the package presented to the post office and will mail it to the original suspected receiver from the same post office today. We have already assigned a detail to track that package hourly as it moves towards its destination.

Obviously, we will arrest anybody who picks up the package.

But now the hard part begins and so we have two experienced Interpol staff present and two leading American investigators to see if we can arrive at a well-coordinated plan to capture the two major principles in this scheme.

I will start on the right side of the table and go clockwise to hear each of your suggestions. Inspector Bascal, your first."

CHAPTER 30

Special agent Bascal had been with Interpol for almost twenty years and the past five years, because of his extensive experience, his assignments usually involved difficult cases of serious crimes.

"I am glad to hear of our recent success of gathering evidence. However, the hard work must continue, and I would suggest we talk about a series of investigations into several diverse areas where we might possibly unearth additional clues and perhaps the capture of our prime suspects.

The fist thing that comes to my mind is a phycological study of Pauli Zukowski. What was he like when he ran the candy store and the popcorn factory?

What were his peculiar habits and what relationships did he have with his community?

I ask these questions because I have learned that people do not cast aside there habits easily. They tend to stick to what they have experienced for a long period of time, and we know all of us have difficulty in shedding our habits.

Hence, I would suggest we bring in a psychological professional to provide a clearer picture of our suspect."

Perry thanked Bascal and it was now Jack's turn to speak.

"My experience with this type of crime has been primarily related to illegal arms sales within Europe, Russia, and China. They are diverse countries, but the rogue arms dealers follow the same playbook every day. It is because of them all following similar routines, I was always able to catch them. As Inspector Bascal rightfully stated, it is hard to break a habit or a playbook that has yielded many successes.

My suggestion is search out on the street among the thieves and see if we can buy a bomb or two. Then we push for a very large order and see if we can meet with one of the suspects and then we can try to track him to lead us to Zukowski."

"Debra, what do you think?"

"I agreed with inspector Bascal when he stated we need diverse investigations; Bascal spoke of one and Jack spoke of another. But there are other steps that can be taken which have proven to be successful in other crimes.

The first one I think of is the use of rewards and the second approach is media coverage including photos and historical descriptions of the suspects. There are people who might suspect they live in their neighborhood or perhaps the grocer who delivers foodstuff to an isolated cottage may also wonder who lives there.

These people do not relate to the crime being committed because it is not being committed where they live yet, they could live near the suspects, and they could help us find them.

What we have learned today, is a lot of new information, but we are no closer to solving this crime than we were two months ago."

Perry thanked all of them for their suggestions and then called for a forty-five-minute lunch break.

The Interpol Headquarters had an inhouse cafeteria and all four of the members of the meeting headed for the cafeteria.

CHAPTER 31

Fillip had returned after his short trip to the post office, and he expressed to Pauli his difficulty of using proper German pronunciation. He said he felt a little unsure of himself at the post office and maybe the lady clerk was suspicious of him.

"Did she ask you a lot of questions?"

"No, just what was in the package, and I told her it was a gift to my friend."

"Did she accept your answer."

"Yes, and I paid the shipping fees and took my receipt and left."

"Don't let lowly clerks rattle you. They see a hundred of you daily and really don't care what you are shipping, where it is going or who will receive it. What they care about is your payment so German Postal can pay their wages."

"Yeh, I guess your right. Nothing to get excited about."

"Good, now let's get back to work, we have four more packages to manufacture and get them shipped. Remember, your contacts paid a high cost for these items, and they expect quick deliveries."

CHAPTER 32

The Americans and Interpol personnel finished their lunch and as they returned to the conference room, another person entered the room with the group and handed a note to Perry and then left the room.

Perry shook his head and began to speak. "The note just handed to me contained only four words. Three more murders today."

What he would learn later, is they all occurred in different countries in Europe.

"We now have ten deaths, and the numbers will grow larger if we do nothing. I want a couple of days to put together separate teams to study the suggestions provided this morning. This will be in addition to assigning a phycologist to do a detailed description about Pauli.

Jack and Debra, Now, more than ever, we need your contacts 24/7 to provide any lead they can uncover. Every day represents a potential additional death.

We know about the successes of your contacts and their relationships with the underworld. We will welcome any little bit of information they can provide to us.

Thanks for joining us today and I will update you as to our future."

Jack and Debra left the meeting knowing Perry trusted them to provide a lot of street assistance for the ongoing investigations. They intended to draft an email to their contacts updating them with the latest information and emphasizing working every day until Pauli and his nephew are stopped.

Jack would send a separate email to Boris asking for computer help to determine if the internet is used in the purchase of materials and sales of the device.

Debra would also send an email to their American contact informing them that security around key government officials should be increased. They should also warn individuals posting criticism online targeting specific countries and leaders should be on the lookout for packages sent to them.

CHAPTER 33

Jack had sent the email to all their contacts and he and Debra both were hoping some new clue would show up and the investigations would have a new path to travel.

They were all aware of the danger Pauli presented not only to their countries but potentially the entire world. Particularly if he began to sell his invention to many of the dictatorships in the world.

"Debra, I spent a good part of the night thinking of this case and how to approach it from a different angle. I trust our contacts and hope they provide some useful data, but where does that leave you and me? Should we just sit around and hope something good happens. I don't think so.

Remember when we worked alone without help from anyone and had to use our wits and hoped we didn't get shot? I do and here's what I want you and I to do.

Tomorrow, we travel to Kolobrzeg to find out the relationship between Pauli Zukowski and the three people he arranged to have killed who grew up in the city.

There are people there who knew all of them, classmates, businesspeople, teachers, and neighbors They can tell us an important story that could possibly disrupt our current theories and move us quicker towards a solution."

"Jack, you are right. We did not come here to visit all the cafes nearby our apartment. We came because our government trusted us to assist Interpol in getting this case solved. So tomorrow let's start our trip to Poland and begin our own investigation."

"I'll make arrangements, you begin to pack and include our weapons."

After making the travel arrangements, Jack called Perry and informed him of their plans. "Perry, we are leaving tomorrow for Kolobrzeg to do some snooping on our own. I would like the name and ages of the three men killed who were originally from Kolobrzeg. That is all I need to get started and we will keep you informed of our findings."

"That's fine. I'll send you the information in a few minutes. Your help gives me one less thing for us to do. Good luck and if you need help, call.

By the way, I owed you a call about as a follow-up to the package we intercepted at the Halsdorf post office. The item was sent to mailbox in Italy and, nobody claimed it after thirty days and the mail station returned it to the original sender."

After the phone calls, Jack packed enough for a one week stay and they would fly to Berlin and then rent a car for a three-hour drive to their destination.

They had no thoughts on what they might find but they would not leave until they had satisfactory answers to the many open questions.

CHAPTER 34

Jack and Debra arrived in Kolobrzeg in the afternoon and went straight to the hotel Jack had arranged. After bringing their luggage to their room, they decided to walk along the beachfront and visit both the candy store and the Polish Popcorn Company.

Each of the stores were busy serving tourists enjoying a day of ocean breezes and sunshine, and the couple soon realized they could not find out any information from clerks tending to business.

They went back to their hotel to plan for a less complicated day tomorrow.

Back in their hotel studied the names of the three dead men and their dates of birth. He noted they were born within a few months of each other. Jack quickly concluded they went to school together and more than likely had some sort of relationship with Pauli. What kind of relationship between the various dead men and their killer, needs to be answered, he thought.

Pauli was now close to fifty years old and roughly the same age as the dead men. It may be difficult to find a retired teacher who knew them but rather it might be easier to find former classmates. Both he and

Debra had Interpol ID's and he thought it best to go visit the local police and see if they could offer some help.

Visiting the internet, he found the Kolobrzeg police headquarters and knew, it was the logical place to begin the investigation. He called the headquarters and was routed to a detective familiar with case, who welcomed them to meet with him tomorrow morning.

After a long day, they went to bed early and each had thoughts and questions on their mind as the case began to override all other thoughts.

The next morning after a couple of cups of coffee, they made their way to the city police headquarters. There they met detective Andrzej Kaminski who escorted them to a conference room where they met two other local investigators. After introductions, Andrzej opened the meeting.

"I am happy to greet you here today as we learned of your presence here, is to gather facts about Pauli Zukowski. I believe, we can be very helpful to you. The three of us were about the same age as Pauli, and one of us went to the same school as he attended and at the same time.

So, I expect all of what we can share with you will be helpful. Interesting, up until now, Interpol has not requested our help.

Please ask your questions and we will do our best to answer them."

"Thank you for giving us the time to meet with you and your associates. I am sure each question will lead to others and hopefully at the end of our meeting, we will have a more complete picture of this conflicted individual.

My first question is what sort of relationship did Pauli have with each of the three murdered men? Was it a group relationship with the three of them or one individual to another?"

The officer who attended the same school answered the question.

"First, let me try to describe Pauli as I knew him, and it should answer both of your questions.

Pauli was an ok student academically, but he was also sort of a misfit. He was smaller than most of his classmates, an introvert, and a sheepish person. He was the last child with five other siblings and who probably picked on him since he was the runt of the litter.

Well, he got the same treatment in school and maybe even more painful. Each of the dead individuals was known to be a school bully and Pauli being the littlest and easy to pick on, got treated very badly by the bullies. Not as a group but rather individually.

He obviously never forgot how they hurt him and privately vowed to someday get even with them. They may have forgot but he didn't."

"Thank you for that answer and it brought to light other questions which are also now answered.

After he completed high school, did he go on to college? If so, what was his major?"

Another one of the attendees volunteered to answer that question.

"Pauli was smart and went to a major Polish University where he studied chemistry. He graduated with very good grades and shortly after graduation, his father who owned the candy store, died suddenly and of all the children, only Pauli wanted to run the store.

He was successful using his chemistry background to create new and special flavors never presented by anyone else. The store was big hit with tourists and the word spread that it was the place to visit if you were going to the Kolobrzeg beach.

After about five years he started the Polish Popcorn Company and like the candy store, his variety of colors and flavors brought many customers who loved his popcorn.

He was in his mid-thirties when he was introduced to a lady who was also a chemist and they bonded because of their similar educations. They soon married and had two children. She did not want to work but socialize and tend to the children. They had plenty of money, so it was fine with Pauli.

But he still had dreams of being a world-class chemist and he built a laboratory in the popcorn location to try his skill with other chemistry experiments. One of his dreams was to be like Marie Curie and get the Nobel prize.

It was at the popcorn company that he discovered how to make explosives untraceable. We and others in the industry are still unsure as to how he accomplished removing tracers from explosives.

It is obvious his thoughts of retribution against his old enemies returned and the determination to create a product sellable to others. This is how his deadly package was born."

Debra quickly replied, that is a lot of useful information plus an understanding of the complex mind of this person. What's your thought's Jack?"

"Well, they echo yours but now we have a picture of him and it maybe easier to get to him by stroking his ego."

"Where to you people think he would be more comfortable because of language or surroundings?" Debra asked.

Andrzej answered, " We did not think this meeting would last this long and all of us have other things to do today. We think it is important what you are doing, so can we meet again tomorrow morning from eight until noon?"

"Sure, that would be fine, and we heard quite a bit about Pauli today and Debra and I will review what we learned and have more questions for you tomorrow. Again, our thanks to all of you for your time."

They left the meeting and Jack and Debra found their way to a local café for their lunch. After lunch the couple returned to their hotel to discuss and dissect what they had learned.

They now had a better understanding of Pauli and what had driven him to this extreme. They knew, he was no dummy and he would be crafty and sly. Catching him would prove to be difficult and dangerous.

CHAPTER 35

The next morning, Debra and Jack once again met with the three police investigators to renew their conversation and questioning. Jack wanted to know more about Pauli's comfort zone.

"I wonder if one of you can provide information as to where you believe Pauli would reside and feel safer? Would it be here in Poland or elsewhere and would he prefer city or rural living?"

"Here is what I believe from knowing something about his early life. He was a loner and even when he worked in the candy store, he left the sales to his clerks and avoided meeting the customers. Like many Europeans, we speak multiple languages. Many of the tourists going into the candy store came from nearby Germany and Pauli was very fluent in German.

I would think he would prefer Germany since he speaks the language and being a loner, he would prefer a rural setting to avoid people and nosy neighbors. This is my best guess."

Jack felt there was not much more to learn here and now he could direct his contacts in a new direction. He thanked the officers for there helping them and he and Debra left the meeting.

"Debra let's return to the hotel and check out. It's time to return to Germany where I want to go and interview the postal clerk in Halsdorf.

It's a few hours from here and we can try to meet her tomorrow."

About an hour later they were on their way to Halsdorf. They had called Perry and requested if Interpol could arrange a brief meeting tomorrow with the postal clerk who had provided information about the shipper of the bomb package.

Within thirty minutes they received a return call that a meeting could be had at any time from early morning to mid-afternoon. They then arranged hotel reservations in a location close to Halsdorf.

Halsdorf was a small town in a farming area and quite a distance from larger German cities. Jack felt it was just the ideal place for Pauli to settle.

Early the next morning, Jack and Debra went to the small post office and asked to see Frieda. They didn't realize she was the only clerk, and they were talking to her. They all laughed and introduced themselves to her.

Debra began the discussion. "Frieda, have you lived her a long time and are you familiar with the area?"

"I was born about two miles from here and have lived here all my life. It is why I suspected the package guy because I know just about everybody in this town and even in the surrounding areas."

"We noticed there was a lot of farming communities in this part of Germany."

"Oh yes, there are more than a hundred areas like this scattered through out the country. If you like solitude, this is the place to find it."

"I was wondering, when the man came to the post office to mail his package, was there anything that set him apart from the local folk who live here? Asked Jack."

"I thought about that later because his German pronunciation was not very good, and he spoke in a dialect maybe more like you would hear in eastern Germany than here. I wondered about that as well."

"You mean closer to Netherland or France?"

"Yes, they use words differently than we do, out here in the rural areas."

"No more questions Freida, we appreciate your help. Thank you and have a good week."

The pair left the post office and knew they had learned something but nothing usable to find Pauli. As the clerk said, there are a hundred or more areas like this in Germany. Finding the right one will be difficult and if Pauli moves around, it will be even more difficult.

Jack admitted to Debra, they had some good information but nothing to

point in the direction of a location where the suspects could be living.

Maybe I knew something when we signed a one-year rental agreement.

CHAPTER 36

When Pauli and the nephew left Schwerin, they settled in a rural area about twenty miles south of Clappenburg and about fifty miles from the Netherlands border. It was very rural and if they needed a quick escape, it would be easy to cross the Dutch or French border where they again could find suitable hiding places.

Because of the location, they rarely saw other people and avoided them to remain hidden. The nephew typically drove forty or fifty miles to a large city to by groceries or other needs. He always paid cash and rarely returned to the same store, and he altered his disguise for each venture.

Pauli spent most of his days assembling bomb packages for either current orders or to build an inventory. He soon began to study alternate methods of construction and alternative features he could add, to make the devices usable beyond the mailed packaged model.

Several potential customers had asked for devices they could attach to automobiles or plant inside furniture and with the proper electronic hardware and software, which would allow the devices to be detonated remotely.

These models required electronic and mechanical skills and were very different from the chemistry knowledge Pauli possessed. However, he was smart, and the internet had all the information he needed to design future models with numerous capabilities.

Hence, he made the decision to learn how to modify his design with the features customers wanted and who would be willing to pay higher amounts to purchase them.

He quickly learned the basics and found many components he required for future designs were common in consumer goods and had "off-the-shelf" availability at reasonable costs.

He purchased several items from various suppliers, not wanting to raise suspicions about the usage of them. Once he received the items, he began to assemble prototypes in different sizes for specific applications.

Since they lived far from other houses, he could easily test his new devices on his own property. Like all new designs, at first, he had multiple issues but gradually he altered the designs and improved the quality. Soon, he was able to produce very functional units with a wide capability of use.

Although his costs to manufacture increased compared to his earlier models, he was able to raise prices. His previous models sold for approximately 10,000 Euros each and his newer designs started at 20,000 Euros and higher.

His nephew was thrilled with the newer designs and pictured himself getting richer for every sale. He was in contact with numerous customers who sought alternative designs for evil uses. He didn't care about the potential deaths as he dreamed of saving a half million Euros and quitting the business. He wanted to have a normal life without having to hide forever but he did not reveal his plans to Pauli.

Within weeks, he was able to negotiate orders valued at more then 250,000 Euros. Pauli was thrilled and immediately began production on several of the newer models.

However, neither of them considered the effects this would have for Interpol and other national agencies when the killings increased, and more prominent people were being murdered.

The legal sleuths would begin an attack with vengeance.

CHAPTER 37

Two days after their meetings in Germany, Jack and Debra were back in Paris at their rental apartment. Jack had notified all the contacts of what he and Debra had learned in Germany and asked each to concentrate their efforts in Germany in try to find the suspects living location.

He did not have a reply from Boris if he had found where the materials were coming from and if sales being generated via the internet?

Without additional information, Jack and Debra were uncertain of how to proceed.

They spent a good part of the day asking each other, what if questions but none of which led to a possible plan for further investigation. They were about out of ideas when Debra received a text from Ethan who requested she call him immediately. She told Jack, "Maybe, we are about to receive some important information."

She immediately dialed Ethan's private number and the phone was quickly answered.

"Sorry to disrupt your day but I have some interesting information for you. The bomb maker is now offering several models for specific kills. They are usable to plant in an automobile or in different sizes to be planted under or inside furniture. They can be detonated using a cellphone.

The cost is 20,000 Euros and up dependent on design and potential application and they are available three weeks after order and only shipped to private mailbox centers.

I received this information from a former KGB classmate, now making money as a hitman. He told me if I had an interest, he could arrange to get me whatever I product I might need. He also said , if I knew someone who might have an interest, he would pay me a decent commission. Why he told me this I am unsure because there is no way he knows of our association."

"That certainly is interesting and disturbing news for us. It can only lead to an increase in killings."

"That is for certain. What do you suggest I do?"

"Ethan, we have a friend, like my husband Jack. If we give you a story, can introduce him to your friend? Jack speaks fluent Russian and knows his way around the territory. We can quickly work up a story of him being a volume buyer."

"It's a possibility but I want no part of any deal. It would only be my dropping a potential name to this guy, I'm not looking to get myself blown up."

"Let Jack and I talk for an hour or so and we will get back to you in a while. You are our hero today."

"Thanks for that, I'll await your call."

CHAPTER 38

Jack overheard most of the conversation and when Debra finished the call, he said to her, "That sounded like good news honey."

"It was Jack but also fraught with danger. Ethan can drop your name as a potential buyer, but we must figure out how we protect him."

"I have an idea. I'm going to become a Russian agent again who sells arms to some weird dictator. I will call Perry and get a quick ID and some dictator names and countries in need of such devices. What do you think.?"

"It's a good idea. Call Perry now and then we can put together our story for Ethan. So far, our efforts have not got us any closer to a solution, and this might turn things around."

Jack picked up his cellphone and dialed Perry's number. "Perry, Jack here and I need some quick help. One of our trusted contacts has a name of a Russian operative who told him he could buy untraceable bombs for him in many sizes and configurations. If he didn't need such devices, could he give him a name of someone who could possibly purchase them. I've volunteered for the job."

"Jack, you realize you are flirting with danger and possible death?"

"I've been there and done that in the past and I will be extremely careful."

"Tell me what you need, and I'll see you get it rapidly."

"I need two Russian passports with a first name as Vladimir. A standard one and one with diplomatic privileges, which will be used to convince someone, I have Russian government support. I also need some names of dictators and countries who might want these weapons. I plan on presenting myself as a serious volume buyer with a lot of cash,"

"How's two days to get you everything? I need to touch base with a few agents myself."

"Two days is fine, and I will call my contact now to further discuss my plan.

Thanks for the help."

"Let's hope we are on a path that leads to Pauli. Stay safe my friend."

Jack then called Ethan and told him, "I want to assure you my story will not involve you as I have other Russian contacts who I will say supplied me the information. This will remove you from the equation. We will call you in two days and provide you some of our plan.

I would like the guy's full name and contact number. I will have Boris find out who are his associates and figure out how to use one of them."

Ethan was pleased about the news and said he looked forward to the call."

Jack and Debra worked on their approach but could not identify buyers until he heard from Perry. They did agree that Debra would stay in Paris and keep their contacts informed.

As promised, Perry telephoned Jack on the second day.

"Jack, first a courier is on his way to your apartment to deliver the two passports you requested. Now let's talk about possible buyers.

Iran's revolutionary guard is always on the lookout for assignation tools. Next would-be Syria, where opposition groups seek means to kill ranking officials. In Africa, jihadist insurgency centered in the states of Burkina Faso, Mali, and Niger are potentials and of course, there is always Sudan.

Any one of the mentioned countries could buy large quantities of weapons.

Do some homework to get your story factual and you will do well.

How you get info on the big boy, I am not sure, but something may happen that allows you to meet him. Good luck and stay safe. I'll be looking for your periodic reports."

"Thanks Perry. What you have provided is sufficient for me to start my story. I'll fine tune to the point of making it believable. By the way, Debra will remain in Paris and maintain communications with our contacts.

Again, thanks for the support. Let's hope it results in a win for us."

CHAPTER 39

The next few days were spent fine tuning his story. He memorized the names of all the dictators by country, provided to him by Perry.

He had received information from Boris about the Russian agents associates and Jack was happy to learn, he had previously worked with one of them on an arms deal.

Boris also told him he could find no evidence on the internet about the manufacture or sales of the devices in question. He felt they were communicating only through known contacts, possibly friends or past cell mates of the nephew.

He called Ethan to again to assure him he was now clear of this deal as Jack had found a believable substitute.

After talking to Ethan, he called the Russian agent he once cooperated with to try and renew a relationship.

"Anatoli, it's me, Vladimir your old friend from days past."

"Vlad, how are you? It's been a few years since I saw you. Are you back in Russia?"

"No, but I will be there in a few days. I'm looking to restart my career, but I need to find some good sources for weapons. I've spent a few months wondering Africa and there are some luscious deals out there waiting for sellers. Are you still in Moscow?"

"Yes"

"Are you available for dinner in two or three days?"

"Sure, Let's meet in two days. Call me from your hotel and we'll have dinner there."

"Thanks Anatoli. I'll text you my information after I arrive. Look forward to seeing an old friend."

"Me too Vlad. See you then."

Debra laughed when Jack finished his call.

"What's so funny, he asked?"

"You're as smooth a used car salesman and deserve the salesman of the year award."

Jack also laughed and explained the importance of this contact.

"Hopefully, he will direct me to the guy Ethan provided or I will ask for two or three contacts since they usually are selling different weapons."

"Jack, be sure to mention assassinations of officials is on your list. Let Anatoli know there are some people out there who want to overthrow a government."

"Good point. Let's do a rehearsal tomorrow. Tonight, I'm in the mood for love."

Debra smiled and took his hand and off they went to the bedroom.

The next morning after breakfast, they went into the business mode and Jack fine-tuned his Anatoli presentation scheduled in a couple of days.

When they reached a point of knowing it would be acceptable, Jack made his reservations and to leave early tomorrow morning.

He packed his suitcase and included two guns in a secret compartment hidden from x-rays and magnetomer searches.

The next morning, he held Debra close as they both understood he was embarking on a very dangerous trip. They kissed each other goodbye, and tears flowed as he slowly walked out the door.

CHAPTER 40

About five hours after leaving Paris, Jack was checking into his hotel not far from Red Square in the center of Moscow.

He went to his room and texted Anatoli he was staying at the Metropole and if he was available to have dinner with him tonight.

Within minutes he received a positive answer and informed Jack he would be there about seven. Jack then proceeded to make reservations at one of the more expensive restaurants in the hotel.

He waited in the lobby for his friend who he had not heard from or seen in about five years. They had been good friends when he was on assignment in Russia for the CIA, but Anatoli never knew his real job.

Jack recognized him the moment he walked into the hotel lobby and walked over and gave him a big hug.

"Anatoli, you look great and haven't seem to have aged since I first met you."

"Thanks Vladimir and you also look great but a little older."

They both laughed and Vladimir suggested they go to the restaurant, and they could talk about old times after ordering a round of drinks.

Anatoli stuck to Vodka and Vladimir had his usual scotch on the rocks.

"Anatoli, thanks for joining me for dinner. What are you doing these days?"

"I couldn't turn down a free meal." He said laughing. I spend a lot of time in Iran and Sudan these days still selling weapons produced here in Russia. I have a good relationship with several manufacturers here and they know I have reliable contacts in several countries. What about you? What are you chasing these days?"

"For a couple years I did no business. Took some cruises and relaxed on a few beaches here and there but then I got bored and I knew there was unrest in Africa. So, I spent another year in Africa researching if I could return to my old job and make a few bucks doing it. To my surprise, there are plenty of good opportunities for me in quite a few places including Sudan. So now I'm looking to make some good contacts and I first thought of you?"

"Thanks Vladimir, I can give you a few reliable names and then it is up to you to make the deals. I have my channels and the people I will supply you have noncompeting channels which doesn't interfere with my clients or my sources. I'd be happy to help you but first let's eat as I'm hungry."

"Sorry Anatoli. Sometimes I talk too much."

He waved to the waiter and soon they were studying the menu and ordered their meals. They then switched the conversation to memories of years ago until their meals were served, and they were silent while they ate.

After finishing their dinner, they ordered more drinks and discussed how Anatoli could possibly help.

"One area interesting to me. I met a couple of people who told me they had close friends interested in doing away with some corrupt dictators and were looking for the right weapons to do so.

I have never been in the assassination business but if I had the right source and product, I might consider it because it's worth big bucks. That and the usual stuff I do know like grenade launchers and air to air missiles is also something I can easily do with the right sources. Hence any help will be appreciated, and I would be happy to pay you a royalty for your help."

"That is not necessary. I am doing well, and I don't mind helping an old friend. Tomorrow, I will send you three or four names and contact information of people I know who could supply your needs."

"Alright, you earned your free meal and I promise you it won't be the last and it won't be separated by five years."

"Oh good, I won't go hungry. It was great to see you again and let me know if the names I supply work out."

CHAPTER 41

The following morning, Jack had received the contact information from Anatoli. The contact's name supplied by Ethan was number three on the list. He reminded himself to send thank you notes to Ethan and Boris for their help.

He sat for a few minutes reviewing what he would discuss with the contact before making the phone call. A few minutes later, he had decided on his approach, making sure he spoke Russian, and made the call.

"Sergey, my name is Vladimir, and I was given your number by my friend Anatoli. He gave me a brief description of the product you have for sale, and it may be of interest to me."

"Vladimir, I am busy right now, can I call you back later today?"

"Sure, any time is ok."

Jack knew that Sergey was being careful and would call Anatoli to confirm my identity. He figured he would get a return call in three to four hours.

The call was returned quicker than Jack had estimated.

"Vladimir, this is Sergey returning your call and I am ready to discuss your interest. May I ask what part of the world would this product be used? I also assume you are buying it for resale to someone else."

"The market I have in mind is Africa and possibly Iran and Syria. Yes, it is for resale, and I am well connected in many parts of the territory.

If you check with Anatoli, he can vouch for many of my sales in the areas."

"Thanks for the information and Anatoli says you're an expert in many phases of the arms business."

"I have had a few successes."

"Good. Let me describe what I get and then you can decide on how you want to start. I can obtain two or three standard models as well as having the capability of doing custom fabrications.

The standard units are box type explosive devices, typically sent as gifts, and the newer models are designed to be easily attached to an automobile or planted under furniture.

All the newer models are cell phone connected for activation and they are untraceable.

Costs for Standard devices are 12,000 Euros and newer models vary from 15,000 to 20,000 Euros. Custom units are of course a higher cost."

"Your description is what I am looking for now and I believe I can resell them in two or three countries.

I will probably buy one or two of the newer models for testing purposes and if successful, it could lead to larger quantities.

How long after order placement can I get delivery and what sort of down payment do you need?"

"Delivery is about three weeks, and a fifty percent payment is required prior to delivery and balance upon receipt of units.

The units come from Germany now and where would you want them to be shipped?"

"Delivery is fine. Any chance of being able to ship them here in Russia or is it safer elsewhere?"

"Russia is good. You must pay a few hundred extra Rubles to get them through customs, but I can arrange delivery without any problem."

"Everything sounds good and here is what I would like before placing my initial order. I want to know exact sizes of the models, the explosive force range and how far from the device can it be detonated?"

"Vladimir, I have used one of the newer models and they are very compact. Probably a hundred by one hundred-fifty-millimeter rectangle.

The range of the explosive is roughly a one-meter circle but very deadly and detonation can be activated from about one-half kilometer.

For example, placed under a car, front seat, or back seat, it will destroy the entire inside of the car and kill all passengers."

"Interesting Sergey. I'm going to order one like you described. Please text me payment details and an expected delivery date.

Once I have that, I will arrange a ship to address."

"Thanks for the order, Vladimir. You will not be disappointed, and I will text you full details in a few minutes. I do look forward to working with you."

"Thank Sergey, lets get something big going."

Jack was happy with the call and the results and since he was in Russia, he might as well make arrangements to meet with Boris.

He called his friends number and Boris promised to join him for lunch tomorrow. In the meantime, Jack would draw up a plan for getting his first unit and how he could convince Sergey, it had been used in a killing somewhere.

CHAPTER 42

Boris and Jack met for lunch at the Metropol restaurant for lunch and to discuss what was now known about the bombing suspect. Jack provided additional information to Boris and then he told him of his conversation with Sergey.

"Jack, I am warning you to be very careful what you say or plan to do with this guy. He was KGB trained and still maintains contact within the GRU.

Do not make many calls to him of long duration as he may attempt to have the call traced to your location. Do not reveal where you are or where you are staying, as this could put you in danger.

When you spoke to Anatoli, did he know your hotel name?"

"Yes, in fact we had dinner together here."

"Any indication that Anatoli told Sergey where you were staying?"

"I'm not sure, why?"

"He may want to trace your movements while you're in Russia. After lunch, go up and pack and I will take you to a safer place. Again, this guy can be dangerous for you."

"Ok, I will move after we have lunch, and I will start carrying a weapon. I will always use a secure phone when calling him. I must use this this guy as he is the only one, I know who can possibly get me to Pauli."

"I understand and will help where I can but now, I want to keep you safe and inform you about obstacle's trying to disrupt you."

"Thanks Boris. I trust you and appreciate the warning.

When they had finished lunch, Jack stayed in the lobby for a few minutes as his instinct suggested someone was watching him. He raised his phone as to make a call, but it had a feature allowing him to see what was behind him.

A man was eyeing him and talking on the phone at the same time but keeping his eyes on Jack as he slowly walked to the elevator. The elevator door closed, and no one had tried to stop him. He pressed three different buttons to avoid showing what floor he exited the elevator.

He quickly went to his room and packed and called Boris I am being followed and will not leave via the lobby. Meet me at the back of the hotel in five minutes as I will use the exit stairs and find my way to the rear of the hotel.

The exit stairway took him to the hotel rear and as he left the building, Boris pulled up beside him. Jack and Boris were not sure if the seller was following him or someone who recognized Jack from a previous encounter.

Boris drove Jack to a smaller hotel on the west side of Moscow, not far from where Boris lived. "You should have no problems with visitors here."

On his way to the new hotel, Jack had asked Boris if he could trace the payment he would make to Sergey and where it may go after receipt.

Boris assured him, he would try to see where the payment finally ended up and hopefully it would give them a lead to the bank that Pauli and the nephew used to hide their sales.

Jack was now alone in the hotel and tried not to think of the danger he might be facing in the future. He realized he had two or three weeks without much to do, until the bomb was delivered to him.

He thought about whether he should receive delivery of the bomb he ordered of the bomb in Russia or since there is a strong possibility of being watched, it would be smarter to have it shipped elsewhere.

He then decided that once the order had been accepted, he would fly to the Netherlands and then drive to Paris to avoid being followed. He knew that Boris's warning was real and the guy eyeing in the hotel was real. What he didn't know is how dangerous it could become and when it would confront him.

The order was completed the next day and a delivery date was set for three weeks later. Sergey was notified that Jack would advise the delivery destination within a week or so.

He had already repacked his suitcase and once he had the response, he left for the airport to begin his journey back to Paris.

His trip was uneventful and finally he was back in the arms of Debra and safe for now.

He planned on speaking to Perry within one day to plan his actions involving the bomb he had just ordered. Interpol might be able to provide a way from him not being involved in a murder of a dictator.

CHAPTER 43

The next day Jack called Perry and suggested a meeting with him to discuss the issues facing him as a seller of untraceable bomb products. Debra would join him in the meeting.

Perry agreed to meet with the couple in two days and special agent Bascal will also join the meeting.

Debra and Jack left for the meeting on the agreed date and met Bascal and Perry at Interpol headquarters.

Perry thanked them for coming and was glad to see them again. He knew progress on this case was moving at a snail's pace, but it was moving.

After they had been seated in a conference room, Jack opened the meeting.

"I have just returned from Russia where I had a conversation with an arms dealer capable of supplying some of Pauli's inventions.

I learned the seller in question had previously trained with the KGB and possibly still maintains relations with them to keep his business alive.

There is no doubt he had me checked out prior to even suggesting he could sell units to me.

I was warned by my contact to be extremely suspicious of this seller and not to give him an opportunity to locate me. He was right, because I discovered someone watching me in my hotel lobby after my contact left me after lunch.

I was able to get to my room and used the fire exit to leave the hotel and met my contact who had arranged a new hotel for me to try and erase my tracks in Russia.

I realize the danger I have opened myself up to, but it has always been a part of many of the jobs I have had in my career. Hence forth I will remain armed whenever and wherever the search for Pauli takes me.

The reason for my meeting today is to inform you I have ordered one unit and will receive it somewhere, yet to be decided. I also need a cover story about using the bomb to possibly kill a known dictator.

There are probably other needs but now these two are a major roadblock to my being successful."

"Jack, I respect your making this sacrifice and we will try to do everything within our power and capabilities to help you succeed and survive. Bascal and I will personally be involved with you and Debra to create a winning plan. Bascal, any comments?"

"I admire you Jack and you are going to be carrying a heavy load. I am going to tell you something, we might be able to do.

Let's suppose you sell this to a rebel in Mali or wherever, and we plant a bomb in an official's car under the front seat. The bomb is detonated and kills the driver, but bulletproof glass between the front and rear protects the passenger.

This can be played out without any casualty's and hidden from the public, but we can create pictures and stories of a coup attempt on the life of whoever we select.

We have done something similar before and made it appear believable. We just must figure out the who, where, and when."

Debra and Jack smiled and knew it was an interesting approach to make Jack a reliable buyer.

Perry also applauded the idea. "Bascal, what an original thought and a way to not only protect Jack but to further the goal of him working to get larger orders directly from the main source."

"Sir, I can start planning this today and within one week, have a workable approach for Jack and pictures and a story for many news outlets. I have a small team to do this and some contacts in the media who will accept my inputs as real news."

"Jack, this is what I can add to what Bascal is proposing. We have a relationship with a couple of dictators who know they are in danger of a coup. I believe we can arrange one of them to work with us on this stunt with promises of further protections since we know they are being threatened.

I will take responsibility for that effort and will start today."

"Thanks Perry, that would give me a realistic cover and lessen the danger. I will need to know in the next ten days, a delivery location, and a possible recipient of a known rebel group."

"We will add that to our to-do list, and you will have your answer in plenty of time.

You and Debra can now leave us and be assured, your lives are important to us, and we want to catch Pauli. Our plan will work."

CHAPTER 44

One week later, Jack received a text note from Bascal; we are almost there with the media part and will finalize everything in two days or less. Perry is also close to a deal. You'll hear from us again soon.

Jack told Debra the good news. "We have a few more days to be certain but I am confident of a good result."

There was no news on the second day but early morning on the third day, Perry called Jack.

"We have some good news and some so-so news. The media story is finished and ready whenever we get to use it.

The so-so news is we are having difficulty convincing a dictator to work with us. It may take a few days more and a couple of million in bribe money, but we will get there eventually.

I have a name and shipping address for you which I will send by text after we end this call. It will be to a member of a jihadist group we have infiltrated.

In fact, the driver supposedly being killed will be a jihadist."

"That works for me Perry. I can wait a few more days and if a question arises, I can always say money transfer from my buyer is an issue."

"Good answer Jack but I am sure we can get this resolved rather quickly. We have a lot of cards to play, and the game is still in progress."

Three days later, Perry informed Jack that the product is to be sent to the jihadist previous sent to him and the incident is going to take place in Burkina Faso within a week after receipt. He was told not to mention either the destination or target when you exchange details with your seller.

Jack texted the seller and provided the delivery information and he would pay today upon receipt of the payment details.

Within the hour, he received the information regarding payment. Before he sent the payment, he notified Boris how it was being sent and the sender's deposit information. He hoped Boris could track the funds as they moved between banks.

He later received confirmation of receipt and a firm delivery date of approximately six days. His customer should receive the device four days later. There were no other comments.

When he had concluded his business, he phoned Perry to discuss the plan further.

"Perry the seller has been paid and I have one of my contacts trying to trace the money path, The item will be ready for shipment in six days, and I wonder if we can follow shipments out of Germany going to Burkina Faso.

I am not sure how it will ship but I was told it would arrive at the destination in four days.

We know who is going to receive it, but who sent it and from where it ships is certainly of strong interest."

"Good point Jack. Unfortunately, we do not know if it will be shipped by the maker or by the seller. We can find out if it is from Germany but out of Russia there is no chance."

"Just a thought, Perry. Based on shipping and delivery, this could happen in the next two weeks or within a couple of days after the two weeks.

What will be interesting once the news is broken is how the seller will respond and what do I do to take advantage of my success?"

"You may want to sit back and do nothing. Just say you have several interesting buyers looking at their future needs. I wouldn't rush the guy.

until you can dangle a few reasonable orders.

When you are ready, you might say the maker is a genius and you would like to meet him to discuss other possibilities for his designs. You would like is to be more involved so you can bring in more opportunities for everyone.

Assure him , he will remain your seller but a conversation with the maker would increase the opportunities but, right now, I am not sure the maker has the capabilities to supply me what my buyers really need."

"That is probably a good strategy, but let's not get too far ahead of ourselves. I'm not sure how the seller will act after the coup attempt. Once, I know his reaction, we can make our moves then.

I'm just waiting for two weeks to pass."

CHAPTER 45

Over the next two weeks, there were two more killings in separate European countries. Interpol, Jack, and his team had not uncovered any further information about Pauli and his operation.

It appeared sales were increasing the potential of four or five murders per month. The media had daily discussions on who might be next and of course, criticism of Interpol was a constant reminder to the public.

There was no news about Burkina Faso and most people would not even recognize it as a country. All Jack and Interpol could do was wait for the story to break.

It was breaking news the next morning and Bascal did a great job with the story and pictures showing a very damaged presidential vehicle with its front end blown apart.

The dictator survived and the explosion was suspected of being planted by a jihadist trying to kill the dictator, but the jihadist was the only person killed.

Jack did not have time to think about the seller contacting him, because the seller called him a few minutes after the news broke on tv.

"Vladimir, congratulations on your successful purchase. Now, how can I help you? Your success, should get you lots of referrals."

"Thanks for the congratulations, Sergey, you are right about my success getting referrals. I've received three calls already this morning from other contacts interested in purchasing devices.

Meanwhile, I've been thinking about several modifications or different footprints for the devices and if I had them, I could attract even more buyers. Is there any chance I could meet the maker, or at least have a conversation with him?

I am not trying to cut you out of the business because, I need someone to do the grunt work of arranging fabrication and shipping. I got a big price for the Burkina Faso job and based upon my prior deals; I am trusted to deliver on promises."

"Vladimir, this maker wants to remain safe and avoid being on the run. He trusts his nephew to generate business and maybe, I can get him to talk to you."

"Even that would be fine, Sergey. One of the contacts today wanted at least five devices but with different configurations. He wants to do this to give the impression there are copycat devices also available in the market.

Personally, I don't believe in that approach. I'm convinced the devices work as promised and yes, they could use some modifications but who notices after the thing explodes.

My main interest is in different footprints for specific jobs. You know, autos, trucks, furniture or delivered cartons. All different but getting the same result."

"You have good ideas Vladimir, and you did get a good result from your sale. Hell, you made the news on tv. Let me probe around and see if I can get one of them to listen to you. All I can do is ask."

"Thanks, I plan on surveying some of my contacts in Africa as to what they want in terms of quantities and pricing. I'll get back to you in about a week unless I hear from you sooner."

"You'll hear from me soon, Vladimir."

CHAPTER 46

Pauli and his nephew also watched the news and they had known a unit was being sent to Burkina Faso and they were very happy to learn of the success of the device. The dictator didn't get killed but the device worked to perfection.

They talked about the seller getting additional business from the news report and they would remain very busy making more untraceable bombs.

The nephew worried this could prod Interpol and other policing agencies to increasing their investigation into the origination of the devices. Maybe he thought, it was time to move again to a newer and safer location.

He discussed this with Pauli, and he felt secure where they were and to their knowledge, nobody was nosing around or asking suspicious questions. He felt there was no need to move, and he was comfortable where they were located.

The nephew, being an ex-con, was always suspicious of everyone based upon his prison background. He had little trust in everybody because he knew it only took one person to betray them.

The days continued without any incidents and both Pauli and the nephew forgot about the conversation. They were too busy building new bombs for a growing list of customers.

Interpol did not forget, and they had increased the number of agents looking for pair.

After Jack had his discussion with Sergey, he immediately called Perry to arrange a phone capable of identifying location of calls. Interpol had such devices and would send one to Jack immediately.

He was told only to use this phone with calls from people he wanted to trace. When activated, it would trace incoming call origination or location of a person receiving an outgoing call from Jack.

They were optimistic that the success Jack had on his first sale could lead to his having a discussion with the bomb makers.

A few days after the Pauli/Nephew conversation, he received a call from Sergey wanting to talk to Pauli about his conversation with Vladimir. The nephew told Sergey he would talk to Pauli and get back to him later in the day.

Again, the nephew was suspicious, but he talked to Pauli about what Sergey had requested and Pauli responded.

"Hans, you are never to smart not to learn something new. The seller is right that we are building the same old design we started with quite a few months ago. Maybe it's time to rethink our designs or add newer ones.

Our phones are untraceable, right?"

"Yes, they are as far as I know."

"So, what's the issue? I'm interested because the quicker we grow this business, the quicker we disappear into retirement. I'm shooting for two more good years and then poof. We are gone."

"When would you like to talk to Sergey?"

"Any day this week is fine."

Two days later, Sergey connected with Pauli and let him know about some of the ideas his customer Vladimir had suggested to him.

"Pauli, I know he knows the right people and he has good contacts in Africa. Maybe you should consider listening to him and then decide what you might want to do. I'll tell you one thing about this guy; he can double the prices you currently offer."

"New designs are a good reason to listen and double the sell price is even better. Have him call me tomorrow on this line. It's secure."

Later Sergey called Vladimir and gave him the makers information without revealing this name. He told him to call tomorrow.

CHAPTER 47

Receiving the call from Sergey made Jack's Day. In fact, he thought it was too easy or Sergey had checked on him quite a bit and was satisfied he was the real deal.

Jack again called Perry and told him of his luck in getting to talk to the maker who was possibly Pauli. Jack felt he could determine his nationality from his accent, and he planned on speaking to him in German.

He informed Perry, he would make the call at ten tomorrow morning.

Jack and Debra spent about four hours discussing possible variations to the current design and potential usage applications, sizes, and explosive force.

He made a list of possibilities to discuss and would try to keep the phone line activated for ten minutes or more to allow Interpol to do their job.

He dialed the number given to him and waited while the phone rang. After three rings, the phone was answered.

"Hello, who am I talking to?"

"My name is Vladimir, and I was given your number by Sergey."

"Oh, you're the guy who wants new designs. I'll listen, and you talk. Is that ok."

"Sure. I am not sure if Sergey told you that I have several possible customers in Africa. I have sold arms in that area for lots of years and they trust me to get them the best devices I can obtain. They were really happy with the unit used in the Burkina Faso and one guy told me, you are a genius.

I think so too but here is what I would like to have. I want different size explosives for different jobs. I want different shapes to fit more securely where they are being used.

Units with magnets attached will also be interesting as it makes for an easy attachment. I can think of additional needs, but I would like to hear what you can dream up and then we can marry our ideas."

"You have a long list of interesting ideas Mr. Vladimir. I would have to do some serious studying to get what you want. I like what you say and let me study for a couple of days and may be one or even three of your ideas can be easily fabricated. I won't make promises, but I will try to satisfy your needs. Thanks for the call and I'll call you again in three days."

Then the line went dead.

Jack immediately called Perry to see if Interpol had captured the call and figured out the location.

"Sorry Jack, your call was not traceable, just like his explosives."

Well, I can tell you this, it was Pauli I was talking with because I could hear his mixing Polish and German for various answers. So, since he is speaking even lousy German, he is still there. He promised to call me back in three days and we must wait and see what he tells me.

Perry, I just thought of something to possibly help zero in on him. I am guessing he is receiving explosive materials and other needed supplies from two or three countries. Iran, Russia, and North Korea. They have all the resources to supply Pauli or every kind of weapon, any crazy would desire.

Does anybody keep track of stuff coming from those countries and showing up in Germany? What about package delivery services delivering goods to rural Germany within a fifty-mile circle from the Halsdorf post office? The same driver may have a set route and deliver materials every couple of months."

"Jack, that is a good thought about delivery services. Let me talk to a couple of my guys and possibly we could start an investigation. Text me when you expect your next phone call from Pauli."

"I will and I also have a contact who may be able to trace deliveries. I'll be in touch."

CHAPTER 48

Moments after Jack finished with his call to Perry, he called Boris to determine if he could trace shipments entering Germany from the countries known to supply anything to anybody for a price.

"Boris, my computer guru. I'm going to test you just to prove how good you can be."

"You have run out of cash, and you need some quick free money. Am I right?"

I know you can do that, but here is something easier. I want you to learn which delivery companies service a territory within fifty miles of Halsdorf, Germany. Once you have that information, then which ones deliver international shipments from Russia, Iran, or North Korea.

Now here is the hard part, can you determine if one location within the area I specified, gets packages from those or other countries weekly, monthly, or just periodically?"

"The identity part is simple, but the tracking part requires I use my hacking skills. You are challenging me, and I accept. I am guessing you are trying to zero in the bomb makers facility."

"You are hard to deceive Boris and I know you understand the importance of this task."

"It is a good idea Jack, and I will do my best starting tonight. I will warn you that shipments from the countries you mentioned sometimes are shipped to a neutral port, like Hong Kong. There they are repacked and probably mislabeled and then forwarded to where nobody looks closely at them."

"That may be the case , but, if you can locate a place getting frequent deliveries to the middle of no-where, it gives us a starting point. See what you come up with and then will discuss it further. Thanks Boris."

"Debra, we have been proactive on this case for quite a while, and we are still at square one. It's time we become more proactive. I have asked Boris to see if he can get some shipping records of companies delivering to a fifty-mile circle from Halsdorf. It might work but we should consider other off-beat ideas to see if we find clues to lead us to Pauli."

"Let's. sit down and start bouncing ideas around and follow-up on a couple that might be worthwhile. Get me a glass of wine and a scotch for yourself for relaxation and we'll begin our therapy session."

"I'll need more than one glass." They both laughed at Jack's joke and after he served the drinks, they began their search for ways to uncover any possible clues.

"What about mail service. They must get electrical or cell phone bills?"

"What name was on the package return address and did the clerk verify it by, asking for an ID?"

"Whose name was on the registration for the car they bought in Netherlands and was that verified by ID?"

"Where do they buy their food? Maybe we can arrange for cameras in all stores within that fifty-mile circle you suggested, and then look only for a single man by using face recognition software."

"Get me another wine Jack. It's triggering ideas."

Jack returned from the kitchen with drink refills before he asked another question.

"Most of the questions we asked ourselves, involve knowing a name. We know they are using aliases but more than likely, they have stuck to one set of ID's once they moved to the location where they are now hiding.

Our priority is to find just one name, and it gets us two suspects."

"We are on the right track. The answers to questions two and three, should be easy to answer. Question one, rather difficult if not impossible to obtain.

Question four could be a winner. My guess would be the nephew does the shopping and goes to a different store in a different local each time to shop.

If we stick to major food outlets, there could be less than twenty-five in the selected area and more than likely they all have video cameras watching customers shop and pay their grocery bills.

We should discuss this approach with Perry about the possibility of adding software to their video inputs and we are immediately notified when a possible match occurs."

"What else can we ask ourselves about a method of gathering clues?"

"How about posting wanted posters in local post offices and elsewhere seeking help from the local citizens?"

"The problem with that, it encourages Pauli and the nephew to quickly move and then we again are without a clue as to where they end up. I would rather zero in as to where I think they currently live and catch them in the act."

"That's true. Let's get perry involved today and see what he says and what he can do to assist us."

CHAPTER 49

"Pauli I am going grocery shopping about forty miles from here, so I'll be gone about four hours."

"Why so far?"

"Because I don't want to raise suspicions. I go to a new store every two weeks and only use cash to buy what we need. We don't know how Interpol is trying to catch us and going to the same store every time, people will remember me, if shown a photograph. Seeing me only once does not jog the memory."

"Alright, don't 'forget to get me some Polish sausages'."

"Ok. We have been here about one year. I still think it is time to move again."

"I haven't seen anyone nosing around here and if Interpol knew where we were, they would have caught us by now. We stay here until we have bad vibes and then leave as quickly as possible.

In fact, when you come back from shopping, let's put together a get-away package and arrange now for a place for us to go. Even if the place is temporary, we should be planning our exit."

"I agreed and I'll pack some of our stuff and talk to some old buddies about a place in France or the Netherlands. If we leave, it must be out of Germany."

"I'm going back to work as I still have three orders to complete. I also must call Vladimir about some of his suggestions.

"You go shopping and I'll see you later."

CHAPTER 50

Jack had just finished his call to Perry when Pauli called on Jack's secure line.

"Vladimir, it's me Otto calling about your suggestions. I was impressed with your knowledge of my devices and how we might make them better and in line with what your customers require.

Making the devices to a larger footprint is not an issue, nor is adding magnets, if you tell me where you want them, I will place them on the package. In fact, I can do everything you asked, but I expect you to provide a rough drawing or sketch of your requirement.

After reviewing it, you will receive a cost and delivery time from Sergey. Thanks for your suggestions and I hope to see future business from you."

"Thank you for listening, I will contact Sergey with my needs. Goodbye."

Within a minute, Perry called and told Jack the call was tracked to southwestern Germany. An exact location could not be identified but it did provide a specific area to search.

"Perry, that is good news because I felt it was within a fifty-mile area around Halsdorf which is in the southwest. The call tracing is good proof of the location area. It may now be easier to use face recognition.

Another interesting point, when Pauli called, he introduced himself as Otto. He adapted a German name."

"At this point, the name Otto doesn't mean much but it may in the future.

Jack, I like the face recognition idea and now we know a geographical area, we can place cameras in the most logical places. We have worked with grocery stores before and it will be an easy adaption to their current video systems.

Regarding your Otto conversation, be careful how you deal with Sergey now. They expect you to deliver orders and you will need excuses for a while.

I would suggest you tell Sergey you're heading for Africa for a month and will begin the sales process and will let him know when you are close to an order.

Stay in touch and let me know what Boris Finds for us. Regards to Debra."

"Thanks for the tips, Perry. We'll call you when something arises,"

Chapter 51

Jack and Debra had just finished their second cup of coffee when Boris called.

"Jack, I think I got lucky. I checked about twenty big and small shipping companies delivering in a seventy-five-to-one-hundred-kilometer circle around Halsdorf. There were three of them, who grabbed my attention.

I was able to find shipping details over a six-month period in the area and the closer I looked, all three were periodically shipping to mailbox stores in five different small towns within one hundred or more kilometers of Halsdorf.

Each shipment was sent to a different store in the five locations each time and then after number five, the next shipment went to number one. My recollection is that each store was getting a shipment once or twice monthly.

The size of each package for each shipment, regardless of the company or eventual destination, weighted between ten and twenty kilograms. I could not verify where the packages came from because they had been forwarded from a company in Italy and more than likely, a repackaging company, strictly handling suspicious goods and then, forwarding them.

It gets more interesting, only two of the mailbox stores receiving shipments were in Germany. The others were in France, Belgium, and Luxembourg.

Now for the best part, all five mailbox stores received packages addressed to Hans Fischer.

Jack, I will send you the complete details of every shipment by date and destination and I know you'll have enough information for Interpol."

"Boris, you are the wizard of Russia and my friend, your information will make a lot of people happy. I will immediately pass this to Interpol. They will quickly figure it out."

"That's why you pay me such a big salary."

They both laughed enjoying the moment and then they said their goodbyes and Jack would make his call to Perry.

"Perry, are you sitting down and have about ten minutes to receive the most significant clues yet to land on your desk."

"I'm ready when you are."

"First, the bomb making materials appear are being repackaged in Italy, so we don't have a clue where they originate but we know they are shipped to five different mailbox stores in four countries by three shipping companies.

They are shipped in a sequence to the stores. For example, they ship to store one and then two, etcetera and then repeat the sequence again.

Shipments to each store average one to two monthly.

The stores are in a circle, each being about eighty kilometers from Halsdorf.

The shipments weight from ten to twenty kilos."

Now for the icing on the cake. They are all shipped to Hans Fischer, probably the nephew,"

"Jack this is amazing. What are the countries?"

"I will send you full details but two in Germany and the rest in France, Luxembourg, and Belgium. Based on recent ship dates, the next shipment will be delivered to the France store soon.

I will give my computer guy a big bonus once this weird case ends."

"Jack, if all this stuff leads us to Pauli, I will get Interpol to pay the bonus.

Now, I will await your sending the full details and I promise you, no early to bed tonight."

CHAPTER 52

Two days after Boris provided the information to Jack, Hans Fischer was on his way to France to pick-up the latest shipment of materials. He received a call from a jail friend who had arranged the French mailbox store as a pick-up site.

"Hans do not approach the Metz store as Interpol is looking for you. I have a place for you and your uncle outside of Nancy. I'll tell you the story when we meet again but I suggest you move fast."

"Thanks Henri, we will be in Nancy tonight."

Hans quickly called Pauli and told him, "Bad vibes are here now. Gather up what we had packed and any other urgent stuff you need. We will leave within minutes after I return in about one hour."

"I'll be ready."

Pauli had figured that Interpol would eventually show up on their doorstep. The only question, when? Based on the call, he assumed it was now.

He gathered up their important stuff including some partially assembled bombs and was ready when Hans arrived. About ten minutes later, they were on their way to a new home in Nancy France.

They drove the 170 kilometers in about two hours and arrived at the new house where Henri waited for them. After unpacking the vehicle, they all sat down for a glass of cold beer.

Henri spoke first. "Sorry for the bad news but if you had entered the store , you would have been arrested. I use that store because it is owned by my friend who texted me and said Interpol was on its way to discuss shipments waiting at the store for a customer pick-up. He knew immediately, it could be a customer named Hans Fischer and notified me.

I suggest tomorrow, we arrange for new IDs for you two and start to figure out where future shipments go and to who?"

"Henri, you can help us with the identities, and we will handle the rest of the stuff. There is a lot to do involving many phone calls. We are happy you were around to help us."

"No problem. I'll be here tomorrow to get new photos for your IDs. What citizenship do you want to declare?"

"Probably German as it is the language, we know best next to Polish."

"Here, Polish maybe better, there is not much love for the Germans."

"Ok, we will give you Polish names tomorrow."

"See you tomorrow."

Fillip and Pauli went to sleep but their day had been ruined by the storm clouds over their heads. They arose early the next morning knowing that had a lot of calls to make and several changes to their delivery methods and destinations.

Pauli called all his suppliers, and all agreed the materials would be routed to another repackaging house in Egypt. Further details would be given later as to where shipments were to be eventually shipped.

Fillip began a search for safe mailbox stores within fifty to one hundred kilometers. He stuck to his original plan of having at least five mailbox stores preferably in five different countries.

He called a couple of close friends, and they provided information on five stores in five different countries. Once he received his new identity, he would arrange an account in each store.

By the end of the day, they had completed everything they needed to continue their operation. Tomorrow they would have new names and new identities, but they also knew this would not be their last encounter with Interpol.

CHAPTER 53

The data supplied by Jack had been carefully reviewed by Interpol specialists and determined Pauli's nephew always picked the deliveries at the mailbox shops within one or two days after receipt. They knew the next shipment would arrive at the shop in Metz France in one day.

Interpol agents had kept surveillance at the shop for three days and yet Hans Fischer did not show up to collect his package. Finally, the agents claimed the package and delivered it to headquarters for special agents to study.

The package contained a shipment of explosive determined to be manufactured in Iran. It did contain a tracer and the agents knew Pauli had a method of disabling the tracer.

They were disappointed in not catching the nephew and figured he was tipped off by someone probably in the mailbox store. They will be more careful the next time.

Perry called Jack to give him the bad news and Interpol had assumed the duo had moved their location, possibly out of Germany and more than likely quit using the delivery method and material source plus the mailbox stores Interpol had learned about.

"Jack, we believe they will not change their method of material acquisition. They will just get a different repackage source and use different mailbox addresses. Perhaps your computer guy can redo his search in a month or two.

They will also get new identities so Otto and Hans will no longer be around. Who they become is anybody's guess.

We had great input from you, and they still managed to get away."

"I wish the outcome had been different Perry, but we have our spies and they have theirs. It will continue this way until they make a fatal mistake.

Then we will catch them.

We will continue to think of ways to get them and my computer friend will figure out something new to try. We'll stay in touch, and we can only hope the death toll doesn't raise to rapidly."

"Thanks Jack. I know you and Debra would prefer to be sitting on a remote beach somewhere instead of chasing bomb makers. We will try our best to get you to that beach one of these days."

CHAPTER 54

"Pauli, do you have enough material to complete the orders we have received?"

"I always order extra and had a decent inventory when we had to leave. I will continue to build our material inventory to avoid future disruptions."

"I have the names of five mailbox outfits in five countries close by. The furthest is close to one hundred and fifty kilometers. I can drive to it in about two hours.

Once we get our new Polish identities, I will visit each shop to arrange a monthly account."

"I have enough stuff for at least four more devices, and we should receive replacement materials in two weeks. I'm hoping the new guy, Vladimir, gets us some interesting orders out of Africa."

"What do you hear from Sergey?"

"I have heard nothing from him in the past week. He also had promised me some interesting orders.

Maybe something is making it more difficult or risky to sell our stuff. He works out of Russia and possibly he is not paying the right people to continue his work.

He'll call me soon but now I must finish the orders we have, so we can get paid the balance owed to us."

"Remember, we owe Henri a thousand Euros for our new Identities."

""I know, and I have set the money aside for him, when he shows up here. I wonder what Polish names he will give us?"

"Pauli, they all end in ski, so stop worrying."

CHAPTER 55

Pauli and Fillip were not the only ones concerned about Sergey, Jack tried to call him and give him an update on his Africa trip, even though he was still in Paris.

He found out that Sergey's telephone number no longer existed and there were no other explanations. Jack was uncertain how to proceed if Sergey was no longer in the picture.

He figured he would wait a few more days and see if he heard from him again.

Once more Jack and Debra sat down to try and determine what their next steps would be in trying to find Pauli and the nephew.

They discussed calling Pauli if Sergey did not contact them in the next week. They felt it would be a good opportunity for Jack top have a closer relationship with Pauli and maybe find out where he is now located.

Two days after they had that discussion, Boris called Jack with information about Sergey.

"Jack, Sergey has been arrested by the GRU for trying to sell one of Pauli's devices to an undercover agent who told Sergey, he was out to murder the

Premier of Russia. This is a very serious charge and Sergey could be shot or receive a life sentence in one of Russia's slave labor prisons.

He will not survive for very long based upon what he tried to do. Russian courts are not lenient, and it is not uncommon for prisoners to suddenly die from a strange illness."

"I didn't even think of him being in trouble but when I tried to call him, his line was silent."

"Well, he is now officially out of work. You will have to decide how to proceed with Pauli."

"I'll call Perry and discuss with him and see how I can align myself.

with Pauli now that a key buyer has been silenced."

"That would be best and if you need my help, just give me a call."

"Thanks for the information, Boris and I'll stay in touch. Bye for now."

Jack told Debra the news Boris had supplied and then called Perry to discuss it with him.

"Perry, here is another lucky opportunity for us. Sergey is in jail in Russia and more than likely, he will never be free again. He was trapped selling a Pauli device to kill the Premier. Not a smart thing to do in Russia."

"Wow is all I can say. I'm going to check my schedule to arrange a meeting with Bascal and you and Debra asap. What we do next involving Pauli is very important and we must get it right."

"I agree, call me when you have arranged the meeting. We are free to be available any time."

"Thanks Jack. I'll call you later today."

CHAPTER 56

The meeting with Perry was set for the very next morning. Jack and Debra arrived a few minutes before the scheduled time and were met by Bascal who lead them into a conference room.

"Jack, the information you gave to Perry yesterday was shocking. I never will understand why criminals always make a major mistake and, in most cases, never outlive it. But it is good for us, and now, we must decide how we can take advantage of Sergey's big mistake."

"I 'm sure, you, Debra, and myself, have experienced the same thing over and over. The crooks feel like nobody can ever catch them and yet, if they looked at the full prisons, they might change their career path."

Perry had just walked into the room and heard Jack. "Well said, but history says they don't pay any attention to anybody and eventually lose their freedom."

Debra added: "I hope Pauli isn't listening to us. Many successful people will tell you that when you only listen to yourself, you're in trouble and I think Pauli has that kind of problem."

"We could teach a philosophy class, but let's return to the reason we are meeting today.

When Jack called me yesterday with the news, I felt this is great. Pauli now has a big problem without his key sales guy. Then, I thought more about it and realized, we also have a big problem regarding how do we get to Pauli?

Jack now, you are having the opportunity to become number one in Pauli's inner circle. In a few words, what are your ideas?"

"Honestly, I have not given it too much thought until now. I can sell quite a few devices, but I am not in the killing business.

I can buy the units and let Pauli know this one went to Cairo and the other one went to South Africa etcetera. To do this, I will need periodic news reports on a killing that I can claim as a success. Iranian and Syrian rebel groups do this all the time. They claim frequently, it was their guy who murdered the general. Nobody knows the truth because the guy killing the general blew himself up.

I will not get near Pauli without successful claims about my knowing the right buyers of Pauli's toys."

"Interesting response. Bascal, what do you think of Jack's approach and what thoughts do you have on accomplishing what Jack has to do?"

"He is partially correct but what's missing is the sales in Europe and elsewhere. He is limiting himself to a particular area when we know Pauli is selling into many countries.

Somehow, we must think of a way to make Jack a superhero for the entire market, and we know, that will not be easy."

Debra jumped into the conversation. "Jack and I have worked everywhere.

in Europe, Russia, and the Middle East. We speak seven languages, and we know one hell of a lot of people.

We have four contacts working on this case as we speak, and we can quickly add more.

What I am saying is we try to get the nephew out of the sales channel and put Jack in with a force of salespeople in Europe and the Middle East and with his relations in Africa, he could cement the deal.

Doing so, gets us control of the entire market. We can buy Pauli's devices and say we sold them here and there. Pauli doesn't care where they are sold if his cash stream continues.

We know reports of dead people can be faked but only for a short period of time. In that short period of time, we must figure a way for Jack to meet Pauli in person.

Damn, if I didn't just get a thought of a way to do what I said and put pressure on Pauli.

Order more devices of different configurations, then he must order the materials to build the stuff and have time to build the devices. During that time, delivery's destinations can be traced. Pauli's backlog increases and his delivery dates are not acceptable to high Euro buyers.

They begin to complain to Jack, and he demands a meeting with Pauli to solve the sales problems related to late deliveries."

"Very well stated Debra, and I knew if I got the three of you in a room, we could get a workable plan. We don't have one yet, but we have all the ingredients to make it work.

I think we should quit for the day and return in two days. This will give all of us a chance to fine tune the entire process and be able to sign-off on a workable solution."

They all agreed and left the meeting with higher spirits then they had prior to the meeting.

CHAPTER 57

After their meeting, Jack, and Debra, decided to entertain themselves the rest of the day by having a romantic dinner, a few glasses of wine and the rest of the night to make love.

The awoke about 9 the next morning later than usual, had their breakfast and coffee before beginning another round of planning on how to get close to Pauli.

"Debra, I think I should call Pauli now and tell him of Sergey's troubles in Russia and ask him if I can be of any help to him.

My experience includes buying and selling arms in Europe. Russia, China, and the Middle East for more than ten years. I can bring six to ten sales contacts covering Europe and the Middle East very rapidly, based upon my prior history and knowledge of the area.

I can give him referencWes in three countries who will vouch for my abilities.

Of Course, I would use Boris, Franz and Ethan or Anna. They would tell Pauli a believable story."

"It's a plausible story Jack, but I don't think you should rush so rapidly.

First, give him the news about Sergey and tell him you can help if needed.

Tell him you will call him back in a day or two if you get any additional information.

He will check on Sergey and find out what you told him is true. Then you call him again and tell him you have been thinking how you can help him and then give him your pitch plus the contacts to verify your history."

"That sounds good, and I might as well start now."

"Pauli, it is me, Vladimir. I am not sure if you heard about Sergey being arrested in Russia?"

"No, what happened and when? He was to call me two days ago and no call."

"Sorry to tell you, but he tried to sell one of your units to an undercover agent of the Kremlin. He was arrested and charged with trying to kill the Premier. He will either be killed or spend his life in a labor camp."

"Oh my god. I relied on him for a lot of my sales."

Listen to me for a moment. I have more than 20 years of buying and selling arms in Europe. Russia, China, and the Middle East. I know many buyers and sellers in Europe and the Middle East. I can get sales very rapidly, based upon my prior history and knowledge of the area.

Get a pencil and paper ready. Here are four current sellers of arms in the territory who can vouch for me. Boris in Russia, Franz in France, Anna in Belgium, and Ethan in the Netherlands. I will text you their personal numbers and you are free to speak to them about me."

"I 'm not sure which way I want to go Vladimir. Gimme a couple of days to digest the shock of losing Sergey."

"He did a lot of checking about me and he was satisfied he had a good guy to buy and sell your stuff."

"I know but I want to think about it and other things going on right now. I'll call when I'm ready to talk. Thanks for giving me the bad news."

He disconnected the call, but Jack thought he might have a reasonable opportunity to have the relationship.

Jack then quickly called all the names he had given to Pauli and told them to provide a story of success with Vladimir and they would enjoy working with him if you are selling a good product.

CHAPTER 58

The days passed quickly and there was no news from Pauli and Jack could only wait for him to decide. He did not want to push Pauli into a decision since it would probably hurt his chances of getting close to him.

Ten days had quickly gone by when Perry called him with some interesting news.

"Jack, you should like what I have just learned. A seller of Pauli's goods was arrested when he went to a mailbox pick-up point to receive a package from our bomb maker.

The seller was being watched because he had been identified by Interpol as an illegal arms seller. We had no idea he was receiving the package or dealing with Pauli.

Now he is trying to save his skin and is providing some information about his contact arrangement. It is through Fillip the nephew, who he has never met but talks to periodically.

We are examining the bomb sent to him, and it is a little more sophisticated than the first one we recovered. We will provide you the results of our investigation when it is completed.

I am not sure how we can get this arrest news to Fillip or Pauli. I think we allow some time to pass, and Fillip may learn about this arrest from other contacts on the street. Once they know about it, maybe Pauli will want some new people."

That is good news, but have you considered having the guy arrested calling Fillip and trying to trace the call?"

"We discussed it, but it was felt it would ruin our chances of getting to them, once it is known that the buyer got arrested. I believe it would be better to have Fillip or Pauli make to move to hire you."

"Your probably right. We don't want them on the run again as it already is hard enough to find them."

"Sit tight Jack. Let it happen on their time. I know it is frustrating for us and people are still getting killed. You're joining the bomb makers organization could be our only opportunity now. Let's stick to that plan."

After they disconnected, Jack realized he should have asked how the arrested seller paid for the unit. Perhaps Boris could trace the path of the exchange.

He sent Perry a text asking the question, hoping for an answer.

About twenty minutes later , he received the answer, which he immediately forwarded to Boris, asking if he could trace the payment.

Boris sent him a return text; I was wondering when you would use my computer skills again. I'll do my best and hope for a good answer.

CHAPTER 59

More days passed and more people were assassinated by planted bombs.

Jack impatiently waited to hear from Pauli, and he had not heard from Boris. All this waiting frustrated him.

Debra suggested they should take a short river cruise on the Seine which would stop at many wine growing areas along the river. It would only be a four-day cruise which starts in Paris and returns on the fourth day.

Jack agreed as he knew playing the waiting game for much longer wouldn't agree with him.

They left on the cruise three days later.

On the second day of the cruise, Jack did get a message from Pauli that he had not decided and if Jack was still interested. He sent Pauli a return message saying he was in Africa and travelling daily and yes, he was still interested but wouldn't be able to talk or meet with him very soon.

Pauli answered him and they could talk maybe next week. Jack said he would call him probably from Egypt. There were no further communications.

The next day, Boris sent him a message saying the money went from bank A to bank B and then somewhere else he could not hack into. He sent his apologies.

"Debra, Pauli, and his nephew are not stupid. They have made few mistakes and seem to cover their tracks like true profession crooks. I am not sure what it will take to break into their circle."

"Look, they may act professional now, but the day will come when they make a serious mistake. Be patient, remember when we started this gig, it was suggested it might take a year or so. Well, we are now into the seventh month and the trail is still cold. We haven't discovered how to heat up the chase."

"I know and it is frustrating to me, and I am beginning to believe it is one of the most difficult jobs I ever encountered. Let's go to the bar, I need a scotch."

They made their way to the bar and Debra had her usual glass of zinfandel and jack his scotch. At the far end of the bar, a man stared at Jack for a few moments and Jack's instincts wondered who was this guy and why is he staring at me?

"Debra, smile at me and pretend you're in a playful mode. When you have the opportunity take a quick peek at the guy on the right side of the bar. He was staring at me as if he knew me. Maybe you recognize him."

Debra nuzzled close to Jack and playfully kissed him on the check. While doing that she glanced at the stranger and then turned back to Jack.

"Your getting paranoid. That is one of the Interpol agents who we met at our first meeting months ago. Let's go say hello."

"Hi there, we think we know you from a previous meeting?"

"You do and the meeting was held at Interpol Headquarters in Paris, and you are Jack and Debra from America. I assume, you are still involved in the bomb maker investigation. Oh, I am Walter."

"Thanks Walter. I thought I recognized you, but I didn't have your name. The investigation is ongoing, and we are currently in a hold mode waiting for answers from others. Are you still involved with the case?"

"Yes, in fact, I am also in a hold pattern. This person has proved to be very elusive, and it has turned into a very difficult case."

"Those are Jacks thoughts exactly. Both of us are wondering what to do next and every plan we make thinking we are on the right path, leads to failure."

"Don't get distressed. We have at least twenty agents actively chasing down suspected clues and we also are still in limbo. Even being on vacation with my wife, I sit here in the bar wondering, why the case is so confusing."

"Well Walter, welcome to the club. Why don't you and your wife join us for dinner tonight. We have a reservation for table four in the dining room at eight. Maybe we can spend a few minutes on other important subjects."

"Thanks Jack. My wife's name is Celine, and we will enjoy dining with you both. See you at eight.

CHAPTER 60

At exactly eight pm, Walter and Celine were escorted to the table and met by Jack and Debra.

"First, thanks for asking us to join you this evening. It is not often we socialize with others in our business. I say that, because Celine and Debra have a lot in common and may have shared experiences in their respective assignments. Celine is a former member of DGSE, the French Secret Service and I am sure Debra, with her being a former member of the CIA, they both have much in common. So do Jack and me. We could honestly call tonight's meeting, dinner with the spies."

They all laughed as a waiter approached to take their drink orders. After the drinks arrived, the waiter returned to take their dinner orders. Soon, they were swapping old stories of their experiences working for their respective governments.

Celine and Debra soon discovered they had worked in the same countries and spoke the same languages. They also learned; they had similar assignments covering the illegal arms business.

"Celine, when you were in Belgium, did you ever work with a woman named Anna?"

"Maybe, if it is the Anna, I know along with one of her associates, Ethan, an ex-KGB agent."

"Oh my god. Anna and Ethan are good friends of ours and attended our wedding in the USA. We are still in touch with them for our current assignment. Spydom, is a small world."

"Because of my working in the arms field, there a probably more people we know with whom we have had a relationship. What was your area of expertise Jack."

"I also was associated with the arms business but the majority my time was spent in Russia and China. I travelled to many countries, but my home base was Russia."

"Poor Walter spends all his time in France except when we go on vacation."

"I'm just a misfit among you worldly people."

"Your still my favorite husband."

They again laughed and ordered another bottle of wine. They continued to share experiences and, on a few occasions, had been at the same place around the same time.

Jack switched the conversation to discuss the bomb maker project.

"Walter, I am happy to meet you and Celine and possibly, I would like to periodically speak to you and toss some ideas Debra and I might have as we try to bring this case to an end."

"Trust me, Celine and I have had many conversations about the hopelessness you feel when working on a complicated case, we've been there, and it is not fun. Both of us would be happy to share some time with you and maybe provide some guidance for you."

"I thank you for that and I just remembered, we are all on vacation. So, let's have another glass of wine and plan what we want to do and see tomorrow."

"Debra, tomorrow we will be stopping at Dammarie-lrs-lys and there are some lovely cafes and interesting shops. I'm in favor of improving their economy and I can always use some help. It will be a true vacation day."

"That sounds great for me, and the guys can go check out the wine bars."

CHAPTER 61

The party left the river cruiser about 9:30 in the morning and walked around the small town for about thirty minutes.

Walter and Jack found a nice outdoor café and ordered coffees while the ladies had discovered an unusual dress shop about a block away.

"Jack, do you mind if I talk about the bomb maker case?"

"Not really , because I think about it almost constantly. It's a real thorn in my side. I do have some questions regarding the recent arrest of the arms dealer. Did Interpol determine where the package shipped to the mailbox store originate? What country or city? It should be an easy thing to identify."

"I talked to Perry about that very question and nobody seemed to have an answer, Usually, postage amounts, and origination are clearly marked on the package, and it would be strange if it wasn't."

"It would not be strange if it was hand delivered to the shop. Remember, the pair recently moved and maybe the nephew hand delivered the package to establish an account at the mailbox place. Where in France was the guy arrested?"

"I believe it was in a small town named Wassy with a population of about 3000 out in the middle of nowhere. I think the largest city is Nancy about 250 kilometers away. That area is mostly agriculture."

Maybe they left Germany and are now living in France. Based on their prior shipping and receiving mailbox stores, they were all in a circle about 150 kilometers from Halsdorf. Now if we have this one point, it sits on the edge of a circle 150 kilometers or less from where they now live.

Again, thinking about their prior arrangements, they had five mailbox locations. Two in Germany and three more in different countries but in a 100-to-150-kilometer circle. We need a map and knowing one location may give us a clue to where they are located."

"I understand what you are saying and if this one point is in France, then there could be another in France and the other three in different countries but all of them 100-to150-kilometers away from their location."

"You are correct, but the mailbox stores could be in four or five countries which France borders. All we can really assume is they will be 100 or more kilometers from their location.

I will get my friend Boris to start his search again and he should have a good feel where the stores are in a month. It will all depend on how much material is ordered."

"Jack, we have made some progress, but I suggest we quit now as I see the ladies are approaching. Let's find a nice place to have lunch."

Celine and Debra joined them at the table and the discussion shifted from bomb maker to dresses and jewelry. Then, a suggestion to go for lunch.

The two couples left the café and then found a small restaurant where they would have lunch.

Celine asked what they had done while they shopped.

Walter answered, "Just man talk. That's it."

"Boring" Debra replied.

CHAPTER 62

After another day and a half, the cruise had returned to Paris and the couples exchanged addresses and promised to meet again soon.

A few moments after Jack had entered the apartment his phone rang, and it was Pauli.

"Vladimir, do you have time to talk?"

""Yes, I am in an airport, but I have about an hour before my flight. How can I help you?"

"I have given some thought to your proposal, and I am at the stage where I could use your help. I need some one to oversee the entire sales organization. How does that sound to you?"

"I like it. Will I get a percentage of sales, or would you prefer I buy the units and resell them to the various agents?"

"It will be better if you buy the units and then you decide on how much profit you want to earn."

"When do you want me to start?"

"As quickly as possible."

"I will be back in Europe in three days and will start then. Perhaps once I start, we could possibly meet to plan our strategy."

"I will not commit to any meeting at this time. Let's see the results first."

"True. I'll call you after I return. Thanks for the offer."

Jack was elated and quickly phoned Perry.

"Perry, the fish has taken the bait. I suggest we meet asap to develop a strong plan for the near term and future. There are a lot of pieces to this puzzle, and I better make sure the pieces fit together."

"How is tomorrow afternoon around two pm?"

"That will be fine. I'll see you then."

He informed Debra about Pauli's call and the subsequent meeting with Perry.

"I suggest you and I sit down in a few minutes and begin to envision what path I should take to remain safe. I must put together a list of possible sellers from various countries and stake out territories for each one.

One mistake and Pauli and the nephew disappear again. Fortunately, Pauli does not know my real identity or where I call home. I plan on keeping it that way."

"You and I know; we are in a dangerous business and never forget it. I want you around when my hair turns grey."

"Mine will turn before yours."

They both laughed and went to unpack their suitcases from their four-day cruise.

They later had lunch and began their discussion about Jack's strategy; not only to satisfy Pauli, but to capture him and destroy his bomb making business.

Chapter 63

The meeting with Perry and his staff started promptly on time and Jack and Debra had reviewed several items for Jack to follow in his guise as Pauli's sales director.

Perry opened the meeting providing his staff a few details of what Jack had chosen to do to catch the bomb maker.

"There is not any misconception as to how dangerous this role is for Jack. He will be putting himself amid a bunch of killers whose interest is killing others by any means possible. Under no circumstance is his presence to be known by anybody outside of this meeting room.

He will be operating solo and will provide his status to me or Bascal and we will determine when it is appropriate for our involvement. Jack will now let us know certain events he has planned to gain trust from the bomb maker."

"Thanks, Perry for your comments and support.

I realize some of the actions I am about to take are dangerous and I will take numerous steps to protect myself and my identity. My objective is to set the stage, where I cause enough problems for Pauli, that he agrees to meet with me.

To begin, I will be informing Pauli of my aligning myself with ten to twelve associates to sell his bombs within multiple countries in Europe, the Middle East, and Africa. These people will all be fictious and will be impossible to trace.

I will begin to supply orders to Pauli worth thousands of Euros for his products, which he will deliver to me. I will not reveal my associates nor the purpose of the purchase.

He will be paid by a bank of my selection, where we can trace the distribution of funds to their destination. This will be monitored closely using advanced previously unknown technology.

Within a few weeks, I will gradually increase the order amounts and the requirement for improved deliveries.

Working with Bascal, he will create media stories of deaths in faraway places with strange names and killings of people unhappy with their governing system. We do this to avoid suspicion by Pauli.

Also working with Interpol, we will try to disrupt deliveries of key materials, forcing Pauli to be unable to deliver to a schedule.

If Pauli starts to miss delivery dates, I will complain on behalf of my customers and suggest a personal meeting with him on the pretext of solving his delivery problems.

From then on, it will be your turn to act, and I assure you, you will have ample warning of my intended destination and meeting.

Thanks for listening and I am open to questions or concerns."

"I think you have spelled out your approach very well Jack. There maybe some hiccups but we will work with you to smooth the path you have chosen.

It is a good start and let us all hope your actions result in a good outcome for everyone."

The meeting ended and Jack now faced a lot of work to get his plans started and he only had a short period of time left to do it.

CHAPTER 64

The couple left the Interpol facility with full knowledge of the danger it presented to Jack and Debra. Over the next two weeks they would take several steps to convince Pauli of Jack having the sales organization prepared to begin doing business.

Interpol and the CIA had established an account for Jack of five million dollars equivalent to six million Euros.

Jack with the help of Boris opened an account in Estonia in the amount of one million Euros to begin buying devices from Pauli. The Estonia bank assured the depositors, the bank would take special precautions to hide all transactions.

We are ready he told Debra and using his encrypted and non-traceable phone he called Pauli to place orders for several units.

"Pauli, I have good news for you. I have arranged deals with several sales agents in a few key countries. Two of them have already given me orders even without knowing the final price."

"How do you know my name Vladimir?"

"Just about everyone knows your name after you arranged the killing of three Kolobrzeg residents. It was on the news and in a lot of newspapers.

Since I don't know any other name, what name would you like me to use?"

"Otto would be fine. Now tell me about the orders you have received."

Jack proceeded to provide the information about the devices, and he then asked Otto to give him a price and delivery estimate.

"Vladimir, thanks for the orders. I will calculate the price for each one as they have some custom features. I will also provide a reasonable delivery date. The information will be texted to the number I have for you."

"Thanks Otto and if I have further questions, I will also text you. Bye for now."

Jack disconnected the call and sat down to think about the commitment he he was imposing upon himself.

Think twice about every action you are about to take and the consequences of that action. It not only affects you, but it also involves Debra's future.

You will never know when your life is close to danger, so always be prepared for the worse. From this day forward, never leave home without your weapon.

Remember, you have taken the nephews job away and he may harbor deep resentment about you. Do not underestimate his ability to kill you.

He silently told himself all these things and the many possibilities of being in danger.

As he continued to review the perils, he was facing the phone rang, and he could see it was Boris.

"Hello Jack. It's your friendly hacker with some stolen news for you.

"And what trouble have you gotten into now?"

"The usual stuff. The bank in Estonia has a system in place that can trace multiple transfers worldwide. There is minimum fee for the service, but it is worth the cost.

I developed a program to track fifteen companies who deliver into the 100-to150-kilometer circle encompassing five countries. This program will give me a daily look at about forty mailbox stores in the area and not only who sent the package, but who is to receive it.

Whenever a name or address occurs more than once, it is highlighted. If the same receiver shows up in multiple locations, it is saved to higher priority folder, and I am notified immediately.

I am confident that between the bank actions and my delivery program, we will have a clear picture of the bomb makers activities and locations.

"Great job Boris. I would guess, there will not useful information for about two to three months if they keep their prior operating procedures in place."

"Jack, we went this route before, and the information was tipped to the suspects, and we ended up empty handed. This time, I want to information to remain between you and I until we have enough concrete information to bring about arrests.

I will keep you in the loop as data is slowly gathered."

"I one hundred percent agree with you. I am walking on a steep cliff, and I do not want to fall. Gather the data and you and I can discuss its relevance and only when we have ironclad information, from the bank and the deliveries, will it be presented to Interpol."

"Thanks, my friend. I will talk to you again in a few weeks."

For Jack, the day had its highs and lows but after his conversation with Boris, he was more confident of a successful ending this time around.

CHAPTER 65

Four days after Pauli received the orders from Jack, he texted with quotes and delivery dates. The pricing had increased from a similar order previously placed, but it was not a deal breaker.

The delivery dates suggested Pauli did not have inventory to quickly assemble these orders. He immediately texted Boris to inform him that Pauli would be purchasing materials for orders Jack had provided.

Jack answered the Pauli text asking him about payment terms. Within minutes he received a reply simply stating sixty percent in advance, balance upon notification of delivery.

Another text then asked where to send the money. Again, he received a quick reply. Funds are to be sent to Polish Munitions, care of Privatbankia a.s.

Jack was somewhat surprised by the name of the company and a bank in Slovakia. He again texted Boris the information and asked him to arrange a transfer of 24,000 Euros to Polish Munitions and to start the tracing process.

Jack waited another ten days before he sent texted Pauli again. This time he ordered three standard units and a custom unit with magnetic attachments suitable for a large vehicle.

He received confirmation of the orders and was promised pricing and delivery within a few days. Pauli also thanked him for the most recent payment, and they were waiting for material deliveries to start assembly.

Boris was again informed of the order placement and possible increased deliveries of vital materials.

During the time he was waiting to hear from Pauli, he received a cryptic message from Franz. Be careful, you are being watched. Call me.

He had not heard from Franz in over a month and his note sounded scary. He immediately phoned him to learn more about the message.

"Jack, a friend of a friend confided to me about a Polish Munitions company selling untraceable bombs. This person was not interested but just in case, he was given the name of Vladmir and if he could have him checked out by other friends.

I don't know what name you are using during your investigation and if it is you, be very careful who you meet or talk too. Some of these guys are thugs and have no concern about killing anyone."

"It is me Franz and thanks for the warning. I am supposed to be the exclusive seller but maybe the nephew doesn't agree.

I will take additional precautions immediately. Thanks for the warning."

After his conversation with Franz, he began to wonder how he could get the nephew out of the sales business. Maybe, I have cut off his way of earning decent money. Perhaps he is trying to prove to Pauli, that my appointment was not a good decision. I should talk to Debra about this subject.

That afternoon after they had lunch, he asked Debra to come to the living room of their apartment to discuss a possible problem,

"Honey, I have a rather large dilemma confronting me. I believe Pauli's nephew is unhappy for me to be the major supplier or orders to Pauli and the nephew has lost his source of income.

I am assuming this because Franz called warning me that dangerous people would try to find me and learn about me. The people that told this to Franz referred to me as Vladimir. Only Sergey, Pauli and maybe one other person besides the nephew, know me by that name.

I have a thought about how I can get the nephew on my side. Hire him. I willi offer him a job as my assistant and pay him a good commission on all sales from the people I supply to him.

These people will be undercover Interpol agents acting as middlemen to sell the product to bad guys. I have not presented this to Perry yet, but I believe he will approve it.

We must gain inside knowledge to the workings of Pauli's operation.

CHAPTER 66

Debra liked Jack's solution to the issue and told him to now discuss it with Perry.

He dialed Perry's number, and the phone was quickly answered.

"Jack, I was just wondering how you were doing. How is the relationship going?"

"It's the reason I am calling you. I have heard from a reliable source that Pauli's nephew may be trying to get rid of me or change Pauli's impression of me.

I think I stepped on his toes taking over what was his exclusive territory and thereby cutting off a major source of income for him.

Here is what I propose. I would like three agents from Interpol who can serve as either buyers or resellers of Pauli's devices. They should operate in three separate countries.

I will ask Pauli if his nephew would become my assistant for a piece of the action, and he would work with the three agents mainly by phone, email, or text. Periodically they would provide orders and I will set up a means of payment for their orders.

"Do you think we can make it work?"

"Absolutely. We have a lot of agents with a lot of experience with the illegal arms trade. They will fit in perfectly for this charade we are about to create.

"Great idea and eventually, we will catch them. I'll call you after a locate the players and brief them and then we'll meet with you. Stay safe."

"Well Debra, once we have an Interpol team together, I will approach Pauli and ask if the nephew wants to assist me. This opportunity might bring us closer to an end of this case."

"Don't get your hopes up. Just make sure you dot all the I's and cross the T's. It is far from being over, and maybe it will last another six months."

"I have to be optimistic, but you may be a better guesser than me."

Two more orders were given to Pauli, and he praised Jack for his success. Pauli confided his suppliers were sending larger batches of materials on a more frequent schedule and his deliveries should improve.

Jack was happy with the response as it presented a chance to identify the destination and pick-up points. Boris will like it and it should make his job easier.

As that thought entered his mind, he received a call from Boris.

"Well sir, in a short period, I have been able to identify two additional points on our circle. I am guessing within one or two months; I will have five-points verified."

"Maybe faster, Boris. I just learned Pauli has increased his ordering of materials and therefore you should experience a higher level of activity. I will help you as I order three more units over the next four weeks."

"Good news Jack and I will keep a lookout for the areas I am watching. I was disappointed the bank could not trace your funds beyond Slovakia.

They promised me they have hired a couple of hack wizards to try and overcome the blockages. I'll advise you if they find anything new.

You stay safe and let you and me solve this case soon."

CHAPTER 67

Perry had selected his three agents to now serve as bad guys trying to sell killing devices. He arranged a meeting for later in the week.

Jack decided initially, he would require one agent in the Netherlands, One in Hungry and the third person in Bulgaria. Should the nephew want some location changes, it would always be available to do.

Perry began the meeting by introducing the agents and assured Jack, they had the latest information available about the case. It was then Jack's turn to say what he expected from the agents.

"For discussions concerning me, I am known by Pauli and his nephew as Vladimir. I was vetted by a Russian on behalf of Pauli,by the name of Sergey who made a major mistake in Russia and is now in jail for a longtime.

My plans are very simple. I want to give the nephew a job as my assistant and let him oversee your activities. Remember, our object is to learn where they are located and manufacture their deadly devices.

The nephew is an ex-con and appears to know his way around the illegal routes to move materials and completed devices. Both he and Pauli can disappear rapidly as they have done twice before to avoid capture.

I would one of you to try and become true friends of the nephew as every bit of information we can gather will be usable.

I would like you to be in the selected countries early next week and I will work on arranging the hiring of the nephew. From then on, he will be your primary contact and you will provide your whereabouts to Interpol, and they will notify me. Any questions?"

"Where do I get orders for these devices?"

"I'll leave that to your imagination. If you come up with a good idea involving an assassination attempt in Europe or elsewhere, keep it secret. Just tell the nephew you have an order to be delivered by such and such date. Never reveal the buyer or where it is going."

"How many orders are you trying to get?"

"All of you should try for an order about every six weeks Do not exceed two or three units for any order. Typically, it is one device per order. Text me and I will arrange payment.

Remember, they will trace to equate certain units with assassinations with make for good TV and newspaper headlines. We can only fake a few of these before they realize someone is getting close to them."

"How savvy is the nephew?"

"He has been in prison a few times and it should be assumed he has a few prisoners he probably contacts to get input on various people and that includes you.

He is not dumb, which means you have stay alert. Don't provide him any information about your current or previous life as an arms dealer.

I think I have provided you enough information to het you started. The rest is up to you. Everyone here wants to end this case and put he bomber and nephew in prison for a long time.

We hope with your efforts and other things we are doing; this will be the end of the bomb maker. Good luck and stay safe."

Perry than thanked Jack and added several more caveats.

"This is a joint CIA/Interpol investigation. There are many lives on the line which we can only save by doing the best job we can do. Even small mistakes will threaten closure. I know the capabilities of the four of you here today so just retain the level of professionalism you have demonstrated throughout your career, and we will succeed. Thank you."

CHAPTER 68

Jack let a few days pass for the three agents to get themself settled before making the call to Pauli.

"Otto, how are you today?"

"I am busy Vladimir, trying to get your orders assembled. What do you need now?"

"I'm looking for an assistant to help here in Europe and I wondered if your nephew wants a good paying job?"

"Can you give me more information?"

"I need someone to manage three or four arms dealers in several countries so I can have more time to concentrate on Africa which is an extremely promising area for big sales.

I can promise him expenses plus thirty percent commission on sales. I really need help."

"Let me talk to him and I'll get back to you."

"Thanks."

Jack thought: "the trap has been baited and we will see if the rat goes for the bait."

After he had talked to Jack, Pauli called his nephew into his lab to discuss the offer being made. Pauli saw it as an advantage for the business and the possibility of Fillip getting experience from a pro.

It would also reduce some stress on Pauli as the nephew complained quite a lot about his loss of income.

"Fillip, I know you are unhappy about losing your sales in Europe and the associated money. I called Vladimir and convinced him that I wanted you to work with him in Europe. He has agreed to assign three or four arms dealers he knows for you to manage.

He also agreed he will pay your expenses and give you a thirty percent commission on European sales. I am not just a chemist; I can also negotiate."

"Pauli, you told him that and he accepted?"

Yes, and why not. I want the business and he can get it. But I also want you to succeed, and I think you could learn a lot from Vladimir. He is very knowledgeable of many countries and areas. Sergey told me all about him and how good he could be to our business."

"You told him all that and it is really happening?"

"I called him and told him what I wanted, and he understood, I was the boss. He finely agreed to my terms and now you must decide if you want a good paying job, within my company."

"I see it as a good chance. Should I call him, or do you want to do it?"

"No, you call and get the details when you can start."

Fillip waited about an hour before he called. He thought what he could do with the money and a shapely lady came to mind, she certainly will play with me if there is money available. He then dialed the number.

"Vladimir, it's me Fillip. My uncle told me he got me a new job with you, and it will pay me some good money. When do you want me to start?"

"That is good news Fillip. How about next week because I want to notify the dealers and let them know they will report to you. You and I will become two-man team and our target is sales in many places for big Euros."

"I like it and I'll call you Monday."

The rats took the bait thought Jack as he smiled.

CHAPTER 69

The agents posing as arms dealers had settled in the countries previously selected and each one had called Jack using untraceable phones and provided contact information for his use only. They also provided contact numbers to be used by the nephew.

As planned, Fillip called Jack early Monday was given the names and contact numbers of the three dealers. It was suggested that Fillip contact them as soon as possible to begin the search for customers for the deadly devices.

Fillip may be able to give them leads about other dealers in the area who might also support their sales efforts.

Feedback to Jack suggested all the calls went well and the dealers acted enthusiastic about having the nephew as a member of their team. They all hoped to eventually have significant information about Pauli's illegal activities.

It was time for Jack to give Pauli two more orders destined for Sudan and he shared with Pauli that there would be more larger orders from his buyer. According to Vladimir, there would soon be a brutal attack on the governing body of Sudan and Pauli would be the main beneficiary.

Pauli immediately increased his ordering of essential materials but working alone, his delivery commitments were not being met.

This was all in Jack's plan, and he intended to gradually overwhelm him with orders he could not deliver.

Within two weeks of placing additional orders, Boris had been able to identify every delivery point in five countries.

Pauli was also experiencing another problem. Fillip now being unavailable to timely pick up necessary materials and it was contributing to late deliveries. Pauli began to consider picking up deliveries by himself or arranging the mailbox stores to set up deliveries to him.

He knew, this could result in exposing his location, so he had to think of another way of getting the materials safely. He knew Fillip was earning more Euros than he ever had and would be reluctant to have to continually drive a few hundred kilometers for Pauli and perhaps lose a sale.

He thought maybe he could arrange for Vladimir to periodically pick up some materials and Fillip at other times. he wondered if this would put him in danger of being exposed.

He finally decided he would arrange to have all the materials arriving at different locations be sent to one facility where he could easily pick them up himself. He would continue this practice for one month and then change to have the materials sent to another location for him.

He would begin testing this decision immediately.

CHAPTER 70

Jack was still happy with his success luring Fillip to join his team of illegal arms dealers and he had been thinking of it as he took his evening walk in his neighborhood.

He knew there was some danger of Fillip learning how the dealers were getting their sales, but his income had risen dramatically. Hence, he probably didn't think where or how sales happened because he earned money on every sale.

One of the agents working with the nephew told Jack that Fillip now had a steady girl friend who previously had been a hooker and wining and dining her was now a steady occurrence.

He certainly is not saving his money thought Jack. As that thought entered his mind, his instinct sensed someone was following him. He took his phone from his pocket and held it up as if he was reading something on the screen, but this camera showed what was behind him and it was not a friendly neighbor.

He quickly called Perry and told him his location and he would pass his apartment building in about five minutes. He would not stop, and he had already released the safety on the gun he carried in his pocket. Perry told him help was on the way.

He then called Debra and told her to arm herself and not to allow anyone into their apartment.

As he approached his building, he noted another man lurking at the entrance but not looking at him. He increased his walking pace and passed within two feet of the man at the entrance. He continued down the block and made a sudden turn between two cafes and ducked under an open umbrella.

The man following him stopped but did not see him and slowly started into the space between the two cafes but now he held a gun in his hand. The second man also appeared at the same spot but just stood there waiting to see what would happen.

It didn't take long before Jack shot the first man when he was about three feet from him. The second pulled out a gun but he was suddenly tackled by two large men who threw him to the ground. One of the men pointed at Jack and gave him a signal to get out of there fast.

Jack understood the cue and hurried back to his building avoiding a crowd who had heard the shots. He did not use the elevator but took to the stairs two at a time.

He put the key in the door but before opening it, he said "Debra, it's me and everything is ok." He then opened the door to see her standing with a gun in her hand.

He approached with open arms and she quickly per her arms around him. She was shaking as she hugged him.

"Let's sit and I'll tell what happened.

"I sensed someone was following me and verified it on my phone. I called Perry to tell him my location and I would pass our building in five minutes. As I neared our building, there was another man waiting for me to pass. I walked a little slower and ducked between the two cafes down the street.

The gunman did not see me immediately and I shot him. The second man standing near the opening between the cafes was quickly tackled by two men and throw to the ground. One man signaled me to get out of there and I made it safely back here."

"Oh my god Jack. I am glad you are ok. I was ready for anything after you called me. Who in the hell is looking to kill you?"

"My first guess is Fillip. He resented my taking his job away from him, which could mean, Fillip lost his influence over Pauli. Maybe it is time we put Fillip behind bars."

CHAPTER 71

Perry called Jack the following morning and he was happy to learn Jack was fine. A little shaken but unharmed.

"Jack, any idea who would be looking for you and want to kill you? We tried to get information from the guy we captured, but he acted like a clam and shut his mouth."

"There is only one name I keep thinking about and it is Fillip. He must resent I took away his plush job in Europe and perhaps he doesn't like me having a close relationship with his uncle. I am sure he has several former prison friends ready to kill for Euros."

"I think you are right, for everything you said, and we know the guy we captured did time with Fillip a few years ago. We could arrest him at any time for lots of charges. The problem with that is, we lose a key source of locating Pauli. I am not sure we want to give up on that opportunity yet."

"I agree but I will stay armed and ready because he may have others who feel luckier.

I have been successful on putting the squeeze on Pauli to deliver faster and I know he may have pick up problems getting his materials since his nephew is working. I plan on placing more orders later this week to see how he responds."

"Any info as to where the suppliers deliver their goods?"

"Yes, five sites in five countries have been verified and over the next month, we should be able to provide exact data as to when we can expect material to arrive at all the five locations.

At that point, we would request Interpol to plant people near these locations and see if we can tag Pauli's car or whoever picks up a package and follow the vehicle to his location via GPS."

"That is good. Let me know when we can do it and where, without tipping off the mailbox sites. We may only get one chance to catch this guy."

CHAPTER 72

Pauli was unaware of his nephew's attempt to have Vladimir killed and if he did learn about it, what would he do? Besides, he had his own problems getting materials he needed to complete the orders he had received.

At this point, he was alone, and he had nobody he could trust to help him solve the problems and he wondered how long he could operate this way before his customers lost interest in him and his products.

He had a nice stream of money flowing into his account and he knew, another year this good, he can retire and live a normal life.

He understood, he had to solve his problems and he could only think of a few ways out of his dilemma.

There was Fillip, now hustling orders and shacking up with a hooker. He suddenly became a lose cause. Maybe I should not have gotten him the job with Vladimir.

What about Vladimir, getting me decent orders worth a lot of money, but could he be trusted? The other street crooks he knew would slit his throat for a hundred Euros.

Lastly, there are the guys who run the mailbox stores and maybe for a few more Euros, they could arrange delivery to my place. The problem with that is, I don't know any of them. Fillip's friends arranged the locations, and can I really trust a bunch of street crooks?

He had been pacing back and forth in his lab and tiring himself out. He sat down to rest for a while, but he couldn't avoid the continuous thoughts of his problems without solutions. Then he got an idea.

He called Vladimir and asked him if he would pick up some materials for him at a mailbox site in Belgium. He would then meet him at a restaurant at the junction of A4 and A26 in Reims. Jack was thrilled of this turn of events.

He agreed to help him, but it would have to be tomorrow for lunch because he was just returning from Spain. Pauli accepted his help and would meet him as scheduled.

Pauli travelled the short forty kilometers from his lab to Reims to meet Jack for lunch. He arrived two hours early to observe the cars coming or going to the restaurant and watch for any suspicious actions by anybody. He did not want to get caught.

Interpol was aware of what Pauli might do to avoid detection. They had parked a delivery truck at on corner of the parking lot with camera visibility of the entire area. Inside the rear of the truck sat two agents with their eyes glues to a large screen watching every car that parked in the lot.

They had the capability of zoom technology and could zoom into every vehicle and judge how many people were inside. Mostly, all drivers exited their vehicles soon after arrival and some waited until another vehicle arrived and then both drivers left their cars to go for a meal.

Pauli parked near the back of the large lot, but his windshield faced the truck. The agents noted that this driver did not leave his car and after one hour they photographed him and sent his picture off to Interpol.

Ten minutes later, they knew they had their man.

About forty minutes later, Jack drove into the lot and parked not to far from Pauli. Jack exited the car and walked towards Pauli's sedan and Pauli also exited his car and met Jack.

Vladimir, it is nice to meet you and thank you you're your help. Let's go to lunch and we can talk inside the restaurant.

While the two walked to the restaurant another vehicle was parking almost besides Jack's car. The pair entered and were quickly seated towards the back of the restaurant where they could not see their cars.

A person exited the car and seemed to disappear as he approached Pauli's car. He had slid under the car and skillfully planted two GPS tracking devices at the front and rear of the car. He was done in less than a minute and was back in his car and drove away.

All of this was being digitally entered on a high-tech video recorder and it was shut off after the known agent left the lot. It was turned on again as Jack and Pauli left the restaurant.

Pauli walked with Jack to his car and together they carried Pauli's materials to his car. They said their good buys, and each left the restaurant lot to go their separate ways.

The GPS data was already displayed on the large screen as Pauli headed back to his lab.

CHAPTER 73

The surveillance truck parked at the restaurant finally left and would return to an Interpol office. The tracking was now being closely monitored in a central location in France.

The GPS route tracking showed the car had travelled about twenty Kilometers East from the original location and had parked at a petrol station for a short period before continuing North towards Germany. It finally stopped at a location ten kilometers past the German-France border.

Within thirty minutes, Interpol agents arrived and found the vehicle was empty and parked in a farming district a long distance from any building or home. There was no indication of any damage to the vehicle, and the GPS units were still attached to the car.

"Pauli had arranged for another contact to meet him at the petrol station with another car, load the materials into the new car and then the person would drive the car North and park it away from the direction Pauli would take to his lab. Once more, Pauli had successfully outwitted Interpol.

Perry was shocked when he got this news and immediately called Jack to tell him about the latest saga of Pauli.

"Jack, this is an unreal scenario and we have been stymied once more. We tracked the car from the moment it left the restaurant. Twenty kilometers later, Pauli switched cars at a petrol station in France and disappeared. The original car with the GPS, headed for Germany. It was found sitting empty next to a field of flowers, just over the German border.

I am guessing he will now move to a new location and since you know of one delivery point, he will probably change them as well."

"Perry, this is unreal. We do everything right but so doesn't Pauli. He is thinking about what can go wrong and makes the corrections.

Whenever we get close to closure, he has a way of eluding us."

"The next time we get close to him, we make an arrest. We'll find his lab eventually and without him, it can't function anyway."

"I agree, let's just concentrate on catching him or Fillip."

"I'm going to call him and attempt to set a future meeting and I'll let you know if it ever happens."

"Good idea and we will talk later."

After talking to Perry, Jack placed a call to Pauli who answered the call on the third ring.

"Pauli, I want to thank you for the lunch, and it was nice to finally meet you. I hope you got home safely."

"Oh yeah, no problems and what about you?"

"Just a lot of traffic, but I am fine. I talked to another dealer today in a remote part of Africa. He knew of the products I have previously sent to other areas and wanted to do some business. Are you beginning to catch up on deliveries?"

"Yes and no. I am still trying to solve getting the material deliveries sent somewhere else, so I don't have to travel to far to get them. It delays my efforts to get you the devices you require because to retrieve my materials, I lose almost a full day. This is not good, but I have yet to figure out how to solve the problem."

"Let me think about it and I'll let you know my ideas. Again, thanks for lunch. Let me treat the next time."

"You're welcome, Vladimir, it was my pleasure. Thanks for the call."

Jack sat for a moment and thought to himself. How in the hell am I going to catch this guy?

CHAPTER 74

Jack thought a lot about how he could entrap Paulin and catch him. I know he has a problem retrieving his deliveries and his pickup locations are scattered in four different countries.

Why doesn't he just look on the internet and he would probably discover, most of the mailbox stores offer delivery to a home or business. Maybe, he doesn't have internet services to avoid be found.

Once more, Pauli has figured out another way of protecting his lab location.

I don't think any suggestion from me would be acceptable to him, but it may if it came from Fillip. Now the question is, how do I get him to convince his uncle, there are smarter ways to proceed.

Jack spent a good portion of the day thinking of ways to trick Pauli and although he had a few cleaver ideas, none of them will work unless they are given by someone he trusts, one hundred percent.

He decided to see how far he could get with Fillip by being friendly and building his ego, so he decided to call him and run a test.

"Fillip. I am calling you to congratulate you on the last two orders you sent to me. A great job and the buyers and may buy a lot more devices. I hope your uncle can deliver on time.

I've talked to him in the past two days, and he complains he spends to much time retrieving deliveries. Wasn't that your job once? I look on the internet and most mailbox outfits offer delivery. Why won't he do that?"

"Vladimir, he is a stubborn old man. He won't use the internet except to study chemistry issues. He is afraid someone will trace him."

"Well, you know him better than I do, but he needs help. Our customer doesn't want to hear about his problems. They want what they ordered delivered on time."

"Let me see what I can do because some of these customers are mine and will start yelling at me."

"Okay, let me know if you feel you have made some progress, because it's affecting me as well. Thanks again for your good work and we'll talk again soon."

That was interesting and I did learn something useful. Pauli uses the internet for studying chemistry. Maybe Boris can find him?

He called Boris but the phone was not answered, and he left a simple message for Boris to return his call.

Within a few minutes, Boris returned his call.

"Thanks for returning my call as I have learned something interesting today which should be useful to you. Pauli uses the internet to solve chemistry issues. Is there a chance of being able to locate him on the net studying chemistry?"

"It's very doubtful as there are thousands of sites, and I would not know where to start."

"I Understand, but he is the bomb maker and maybe he just looks at explosive materials and how to use them or detonate them. I know, I am grasping at straws, but I am trying hard to find a way to catch this guy."

"I'll try a couple of things, but I have my doubts about success. I'll let you know in a few days. Thanks for the call."

How can one guy outthink fifty plus experienced investigators, with all the latest gadgets, who are trying their best to catch him?

CHAPTER 75

The killings increased and Pauli continued his bomb making activity yet paid no attention to complaints of late deliveries. He knew from experience; his buyers had no place else to obtain his secret weapons.

He saw his bank account rising and figured that one more year of good sales will allow him to close the business and he would become untraceable like his bombs.

Hence, he figured out, by taking a day off every other week, he could collect his packages of materials needed to fabricate his deadly devices.

Based on Boris's study of shipping destinations, the stores receiving deliveries were monitored by Interpol to see if Fillip or Pauli ever came to collect the materials. Again, Pauli was one step ahead of them.

He had hired a small parcel delivery service to visit each store and obtain his packages. The parcel delivery service had many trucks and was a frequent visitor to each of the stores, almost daily, and hence was never questioned. Interpol never determined whether the vans were delivering shipments or picking up shipments and therefore, it was a legitimate business relationship.

Every two weeks, Pauli would meet the van on the outskirts of small French villages and exchange incoming materials and give the driver devices he required to be shipped per buyer instructions.

The owner of the delivery service drove the van being used for this questionable service and was paid double the normal price. The driver realized the money he was receiving for his service, kept him from asking questions.

With no knowledge of material or bomb shipments, neither Interpol nor Jack and Debra and their team had any new clues and there was little progress towards a solution.

Working on this case for many months now, Jack, Debra and the team were all frustrated with their inability to stop the killings and capture Pauli.

CHAPTER 76

Interpol and the FBI wanting better results and they had voiced their unhappiness with top officials of Interpol. Perry was called before his

Superiors who expressed their displeasure with the lack of clues to bring the case to a close. He was instructed to apply more people and an expansive investigation to get a solution faster.

Perry arranged another meeting with the entire team to try and map out a new strategy as the pressure from within Interpol and the FBI wanting better results. The meeting took place two days after top officials from both organizations expressed their unhappiness over negative results.

"Thank for attending today. It is a meeting I never thought would happen. We all know, until now, Pauli has out foxed us and for now, safely keeps delivering his deadly devices. He feels he is untouchable and maybe we will eventually give up the chase.

He is right for now, but he is wrong that we will give up.

The whole purpose of this meeting is to look at steps we could possibly take to catch him. He may be invisible now, but he is human and as a group, we should be smarter than him.

Let's put our ideas and theories on the table and separate the good from the so-so and leave here today positive strategy of finding him and putting him prison.

I implore each of you to give us your ideas and thoughts regardless how crazy they may sound. Who wants to begin?"

Bascal, Perry's trusted assistant, began by reminding everyone that from day one, we all knew this could be a long and dangerous case. It is now much longer than we originally assumed and the guy we are chasing seems to have outguessed all our attempts to capture him.

I am going to question what we are now doing or not doing. If we are doing it, can it be improved? If we are not doing something, why not?

For example, we are trying to identify Pauli or his nephew Fillip at mailbox stores where we know shipments are arriving for pickup by either of them or accomplices. What we are doing is not working, and he still is getting his shipments and he more than likely is shipping bombs in response to sales.

So, what are we missing? Every day various delivery vans arrive at each of the mailbox sites, but we never investigate them as to whether they are delivering goods or picking them up. A member of Jack's team knows the name of those that deliver the basic materials to Pauli. We have never investigated them in detail as to where their shipments originate.

What if a different parcel service is picking up the material and delivering it to Pauli. When they deliver to Pauli, does he give them shipments to forward? We must begin to answer these questions if we expect to succeed."

Jack was next and wanted to add what Bascal had stated.

"I have real experience in picking up shipments specifically sent to Pauli and yet I went into one of the sites and asked for a delivery for Otto Weber, Pauli's fake alias, and I was given his packages without question.

The point is, we can not rely on others to do our jobs. The clerks in these places see 50 to 100 people daily and all they do is try and satisfy their customers request, they have no idea about who is bad and what packages are being shipped to them or what they might be shipping to someone else.

The last time Interpol asked about shipments for Otto Weber at a delivery site, he was tipped by someone, and they quickly changed sites. We must think about what more we can do as an undercover investigation to get this information.

Here is another possibility. What have we done to shut off Pauli's sources of supplies?

I know he probably can get his stuff from a few sources, but we could put the squeeze on them one at a time to really screwup his fab and delivery cycle. Who is the trans-shipper in Italy who accumulates and repacks his materials and ships them to the mailbox stores?

That's it for me at this stage but we must do something to reduce the constant stress."

Walter, a newer member of the team from Interpol wanted to speak next.

"I spoke to Jack on occasion regarding this case and here is my concern.

I know we keep tabs on Fillip. Pauli's nephew, but how much do we really track him?

It seems to me; he could be a vital link to get to Pauli and yet we are not using him to the full extent of our possibilities.

For example, have we added tracking GPS to his vehicle? Can we track him by aircraft or drone?

We know he is typically shacked up with a hooker, what do we know about her and how much does she know about him?

I believe we are missing an opportunity by not getting more involved in his daily routine."

Perry then suggested a break for lunch in the cafeteria and they would meet again in an hour.

The meeting resumed about an hour after the break and again Perry had comments to add what had been said thus far.

"What each of you has said thus far is all true. We have failed up to this point because we assumed the villain would make mistakes and we also assumed this case would be solved rapidly.

Well, we were wrong on both counts and now we will start towards solving this mess we partially created.

Here is what I am initiating starting today. Bascal, you are to form a team dedicated to the delivery of materials and shipments of completed devices. This team is to apply one hundred percent of it's time on this one factor until all questions are answered.

Jack, I know a member of your team also has important data concerning the companies involved in the shipping business. If possible, I would like him to work with Bascal on this one item.

Next, Walter. Although you are new to this case, you have a history of experiences which will be beneficial to another team which I want you to lead. I want you to also form a team exclusively to investigate and focus on the nephew, and those he may be in contact with at this time.

You are to gather data only and prepare a plan of action to bring him to justice. In no way is he to learn of your efforts until we are ready and able to arrest him. You and your team are to use every resource available to this organization to accomplish your objective. As I told Bascal, your team will also spend one hundred percent of time and effort to reach your goal.

Jack you, and Debra will work with both teams as consultants and critics to make sure we are not missing anything as we begin this highly focused investigation phase.

We would appreciate if your team members could provide input and help when requested.

I expect this phase to be our sole and maybe last attempt to end the reign of terror this monster has created. I would like to have weekly updates as to your findings and I am setting a target completion date, two months from now.

If there are no further questions, and remember what I said to begin, we will not give up until we catch them."

The meeting room quickly emptied as everyone now had there marching orders. It will be a parade ending at Pauli's residence.

CHAPTER 77

Within hours after the Perry meeting, Bascal had assembled his team and had received delivery site information from Boris. He began to prioritize the actions he would take in a chronological order.

First and foremost, he assigned two people to seek information on each of the delivery firms Boris had identified. Bascal expected complete and detailed information on each firm using public data. None of the firms were to be contacted.

Delivery services frequenting the know mailbox sites being used by Pauli were to be always tracked as to their destinations and type of packages being delivered. Interpol had good ideas of the size packages being received and even a better idea of packages being shipped by Pauli.

Agents were to provide a daily report to Bascal for every firm suspected of transporting questionable materials.

He also assigned a person to track delivery services identified who pickup packages at the known sites and then deliver into the French countryside. The known delivery services engaged in suspected deliveries are to be under surveillance by planted GPS monitors, aircraft, or drones if possible.

Information is to be carefully checked daily and firms only eliminated when proof of legal deliveries are found. Again, all actions are to be taken without spooking those who are under investigation.

Walter had established his team quickly after the meeting ended. He would use three agents who currently have a sales relationship with Fillip and a fourth person to investigate known contacts of Fillip, including the new girlfriend.

Daily reporting was a priority and a necessity for monitoring Fillip's movements.

Lastly, Jack and Debra had reviewed each of the proposed activities of the two teams and would receive daily reports concerning results. Jack had spoken to Boris about providing the latest information on the shipping firms and Jack requested if he could take a close look at the repacking outfit in Italy. He also questioned Boris about the bank's results of tracking the money flow.

For the first time in a long time, Jack and Debra were optimistic about the steps now being utilized to entrap Pauli on many fronts. They knew it will take time, but every little success will begin to close the circle around the menace to society.

The weekly reports will tell the story, chapter by chapter, until the conclusive ending.

CHAPTER 78

Pauli was happy with the arrangements he had made to improve his deliveries of required materials and shipments and customers complaints were slowly going away.

He may never get the Nobel prize for chemistry, but he was proud of his ability to successfully function in the illegal weapons arena. Feeling confident of his ability to avoid discovery by Interpol and his growing backlog of orders, gave him the feeling of being invincible.

He felt it was a good time to begin offering larger and more dangerous devices. He had learned enough about explosives to safely build newer designs possibly capable of taking down buildings and other large structures.

He figured there would be a good market for these products where rebel groups wanted to disrupt local and regional infrastructure. He pictured selling these items for 50,000 Euros and higher dependent on force of the device.

I must first catch up on my late deliveries, he thought, and once that is close to being satisfied, I will move to more destructive items. Maybe I can accomplish this in the next few weeks.

He had not heard from his nephew in a few days and decided to call him and get a feeling about possible future sales.

"Hello Fillip. I haven't heard from you this week and wanted to know how you are doing."

"I'm fine. I'm with my girlfriend now, so can I call you back in an hour or two?"

"Sure, I'll be here."

Within the hour, Fillip called his uncle to provide him a look at future orders.

"Pauli, I am living a good life now thanks to getting me this job with Vladimir. We may book at least on order per week over the next couple of months and some will be for multiple units."

"That is good but keep me in the loop as I will purchase sufficient materials to cover the new orders. I am fine and thinking of expanding the product line to include larger explosive units. I hope, I can begin design and testing in two month and then you can earn some very big money."

"Sounds good Uncle, my girlfriend is making us dinner now. I will keep in touch with you and let you know what orders can be expected and the delivery dates. Stay safe Uncle."

"You stay safe and enjoy your evening."

Pauli set the phone down and was happy to hear Fillip was enjoying his life. He knew he had a rough start and spent a few years in jail. Now he was making money and had a girlfriend. I'm glad for him.

He then returned to his lab and immediately resumed fabricating more devices.

CHAPTER 79

Pauli wasn't the only busy person, Bascal and Walter were working with their teams and had prepared a week-by-week schedule of specific actions. Plans had been sent to Jack and Debra for approval and they quickly signaled, everything was a go.

Bascal's team had carefully reviewed the data supplied by Boris and had identified four delivery firms to investigate and track daily. This action would start immediately as they knew materials from Italy were being shipped at least twice a week.

Interpol SUV's and small cargo trucks had been situated at the five known sites where materials were being received. Video evidence of the of the questionable delivery vans coming and going from the targeted sites was being collected.

When an opportunity presented itself, agents would try to attach GPS tracking devices to the delivery vans. Once they were able to discover a van traveling to various French villages, aircraft or drones would be added to the surveillance routine.

Walter had a more difficult assignment as Interpol did not know where Fillip or his new girlfriend resided. The sales agents working for Interpol had never met Fillip and only communicated to him be phone. They figured he was using untraceable burner phones usually discarded after a few calls. Trying to locate him even within a small area would be a difficult job.

The agents wondered if even Pauli knew where his nephew lived or the area's where he might contact buyers. They thought they might be able to trace a call to a known location of a cell tower. That would at least place him within a mile or so within a certain area.

Walter knew Jack had hired Fillip and maybe he can contact him a couple of times within a few hours and Interpol using advanced triangular technology, pinpoint him within a specific location relating to cell towers.

Shorty after his thoughts of trying to locate Fillip, he phoned Jack.

"Hey, I need some help. Can you call Fillip with a story to keep him on the line for at least five minutes and then disconnect for a reason. Then call him back with an excuse for the disconnect and try to keep him engaged for another four or five minutes.

We have some new technology which allows us to triangulate phone calls and identifies cell towers within or close to an area where the call is being answered. It would be a good thing to know, as there are no clues as to where he operates."

"Sure Walter. Give me about ten minutes and I will make the call from the apartment, and I am confident, I can keep him on the line long enough to do your thing."

"Thanks, I appreciate your assistance."

Ten minutes later Jack clicked on the number he had for Fillip, and he quickly answered the phone.

"Vladimir how are you. I was just talking to my uncle yesterday and told him we expected to get a lot of new orders soon."

"I am fine. How is your uncle and did he ever solve his delivery problems?"

"Yes, he did. I'm not sure how he did but he says it is working well. He told me as he catches up with some late orders, he will soon begin designs on larger units. I believe he wants to sell them to rebels who want to blowup water and electricity sites. He says, they would sell for thousands of Euros.

I told him I would speak to you about possible customers in Africa."

"Thanks, Fillip, I'm glad to hear he is improving his deliveries and Interesting enough, I had an inquiry for such large units just last week and tuned it down, because I had nothing I could offer.

How are your guys doing and what orders are you expecting in the coming weeks? Is there anything I can do to help you?"

"No, not now but if there is an issue, I will contact you."

"Fillip, I have another call on my phone now from an African group. Let me call you back in about fifteen minutes as I want to talk to you about money."

"I always like to talk about money Vladimir. Call me you are finished with your customer."

"Thanks Fillip. I'll call you as soon as I finish with the other call."

Jack called Walter to tell him he would call Fillip again in about fifteen minutes. He asked him to inform him if they were able to figure out where the call had been received.

As Jack waited to make the call, he thought of how he might entice Fillip to meet him. A thought came to him, and he made to call.

"Fillip, sorry I had to interrupt our call before, but I have been trying to talk to the person for about a week. Let's talk about us now.

I hope you feel comfortable in your new job, and we should begin to have more success as time goes on. With that in mind, your commission rate is now twenty-five percent of each sale.

I am going to increase it to thirty percent when you achieve sales of 100 thousand Euros and thirty- five percent after you exceed 250 thousand Euros.

This might become easier if your uncle begins to produce larger and more explosive force units. I don't expect this to happen soon, but I am sure it will eventually happen.

Does my offer sound okay to you?"

"Vladimir, it is a very kind offer you made, and I promise you I will work hard to achieve the goals you have set."

"Any chance w can meet soon and pinpoint some sales we both can work on? I am currently in France, and we could find as convenient place for us to meet."

"Sorry Vladimir, I am now in a different country, but I could be in France in about ten days. How does that sound?"

"That would be good Fillip. I'll call you in a week to confirm where we can meet. Thanks for talking to me and start beating those sales goals."

"I plan too. Talk to you soon."

Within a minute after Jack had disconnected from Fillip, he received a call from Walter.

"All systems worked well Jack and we were able to locate Fillip in the Netherlands within a twenty-mile circle. We are analyzing the data now and believe we can eventually discover his location within a five-mile circle. We could probably trap him in an area if he stayed at that location."

"During my talk with him, we planned on meeting in France in a couple of weeks. No sense in trying to capture him now as he promised to meet with me, and we can easily arrest him then."

"That sounds even better than trying to get a lot of agents to find him in a five-mile area. Keep me informed and we will arrange support for you."

"Thanks Walter, the trap is set, and we should catch him in a couple of weeks. Bye for now."

CHAPTER 80

Fillip left the area where he had received the call and returned to France where he would spend the rest of the day with his girlfriend Francine.

The met and went to dinner to a small café and enjoyed the meal and the friendly conversations. They then returned to Francine's apartment for the remainder of the evening and night.

They were sitting in the family room having an after-dinner drink when Fillip set his glass down asked Francine if they could have a talk. Francine agreed but wondered what he was about to say.

"Francine, I care for you a lot and perhaps more than I ever cared for anybody in my life. I am nervous because what I am about to say may shock you and I do not want to hurt you.

I must tell you my name is not Hans Fischer, but the real name is Fillip.

Chakowski: born in Poland and raised in the city of Kolobrzeg. I have served more than four years in prison for stupid crimes and now I am involved in selling deadly devices to known killers.

Today, I talked to my major contact, and I sensed I was being set up to be captured. I do not want it to happen to me and I would not want any harm to come to you.

I have more than fifty thousand Euros saved, and I want to abandon my old life and begin anew. I can only do this by leaving this area and resettle in another country. I don't want to lose you as you are the best thing that has ever happened to me."

"Whether I call you Hans or Fillip, the feelings I have for you are also real. I have also led a life I am now ashamed about and I often wondered if I could ever survive in the real world.

You and I are like rotten apples fallen from the tree and we slowly rot on the ground until we turn to dust.

I don't want to lose you from my life, and I also want to start to become a better person. I have some money and I have a plan not well thought out yet, but together we can make it workable."

"Francine maybe we can make it together, but I am certain I must be somewhere else within the next week to ten days or Interpol will get me. Then I will probably go to prison for a very long time."

"We can do this quickly. Here is what I am thinking. I have an aunt and uncle living in Germany on a very rural farm. They have often asked me to come and live with them and help them with many things.

They are older and do need help. Have you ever worked on a farm?"

"No, but for freedom, I can learn fast. I will need new identification papers, but I can arrange to have those in two to three days."

"Get German papers quickly and we can leave here in five days. Do not tell anyone about this and neither will I. We are two lovers escaping to a new life and if we support each other, we will make it.

I will call my uncle tomorrow and tell him we will arrive in six days to move in with him and his wife and to help them on the farm."

"If I didn't say I love you before, I am telling you now. I want to begin my life over and to do it with you by my side, is fantastic. I will arrange to get new papers tomorrow and I also want to get rid of my car. We can use yours because you are not being hunted."

"What's your car worth?"

"I paid 8000 Euros for it about a year ago."

"I can sell to a friend who I know needs a used car. Is 3000 to 4000 Euros, ok?"

"Its better than nothing. Whatever you can get is acceptable."

"Fillip, come to me, I want to hold you close and think of all the days ahead of us and no more lonely nights."

They hugged for a few moments and then one romantic kiss led to another, and they slowly walked to the waiting bed.

Fillip arose early and arranged to meet his friendly forger to have new documents prepared for Germany. The task would take about three days.

He returned to the apartment and Francine had already spoken to her uncle and she told Fillip, the uncle was thrilled they were coming to live in their home and to help with the farming chores. She had also talked to her friend who needed a new car and she agreed to buy Fillip's for 3500 Euros.

"Francine, I think we should plan on leaving here in four days and we can drive straight to your uncle's farm. It should only take about seven hours and we can share the driving. I have very little to pack and I will help you to pack your things."

"I will only take what is necessary and I will give the rest to my friend who is buying your car. She does not know where we are going, and she doesn't know your name."

"I must call my uncle Pauli to say goodbye and I will tell him we are going on a short vacation. No further information is necessary."

They were anxious for the time to pass quickly, and their enthusiasm grew as each day passed. They had high hopes for the life they would begin to share and were ready cast all old sins away.

Fillip could only hope that his new life would keep him hidden from Interpol and others who may be looking for him. He promised himself, he would become a loving partner and try to become a model citizen.

Francine had similar thoughts and she hoped that by supporting each other they would accomplish their wishes.

Time would tell how their wishes would turn into reality but with love and the support of the uncle and aunt, it could very well happen.

CHAPTER 81

Jack waited a week after talking to Filip to call him again and to see if he could convince him to meet a village in France he had coordinated with Walter and Interpol. The trap was set, and it was now up to Jack to pull Fillip into the trap.

He clicked on Fillips name on his phone and after two rings, he heard the following message. "This number has been disconnected and is no longer in service."

He immediately called one of the agents who worked with Fillip and asked if he had heard from him recently. He received the news that Fillip was on vacation for the next two weeks.

This was surprising to Jack who was unaware of Fillip taking a vacation.

He then called Pauli to see if he had heard from his nephew only to learn he had not heard from him in a while.

Finally, he called Walter to advise him of the information he had received and asked him, what is plan B?

"We have no knowledge where he is and where he might be headed. I wonder if something spooked him. Maybe he is on vacation and just doesn't want to talk to anybody at this point.

I just don't know, and it makes my job suddenly much more difficult."

"Walter, I'll try calling him again in a couple of days as I am not sure as to what is happening. I know he was very pleased when I told him I was increasing his commissions and his sales goals were relatively easy to meet. Hence, all I can do now is to take a wait and see position."

"I agree, as there is not anything I can do to change the situation.

CHAPTER 82

Francine and Filip packed the car and they left early in the morning of the fourth day, They, had no problem selling Fillip's car nor giving away furniture and clothes to those who wanted them.

Their wish was to drive for seven hours safely and after the long drive to see the place that they will now call home. They stopped only once for gas and to use the restroom.

Three hours later they spied the house sitting all alone on a large parcel of land and within minutes they entered the driveway and saw Francine's aunt and uncle on the porch waiting to greet them.

To the couple it was a great relief and one they would remember forever. They had finally broken the chains that had bound them for as long as they could remember and stepped out of the car into the outstretched arms of those who would now shield them from danger.

Fillip marveled at the landscape surrounding the house and he was so happy with the greeting from people he had never met. He wondered what kind of jobs they would give him on the property because he had never even visited a farm until now.

Together, they unpacked the car and carried their belongings to the room they would share in the house. The aunt had told them to take their time in unpacking and dinner would be served at six promptly.

After putting all their clothes and personal items in places where they could easily find them, they decided to take a short nap before dinner. Each set an alarm on their phone and laid down to a very comfortable bed and quickly dozed off.

The alarms waked them in time to wash up and head down the stairs to dinner in the dining room. The aunt and uncle were already seated, and Francine and Filip took seats on opposite sides of the table.

The aunt welcomed them to their first dinner and then arose and went to the kitchen to bring the food to the table. Francine offered to help but the aunt assured her everything was under control.

In less than a minute, the room was filled with the aroma of hot meats and vegetables to be enjoyed by the four people.

"She always cooks way more than we can eat" The uncle said.

Filip was not used to so much food being put before him on one table. He raised his plate and took a portion of almost all the dishes and when he began to eat, he marveled at the taste of each of the different foods.

"Wow, this food is wonderful. Can we expect such good food from now on?" asked Filip.

"Frau Eva has been cooking like this for almost forty years and I doubt if she will ever change. You can call her Eva and I'm Gunther. Tomorrow, I will give each of you a tour of the farm and point out to you, the things I now need help doing.

It probably will be better if Fillip works with me and Francine helps her aunt Eva with the cooking and house chores,

Fillip. Have you ever drove a tractor, plowed a field, or milked a cow?"

"No, I have never done any of those things. This is my very first visit to a farm and I am ready to learn and help you."

"Thinks for that comment because as I have aged, it has become more difficult for me to do many of the things I used to do every day. I think the same about Eva because she could also use some help.

It was the main reason we were so happy that you were coming to live with us. We always wanted to stay in our home as we aged, and we are blessed to have you to assist us."

"Uncle Gunther and Aunt Eva, we are happy to have found a place where we could be helpful and happy. We dreamed of escaping from the rat race,

and I remembered the offer you once made to me.

We are so happy we can be of help to you, and we thank you for the opportunity you have given us. We promise we will not disappoint either of you.

CHAPTER 83

Things may have gotten bad for Walter and Jack with the disappearance of Fillip. Interpol put out an alert to all their agents, posted wanted photos in postal facilities and had given some information to various news and television bureaus.

Unfortunately for Interpol, the only photos of Fillip were ten-year-old prison mug shops, and his image today was very different.

For all the problems Walter and Jack had regarding Fillip, Bascal had a few small successes in tracking the repackaging and shipments of key materials needed for bomb manufacturing.

Interpol had located the facility in Italy responsible for repackaging the materials and specifying the content to ensure it passed easily through customs inspection. The factory was ordered to be closed immediately and several executives were arrested.

Pauli learned about this problem from a Russian supplier, who was able to redirect materials from Russia and other areas to a similar operation in Hong Kong. There would be a gap in receipts of material, but Pauli had stockpiled some excess on the chance that something like this would happen.

Bascal's team also had been carefully tracking a few delivery vans and found there were at least seven different meeting points where packages were transferred from one van to another. They were not sure whether this was a normal business practice or a way of hiding actual shipping destinations.

Thus far, no enforceable actions had been witnessed and although the vans exchanged packages. It might be just a way of getting packages to a van that covers a specified territory. Interpol agents had not quite figured it out.

Meanwhile Jack had reported Pauli did not appear to have a problem meeting his delivery schedule, and even he wondered how Pauli was getting his materials used to manufacture, and how he was arranging shipments.

The guessing game continued for some time as the tracking of delivery vans seemed to elude Interpol's investigations. It was almost as if Pauli had an inside source to Interpol's strategy and planning.

Deaths continued to happen because of package bombs. Pauli must have other sellers and buyers totally unknown to either Interpol or Jack and his team. It also appeared that even Fillip never had any awareness of these people continuing to buy from Paoli.

Jack thought about the possible connections a long time and discussed it extensively with Debra. During one of their most recent discussions, Debra asked Jack an interesting question.

"Do you remember the first killing that occurred in Finland it was assumed caried out by Russian agents. Well, think about this. What if the Russians are assisting Pauli and helping him find buyers?"

"I never gave that a thought. We know he gets some materials from Russia and what if they are arranging the repacking and controlling shipments that avoid Detection?"

"Maybe you should get Boris more involved."

"Your right and maybe he can find how materials and shipments are now moving. I will call him now."

"Boris, how are you?"

"What do you need now Jack?"

"You know me too well but yes; I do need some help. First, Fillip has disappeared, and nobody has a clue as to his hereabouts. Second, Interpol and the rest of us are stymied as to how Pauli is receiving his materials and And shipping his goods.

People are still dying from package bombs with untraceable materials. Do you remember the fist known killing happened in Finland and at the time it was suspected that Russian agents were involves as the victim was a harsh critic of Putin?

Based upon that event, there may be a chance that Russian sellers or buyers are assisting in the sale of devices, and they could also be arranging shipments to Pauli."

"Jack, until now, I have been focused on the money trail and I also have not made enough progress to really help in that area. I can try speaking to some friends to try and determine if Pauli is being helped by people here in Russia.

I can also look again at several delivery companies and try to understand if their business has increased or fallen at the sites, I assumed were receiving the material deliveries.

Beyond that, I am not sure how helpful I can be for you."

"Thanks Boris, understand, but see if you can help us."

CHAPTER 84

Boris knew if Interpol and Jack and Debra were having problems, it meant there some smart people steering Pauli in a direction to avoid capture. It had to be people who understood the internal workings of law enforcement, Interpol, and even the CIA.

Boris suspected the Russian GRU probably because Pauli was a lone wolf who had a powerful weapon to sell. Nobody understood his secret formula which allowed him to take anybody's explosive material and make it untraceable.

If it is Russian agents helping him get his material and helping him sell his devices, they are probably helping him hid his money in banks controlled by crooked Russian bankers outside of Russia. This is where I should begin my search.

Tomorrow I will call a couple of friends I trained how to hack banks and see if they could point me in the direction of the crooked bankers.

The next morning, he called a friend in Poland and was able to get the names of a bank in France and one in Slovakia his friend knew that were being controlled by Russian bankers. He was told these bankers are dealing with Russian and European millionaires trying to hide money from either corruption or illegal sales of banned goods and of course, to avoid paying taxes.

He then called another friend he had also trained and helped a few times and asked the same questions he had asked the first friend. He was given the Slovakia bank name again and a newer bank in Germany working mostly with smaller illegal arms dealers and other questionable startups. It was also controlled by a Russian banker.

He suspected the Slovakian and French banks were looking for big dollar evaders and probably would not work with a small guy like Pauli. He then decided he would study the German bank and see what he could learn.

It was lunchtime and his wife had prepared him some food and after eating, he went to his computer lab and loaded newer software he had developed on to his most powerful computer, The bank he was looking for was named, Carton Commercial Bank and located in Munich.

A few keystrokes and he was looking at the internet site for the bank. He clicked on new accounts and provided the requested information to open an account. He quickly transferred a thousand Euros into the bank and within minutes, he had a legal account and password to enter the website.

Having an account number and password would make entry and the job easier. He would now wait a day or two, and work on other items related to the case, before trying his hand at hacking.

The next day he contacted a few more people trying to determine if Russian agents were guiding Pauli. He talked to four, known illegal arms dealers he knew, and asked about the possibility of Russian agents being involved in the bomb incidents.

Two of the four told Boris, they had knowledge of agent's involvement both in guiding the maker and having a direct financial interest in the business.

This would be interesting news to Jack and Interpol, and it would complicate the ability to find and capture Pauli.

Within minutes of learning this information, Boris called Jack to give him the bad news.

There was not any hurry for any further bank hacking at this time. Maybe it will come in handy in the future.

CHAPTER 85

Back on farm, Francine and Fillip had established a routine.

He had learned how to use the milking machines and every morning around six am he would be out in the cow barn attending to the milking chores. After that he would take the tractor and check the irrigation systems on the land where crops were growing, to ensure no breaks had occurred.

At eight am, he would join Francine who had cooked the breakfast and along with Gunther and Eva, they would have their morning meal.

Gunther was amazed as how quickly Fillip had learned and how happy he appeared while doing his chores. To Fillip, it was a dream come true and he reminded himself of the days, months, and years he had wasted in prison and the time he had spent with Pauli and how they were always planning for their next move to avoid Interpol and now he was free.

Eva had similar thoughts about Francine and how she listened to Eva as she cooked and then Francine cooked almost as good as Eva.

At times, Fillip would take the tractor and ride around the entire perimeter of the farm and marvel at the wonders of nature. This is something he never envisioned in his life until now and he knew, he would never tire of enjoying the life he now lived.

Francine had similar thoughts of how she hated her life as a prostitute and through fate or for fortune, she met a man who loved her, who also had a past he longed to forget.

By moving to the farm, they not only helped themselves, but they also made Gunther and Eva's life much easier.

As the days passed, their previous lives gradually were erased from their memory. They enjoyed their meals with Gunther and Eva and learned about the life on the farm, and they had endured over the years. Gunther and Eva never asked about Francine and Fillip's past. They only assumed it was not good.

Everyday Francine and Fillip were thankful of the decision they had made and the people they were now becoming. The bonds of love grew stronger, and they always had a smile on their faces.

Chapter 86

After Jack had spoken to Boris and received the bad news, he called Perry to arrange another meeting with the staff.

He explained to Perry, the truth was now evident, Pauli was a Russian puppet. They gave him easy access to the materials he needed and through various means, he was able to ship his devices to customers in faraway places. They will continue to manipulate him for their advantage if they need his devices. When the need goes away, they will kill him.

Later in the day, Perry confirmed a meeting on Monday morning.

Jack and Debra discussed the news given to them from Boris. It would not be easy to outsmart the Russians, but Jack had done it before. It would now become a chess match between the Russians and Jacks team.

He told Debra he thought he might have a way to Pauli if he could convince him, Vladimir was one of their agents. Of course, he realized he could also be killed once the Russian agents they learned of his plot.

"Jack it is a big risk for you to take, but I cannot envision another solution."

"I understand the consequences of my actions and will think twice of every step I take while I am playing the part. I will ask Boris if he can get me an agent's name and I will try to befriend him. Remember, I passed the test with Sergey, and it worked then; Pauli accepted me."

"Your moving into a different league and the rules are very different than what Sergey used."

"Listen to this approach. I tell them I am selling Pauli's devices in places your people are not active. I know my way around but would feel more comfortable being a part of a larger and better financed group.

Pauli doesn't understand the questions raised by late deliveries or his inability to customize units very quickly. He only understands the formula for making his single device, but he lacks an understanding of the market and what it takes to grow it into a cash cow.

You people can help me, and we all can get a little richer with more customers, newer products, and higher sales, everywhere."

"Bounce it off Perry and see what he and his staff think about it."

Monday arrived and Jack and Debra were back sitting in Perry's conference room. Almost ten months had passed and although they have gotten close to solving the case at various times. it is still open and under investigation.

"Good morning, all. We all know we are here because we continue to be outsmarted in the untraceable bomb case and we gave credit to Pauli. Well, he doesn't deserve it.

A member of Jack's team has reliable information, Pauli is in the hands of Russian agents, and they had orchestrated all his steps to continuously mislead us. They control his production by providing his materials. They control his customer base with almost exclusive selling rights for his devices within Europe and elsewhere. They control his shipping and lastly, they control his money, as it sits in a Russian managed bank in Germany.

We will now consider what we must do to win.

Jack asked for this meeting, and I assume he has some fresh ideas. Jack, you have our attention."

"Thank you. All Perry just said is true and it raises the bar and challenges our skills. Most of us have been challenged in the past and through experience and perseverance, we figured out how to overcome the obstacles.

This case is different, but the challenges are the same and to succeed, we may have to use an "outside-of-the-box" approach.

Debra and I spent a few hours over the weekend discussing not how we could get to Pauli quickly, but rather, how can we become one of the Russian agents. Here is my suggestion on how I believe I can proceed.

I have spent a few years in Russia as an undercover agent for my country. I speak fluent Russian and would have no difficulty talking to any person in Russian society.

A few months ago, I was able to become an active seller of Pauli's devices because, I convinced a man named Sergey, who I thought was his Russian agent. I told him I knew my way around and he had me checked me out thoroughly by other Russians, I knew in the past. I passed all the tests, and I am confident, I can do it again.

Here is my first step. I plan on approaching a known agent as being a well-known seller of illegal arms and specialty devices such as Pauli's in all of Africa. They have some contacts there, but I can assure them, I have many more and have been very successful. I will remind them I sold the device that almost killed the leader of Burkina Faso.

I should be able to impress them with my knowledge of the arms and munitions business and prove to them I can increase my success in Africa."

If they respond, "if you are so good, why do you need our help? I would tell them, "It has been difficult for me to complete sales when I cannot provide a delivery date. I have no one to push for me and I recognize the potential of being in an organization with similar goals."

"I am doing this to obtain one piece of information to lead us to Pauli. A material delivery date, a shipping of a device date, or anything that would reveal his locale."

"Jack, you are skating on thin ice with that approach, but I think we can add a piece that you don't have, which may get you into their circle rather quickly and keep you safe.

From the time of the murder in Finland, we suspected it was carried out by Russian agents. Within days, we were able to verify it was Russian agents as we thought, but we also learned the names of the agents who participated in the killing.

We cannot identify our source of this information, but we can arrange for him to pass your credentials to the right people and see if they respond. Please hold off any attempt to contact anyone in Russia before seeing what we can accomplish."

"I understand Perry, and it is always nice to have friends in high places. I will wait until you provide the answer to your request, and then we can streamline my story."

The meeting ended without solving any of the problems but with a ray of hope. Jack may be on the right track running directly to Pauli's location.

CHAPTER 87

After the meeting ended, Perry called another executive within Interpol.

"Sir, this call is regarding the bomb maker case, and we have validated information, the maker is being guided by Russian agents. A member of our team from the USA has volunteered to attempt to infiltrate the group of agents under the guise of being an active seller of arms and other weapons in Africa.

He is fluent in Russian and has previously lived there undercover for several years. He also is very knowledgeable of the illegal arms trade within Europe.

My request is to have our contact vouch for this individual as he tries to infiltrate the group now supporting the bomb maker.

At our headquarters, we have discussed various ways of stopping the manufacture and flow of these deadly weapons. In every instance, we have been stymied and now we now the relationship between the maker and the Russian agents, we feel if we can get inside the group, we stand a chance of successfully ending this case.

I can assure you; this person is experienced and holds the highest security clearance of his country. He was sent here by the FBI as the number one candidate to assist us in our investigation. Because of his personal contacts, we have gathered a lot if useful information regarding the suspect.

Sir, we would appreciate your assistance in this matter."

"The description of the American sounds like someone I personally know. Is his name Jack?"

"That is correct sir. Do you know Jack?"

"I know him very well and he used to have direct access to me when I headed up the office in France. He solved a lot of problems for us when he was here.

You've got the right guy for the job, and I'll attend to the matter quickly and give you an answer whenever I hear from our contact. It just dawned on me; our contact may also know Jack.

I think this may work for us. Talk to you when I learn something."

Perry was sort of in shock learning his boss was a friend of Jack. Getting him into the group maybe easier than I thought.

Perry then called Jack to let him know what was happening.

"Jack, I spoke to my boss, and he will contact our plant and will get back to me. He told me he knows you very well. Can you guess who it might be?"

I do know a few people in Interpol but whenever I had a problem in Europe, I would call Dennis Wilson. Is he your boss?"

"Yes. And when he calls me again, I will give him your number. I am sure he will be happy to talk to you."

"I am sure he will. On our last case together here in Europe, my team and I recovered a large sum of money from some bad guys. I recommended Interpol receive $200 million dollars from the US government for their assistance on a special case.

"Dennis was a major source of support and help in solving the case and Interpol appreciated the funds they received. I will never forget him, and I am sure he will not forget me. I'll look forward to his call."

CHAPTER 88

Three days after Jack had heard from Perry about his boss's involvement,

He received a call from Dennis Wilson.

"Jack, how are you and you still haven't retired yet?"

"Yes, I have. In fact, I've retired three times and the government still thinks I should be working."

"I'm happy you are still well and working with us on this difficult case. I contacted our man in Russia, and he knows all about you and your capabilities. You may know him, but you will never meet, and he will remain, nameless to you and others.

He will lay the groundwork for you to cooperate with the group guiding the bomb maker. You will receive a text message with instructions and a cell number to call and to convince them why they should cooperate with you.

Our man believes your strength in Africa will be very favorable towards their acceptance of you. They have little coverage there and they know a lot of rebel groups are wanting the devices and weapons, you can offer."

"Dennis, thank you for the help. It could go a long way towards settling this case. Besides, Debra and I want to go home to retire."

"Well good luck. Perry will keep me informed of your activities."

"Thank you again."

Now that the entry to work with the Russian group had been prepped by an insider, Jack felt he better fine tune his story because he will only get to tell it once.

"Debra, I just heard from Dennis and Interpol's man will arrange for me to speak to a Russian contact about working with the group. He will notify me in the next few days.

I suggest you and I begin to rehearse my story, so I won't miss any details. I am sure this is a one-shot opportunity that I don't want to miss. So, where do I begin?"

"First, you only talk about Africa. Your knowledge of the country, the various rebels seeking weapons, possibly the people they are wanting to kill and the large amount of Euro sales you can make in the next year.

I know you have some knowledge of all of this but not enough to be convincing to me. I suggest you speak to Perry or one of his assistants and brush up on your history, African leaders, rebel group names, etcetera."

"Your right, I'll call him now and get things started. I don't want to screw this up."

He called Perry and they spoke for more then ten minutes about the subjects Jack would need to make his case to the Russians. Perry promised him a report by tomorrow after which would contain many of the details he needs to know.

Debra would help him learn and would question him extensively about his knowledge. They assumed I would take at least three days before he would be confident enough to make the important phone call.

Early afternoon of the next day, Jack received a very detailed study of many of the countries in Africa experiencing rebel activity. He studied the report and keeping notes on countries and known people within the country.

He spent about four hours reviewing all the information and then began to dissect and separate the information for six or seven countries he intended to focus on, and where he had a chance of selling his weapons.

His list included Burkina Faso, where had previously sold a bomb, Mali, Chad, Yemen, South Sudan, Democratic Republic of Congo, and Mozambique. There were at least ten more African countries with rebel activity, but Jack intended to focus on the major few and keep his options open for others.

After selecting the group of countries, where he would concentrate his sales efforts, he had to learn the names of key government officials and rebel groups operating in the areas.

He had now spent over six hours of research and it was time to take a break. I still have a couple of more days to study, he thought and then tomorrow Debra can begin questioning me.

Once I pass her test, I am ready to go.

CHAPTER 89

The next day Jack continued his study of wars or uprisings in Africa. He discovered there were ten to twelve countries engaged in battles with rebel groups fighting for a variety of causes. It included Islamists wanting to establish additional Islamic territories to those only interested in a coup by overthrowing the existing government.

In the countries of interest to Jack, he counted the names of twenty key rebel groups and the Interpol report stated, there may be an additional fifty to one hundred independent unassociated groups also involved in kidnappings and murders.

This was a lot to remember, but Jack would be talking on his cell phone, and he could have cue cards handy to quickly respond with additional information. They can be arranged so I can easily refer to them.

After a few more hours of study, he was ready to have a rehearsal with Debra regarding the future call. She could use the report to ask questions about the countries selected. She would also question the approach being used to join the group.

They worried if Jack would have to travel to Russia to meet with the people managing the process. He would avoid having to go to Russia because of the possibility of someone recognizing him from his prior assignments.

They worked a couple of hours on the project and felt he would be okay after another session tomorrow.

Debra suggested they dine out tonight and find a café with soft music to relax and spend the evening as a couple in love.

They rose the next morning and after dressing and breakfast, they began rehearsing for the call.

"Jack' let me hear your initial introduction to the Russian contact but in English."

"Mr. Rosnovich, my name is Vladimir, and I was recommended to call you.

and discuss how I might help your group by offering my extensive knowledge of Africa. There are many opportunities there for selling numerous weapons including one I currently sell there and which I understand your group also sells.

I have been in the arms and weapons business for quite a few years including selling to Russia and selling Russian made weapons in other places.

For the small, packaged bomb, I was selected by a Russian and verified by other Russian contacts. I have mainly sold this device in Africa.

I would like to know if there is any chance for us to cooperate in the African territory?"

"Thank you, Vladimir. I was expecting your call and please refer to me as Eugenie. I was given information about you by another trusted source who felt we might benefit from a relationship because of your knowledge of the area ad your past successes.

"Can you give me some information as to what areas you might be looking at to exploit? Are you limited to one or two countries, or do you have broader plans?"

"Eugenie, I am currently focused on six or seven countries in different locations of the continent. There is a very large demand for unique weapons of every type, and I know there are several rebel groups vying to get weapons of everything they can get their hands on.

I have studied the areas and groups within the areas for more than six months now and I concluded that my best bet would be with the countries I have studied and selected.

They would be an easier sale, higher margins, and larger orders of various weapons. I am not looking to sell one of a kind every month. I want orders on the magnitude of 100,000 Euros per month or more.

This why I selected this strategy targeted at the minor few who have the need and Euros and are willing to pay the price."

"Why do you need our relationship Vladimir?"

"It is very difficult to be a one-man grocery store. I need a variety of weapons which your group can supply. I know you also have a relationship with the bomb maker. I am wondering if he can keep his manufacturing volumes up and move his deliveries more quickly than he has done in the past.

I am working towards increased business on the continent, but it will be difficult to sell, find suppliers and get shipments expedited by myself. I realize, I need help."

"I recognize your problem Vladimir and at this moment, our group doesn't have the proper resources in place to exploit the area. I believe we can make a deal and I will speak with others about our plans. I will get back to you in a few days. Thank you for the call."

"Thank you, Eugenie. I will wait to hear from you."

Debra told him, she would give him a B rating for his presentation.

"Why a B Debra?"

"You omitted to talk about several important issues. For example, name the seven countries you selected and to mention a few names of the rebel groups, expressing an interest in working with you.

Don't be reluctant to oversell him. You told him you were knowledgeable of the continent so, just assume, he knows far less than you do and show him how smart you can be.

Lastly, I think it is wrong to say you want to get orders of 100,000 Euros per month. That is chickenfeed to the Russians. One point two million a year is blah, so skip the numbers. If you want to drop hints, talk 10 to twenty million a year. That will perk their ears up.

In reconsidering your grade, I am lowering it to a C plus."

CHAPTER 90

"Debra, Your C plus was deserved but the more I look at this plan, the more I dislike it. I am setting myself up to step into a trap without a way out.

"What do you mean, Jack?"

"Here is the problem I am creating for myself. I am promising Russian agents I will be selling weapons for them into countries already armed to the teeth.

They have contacts everywhere and will soon find out, I am full of shit.

Then, I am buying bombs from Pauli and telling him they are going somewhere, and he will know where in a couple of months, but nothing ever happens.

The only explosions you will hear are the Russians and Pauli looking to kill me.

If I am to find Pauli and get myself out of this situation, it must be in less than two months but under my current plan, I have no way to do such a thing. In other words, I am digging a deep hole for myself, which could end up as my grave.

So, forget the C plus and give me a big F for failure."

"Jack, it sounded good at the start but what you are saying now is true. The question is, how in the hell do you get out of the trap?"

"Please call Ethan and Anna and see if they can be here in two days for an urgent meeting. I will call Franz and Boris with the same question. Six minds are better than one and I need to escape from this mess, rapidly.

I am calling Franz and then Boris now."

"I'll call my friends at the same time."

Within a few minutes, they both had confirmation, they would all meet at a hotel in Paris in two days. Debra and Jack will begin planning for the meeting immediately.

Together, they started tossing out ideas one at a time. Some were realistic and others far out of reality. No matter how hard they tried, nothing worthwhile came out of their mouths and then the room became very silent.

They later walked to one of their favorite cafes where their first order was a large glass of Merlot for her and a double scotch for him. Dinner would be ordered in about an hour after another round of drinks.

The next day after breakfast, they started exchanging ideas once more. This time they were more realistic and possibly doable. Debra had a rather unique idea of having Boris monitor the delivery routes of the delivery vans known to frequent the postal mailbox stores. She suggested looking at any one of them, who is consistently delivering packages to small village areas in Western France.

Jack came up with the idea of using Interpol drones to monitor the delivery truck routes and note their stops and, if they stop at what appears to be a small, deserted farmhouse in the middle of nowhere.

From these suggestions, came other ideas which would lead to a capture of Pauli.

Hopefully, whatever idea we select, will be resolved at our meeting tomorrow.

Shortly after their discussion, they left the apartment and went to the hotel to await their guests.

CHAPTER 91

Everyone arrived safely and after they had checked into their rooms, they all left for dinner. It was the usual team affair with lots of greetings accompanied by a drink and then after a couple of rounds of drinks, they ordered their food.

Their typical dinners rarely included business discussions and was more about family and how everyone was doing. When the meal and drinking had ended, they agreed to meet at nine am in the conference room off the lobby.

The following morning after they had all joined in the conference room, Jack began the meeting.

"I want to thank each of you for being here today and it was nice to see all of you last night and hear about your families and your current activities.

Today, I am going to tell you about my problems which I created and soon realized, I was setting myself up for a big fall.

To begin, I had asked Boris to do some snooping and he discovered our bomb maker, Pauli Zukowski was being controlled and manipulated by a group of Russian agents. His manufacturing, sales, and shipments, all under the control of these agents. In addition, his money sits in a German Bank controlled by Russians.

I then had an idea where I would infiltrate the group as an exclusive sales agent for Africa and may be find a way to capture Pauli. With, the help of Interpol, I was able to get an introduction to the leader of the group.

Before contacting him, I studied a detailed report of Africa provided by Interpol. From that report, I selected six or seven countries and associated rebel groups where I would focus my sales effort selling a variety of weapons made in Russia and the untraceable bombs made by Pauli.

I prepared a lengthy presentation to give to the leader of the agents with full details of the countries and groups I would be targeting during my sales pitch.

I rehearsed the presentation with Debra, and she gave me a C plus rating for missing several key points. She gave me a good reason to rethink my approach, and when I did, I suddenly realized, I was putting my life in jeopardy.

How could I sell Russian arms or many package bombs without being discovered in a short period. The Russians would quickly find me, and the rest is history.

It is the reason I needed you here today. How do I safely exit this mess I created, and what would be a safer path to travel?

Lastly, remember, we have been chasing this guy for a few months and we are no closer today than we were when we started.

I have some newer ideas, but I would like to hear a solution from each of you. Then we can decide on a more realistic approach."

Boris raised his hand first and walked to the front of the conference table to begin sharing his thoughts.

"Sorry my information search got you into trouble Jack, but fortunately, you have not made a commitment. I am sure undoing the mess you made will be easier then if you had proceeded with your plan.

Prior to today, I have spent some time thinking about what we could do different to be successful. There must be several solutions to our problem, but we have yet to discover them.

Here is one possibility. I believe in the data I have concerning suspicious delivery vans coming and going around France, I can zero in on a few vans which would shrink the size of an area we have to investigate. Once I do that, we get an Interpol agent to become a delivery driver working for the company delivering to the area under question.

We may rapidly discover the route and van providing service to Pauli for his receipts and shipments. It will not be an overnight solution, as the driver would have to get friendly with other drivers and determine what kind of packages they are delivering and who receives those packages.

My other possibility is rather weird but could possibly work for us.

I drain Pauli's bank account and he now has no money to buy materials unless the Russians finance him.

Jack contacts Pauli on the pretext of placing more orders and wants to learn delivery times. Pauli is irate that his bank was hacked and although the bank is investigating how the hack occurred, Pauli has no money.

Jack asks him about the bank and when he learns the name, he tells Pauli it's a Russian controlled bank and is far as Jack is concerned, he avoids them due to previous incidents. Pauli asks him for suggestions.

Jack gives him a name of a bank he trusts and asks Pauli; can he help him with some funds?

Pauli asks, "If I agree, what do you want?"

Jack responds, "let's have lunch again and discuss terms."

I said it was weird but so isn't this entire case. I'll let someone else speak now because there may be more workable solutions yet to be heard."

Before anyone could begin talking, Jack suggested a fifteen-minute break.

Chapter 92

Before the break, Anna had raised her hand and said she would like to present some ideas. She now began to speak.

"Thanks for your input, Boris. Please stay away from my bank."

Everyone laughed and applauded, and Boris had a big smile on his face.

"I'll be more serious now. We all have experienced mental fatigue from chasing this guy. The fact of his having Russian support makes even more difficult but, we have defeated them before on other cases. This one is just a bit more difficult.

We have tried to find him by following delivery vans, tracing telephone calls and other investigated means. This guy, like all of us, lives in a digital world and it is not as closed or secret as we would wish.

When an email is sent, it is traceable and so is a text message.

Jack, how are you contacting this guy to place orders? Is it by phone or email?

This is just something more for us to think about. Ethan, do you want to speak now?"

"Thanks for the thoughts, Anna and here is another one that could work for us. Jack, I remember you telling us of your lunch meeting with Pauli and how Interpol tried to track him using GPS attached to his vehicle.

You said he drove twenty kilometers East and stopped at a petrol station and then switched cars and the trackable car went into Germany.

We know Pauli and his nephew left Germany and probably settled in France. After his lunch with you Jack, I assume Pauli was in a hurry to get back to his lab with his material deliveries and my guess the distance from the petrol station to the lab is no more than twenty to thirty kilometers southeast of the petrol station to his home in France.

We have a starting point of the petrol station, and if we draw two half circles twenty and thirty kilometers southeast of the station. We end up with a swath of land ten kilometers wide and approximately twenty kilometers along the perimeter.

This should be easy to photograph and then study to find houses without close neighbors. Most of the area I am talking about is agriculture farms and now is the prime time for crop growth.

Find a house which has no surrounding crops, and that may be where you find Pauli."

The group applauded Ethan's suggestion as they all knew what he said could very well be factual. Jack, then spoke.

"I also applaud your insight Ethan, and your idea is certainly worth a try. I will speak to Interpol about suppling photograph images to us. Franz, you haven't spoken yet, and now it is your turn."

"Thank you. I am happy to see, each of you with good ideas and it demonstrates that we are different in our approaches but together we are a strong team.

Like all of you, I have though often as to how we might catch this evil monster, recklessly killing people he knows or doesn't know. I doubt if he ever thinks about his victims except the ones who bullied him.

What he cares about is his great invention and how he accomplished a feat in chemistry nobody had ever done before. His heroine was Marie Curie, who was awarded the Nobel Prize for her work. I am sure Pauli thinks he should also be rewarded.

Maybe, Marie can help us with our problem.

His nephew Fillip told Jack; his uncle only used the internet to study chemistry. Well, that gives us an option to learn how much he follows Nobel Prize recommendations for awards to chemists.

What if we wrote a piece recommending Marie Curie to be awarded another Nobel prize for some of the other things she is known for innovating. We post it on a popular chemistry web site and ask for comments relating to the recommendations from chemists and chemical engineers.

Maybe, Pauli will answer and tell us why and in doing so, he gives away his email address.

As Anna suggested, it's a digital world and once we have an address, it is relatively easy to find the location. It may very well be in the area Ethan predicted.

Debra decided it was her turn to weigh in on the ideas presented.

'We have heard from all four of our trusted team members. Each with suggestions worthy of serious consideration. Regarding Jack's dilemma, I am confident him and I can figure out a successful exit for him.

I also think each one of your ideas is worth pursuing because in all honesty, we don't know what will be successful unless we try it. Hence, I challenge each of you to independently put your idea to a test and see how it works.

Ethan, we will work with you and arrange for Interpol to obtain photos for you to review.

Boris, do what you do best and drain Pauli's bank account.

Franz, you get to research where your letter should be presented, and we will help you get your chemistry terms correct.

Anna, your idea is also worth chasing. Jack and I will work with Interpol to learn what we can trace successfully with the limited data we have obtained.

It's time to end the meeting and I am happy we were able to share our ideas. Now it is your time to turn ideas into action. In closing, Jack and I want to remind you, we are not giving up; we are just reorganizing our thoughts."

CHAPTER 93

Within a few days after the meeting, each team member had begun to implement the idea they had presented to each other. Nobody was sure as to which one would result in the capture of Pauli, but he will get the message, someone is chasing him.

Boris had returned to Russia and knew from experience, the best time to hack a bank is after midnight, He had established an account at CartonCommercial Bank in Munich after he discovered an account had been established by the Russians for Pauli.

He slept most of the day and in the evening, he began assembling the software he would use to try to hack into Pauli's private stash. Shortly after midnight, he turned on his most powerful computer and opened several software packages he had developed.

He signed into his account at the bank and then began a slow process of trying to enter the general account database. It took him three tries before he was successful and then he had to search for Pauli's account.

The only name he had was Otto Weber and he typed the name in search and all the details appeared on his screen. The account showed a balance of almost 750,000 Euros.

Boris quickly had the total funds transferred into an Estonia account and started his exit program which would erase a sign of entry and where the money had been transferred. When he was sure his footprints had been erased, he exited the program safely.

Once he had completed all his work for the evening, he shut down the computer and texted Jack.

Jack, another win for the good guys. 750,000 Euros now sits in my account. I'll buy lunch the next time we meet. Meanwhile, I suggest you wait a few days before contacting Pauli as I am not sure how rapidly the bank will inform him of the loss.

He once again had successfully bested the bad guys.

He wasn't the only one of the team who had good news for Jack. Franz had found the site for nominating people for Nobel Prize consideration and discovered, it is not an easy process.

However, he found another site for discussing the merits of those nominated and others who should be considered for nomination.

He then began his search about the innovations of Marie Curie and discovered several facts suggesting she should have been nominated for at least five chemical processes she had developed.

She had received her first Nobel Prize for her work in Physics in 1903 and in 1911, she was again awarded a Nobel Prize for her discovery of Radium and Polonium.

Her work in radioactivity to assist in the cure of cancer, should have been acceptable for another Nobel.

Franz did his homework and wrote a technical letter suggesting she should be granted another Nobel Prize for her work and the funds donated in her name to cancer research. He posted the letter on the appropriate site and then waited for replies.

Within two days, a response was posted on the site to his letter. The response totally agreed with Franz's thoughts and went on to mention other innovative acts she had performed. The letter was signed by Otto Weber with an email address.

It was sent to Jack the day Franz had seen the reply on the chemistry site.

Having received two positive answers from the ideas brought up in the meeting eased some of the stress he had been feeling for a long time.

He forwarded the positive information he had received to Perry and Jack was sure they would quickly assign an agent to continue the investigation with the new data.

We may be seeing the light at the end of the tunnel, he thought.

CHAPTER 94

Pauli learned of his missing bank funds two days after it had been hacked. The Russians tried to trace how the theft had happened, but no trace could be found. All they could tell him was he lost 750,000 Euros and they could not explain why or when.

Pauli, now had to make some serious decisions. He had very little money for food and no money to pay for materials he had ordered. He would be collecting some small amounts from previous sales but not enough to pay for his materials.

He wondered if the Russians had stolen his money to learn his secret of removing the trace materials. If not them, was it Interpol sending him a message, they were close to capturing him? He could not answer either question and he now felt lost and alone.

He wished his nephew was there with him to at least help him get over the money problem and for him to be able to talk to someone . Being alone was not what he needed now and for the first time since leaving Kolobrzeg he was scared and of what, he didn't know.

He went to the bedroom to lie on the bed and try to think about what to do. Maybe it is time to blow myself up. It would be easy to do. Yet, if I do that, I am letting the bullies beat me once more and I won't let them do that to me ever again.

Maybe I should call Vladimir. He has been friendly to me, and he must have some money. I'll do it tomorrow morning and maybe I can get him to save me.

He continued to think bad thoughts as the darkness of night engulfed his house. Finally, he fell asleep dreaming of happier times and wondered about his children.

He awoke when the sunshine entered his room and everything that happened to him the last few days quickly returned. He had to control himself from crying. He had to talk to someone and the only person he could think of was Vladimir.

CHAPTER 95

The next morning, Pauli called Vladimir's cell but although Jack was at his apartment, he did not answer his phone. Pauli left him a message to return his call to discuss an urgent matter.

Jack quickly understood what Pauli was calling about and decided to discuss his response first with Debra before returning the call.

"Honey, Pauli is calling me with and urgent message. To me, it means he has found out all the money in his account was stolen. He has no money to pay bills and probably cannot get materials any other reasons you need money. How am I to respond while trying to trap him into revealing his location.?"

"Jack, I would guess he is afriad of the Russians because he probably believes, they emptied his bank account. Fillip is no longer available, and he has no friends except you. He needs your help financially and to lift his spirits.

How you do that and get to meet him will be tricky but if you are successful, the case could close rapidly."

While Jack and Debra, were discussing their approach to Pauli, when he didn't contact Jack, he called Fillip's friend Henri who had helped them move to France.

"Henri, it's me Pauli and I have a big problem and need some urgent help."

"What is your problem and how can I help you?"

"Henri, my bank funds were all stolen and I have a little money but not enough to run the business. I am not sure what I should do now."

"You're at the house I moved you too?"

"Yes."

"Stay there and I will be there in about an hour. We can talk then."

'Thanks Henri, thanks. I'll be here waiting for you."

He hung the phone and was happy he would now be able to talk to someone he could trust. If Vladimir called back, he would stall him until after his meeting with Henri.

Jack and Debra had continued their conversation and had selected the approach Jack would take in his conversation with Pauli.

He picked up his cell phone and clicked on Pauli's number. The phone rang twice and then Pauli answered.

"Vladimir, I called you earlier to let you know, I will be a little late in my deliveries to you. I ran into a cash flow problem but solved it earlier today, just before I called you. I'll let you know in a few days when I can ship the devices to you.

Thanks for returning my call."

He had hung up before Jack could even speak.

"Debra, once more he has eluded us, and it sounds like he has made a deal with someone and now doesn't need me. I should have answered his earlier call before he made a deal with another person."

"Every time we get close, the bubble bursts."

Henri had left his house within minutes of hearing from Pauli. He had about an hour's drive to reach his house and he would have time to think how he could now become a partner in the bomb making business.

He had a large stash of Euros in the bank and was sure he could fund the operation almost immediately. He thought because of Pauli's money being stolen, maybe Interpol might be involved.

I have room for him and his lab at my house until we find a more deserted location. If we are partners, he will accept what I have to offer.

Fifty minutes later, he walked into Pauli's house.

Chapter 91

"Henri, thanks for coming to help me. I trust you and I hope we can continue to work together.

All my money, 750,000 Euros was taken from my bank account. It is a Russian controlled bank and I suspect it was them who stole my money.

Maybe they wanted to put me out of business, so they could do it themselves.

I can not run this business without money, so how can you help me."

"Thanks for your trust, Pauli. Maybe Interpol learned about your account and drained it. They have done this before. They can't find you, but they can grab your money to try and put you out of business.

What I would like to do is form a partnership with you and we would each own fifty percent of the new business.

You lost 750,000 Euros, right? I will give you 375,000 Euros for fifty percent ownership. The money is to fund the business until we make profits and then we split them 50/50.

Because I suspect Interpol involvement, I suggest we pack you up and leave here as fast as we can load the car. We can set up at my place until we find a more deserted location.

I can arrange to receive materials safely and to ship units out undetected by others.

Is my offer acceptable to you?"

"Henri, it is more than I could ever expect. My answer is yes, and it's time to move before they realize, we have disappeared again.

They shook hands and the deal was completed. They immediately began packing the lab equipment and partially completed devices. Net, they packed Pauli's belongings and began moving everything to the car.

About two hours after Henri arrived at the farmhouse, they were on the road to Henri's place in the Netherlands. Pauli knew Henri had saved him and he doubted if anyone else would have done the same.

Soon, they arrived at the house and unpacked the car, taking everything, they had moved from the previous location.

Once in the house, Pauli, connected all his equipment and soon he began to work on the partially completed items, he had brought with the move.

Henri, walked into the new lab to help him arrange his equipment.

"Pauli, I moved money from my local bank account and added a personal account, using your name. We will go there tomorrow to create another account strictly for the business and to allow you to transfer funds to your suppliers.

Both our names will be on the new business account, but it mainly is for your use to pay normal costs and to receive funds from sales. When it grows to a safe limit, we can draw excess funds to go into our personal accounts."

"Henri, I will never be able to thank you enough for saving my life. What you have done has saved something I put my life into and only you stepped forward to help."

"Thanks for your trust in me. I also did something for myself. I believe in you and your product and the potential to generate big profits. I hope we can do well enough to retire from the business in two to three years."

"I would also like that Henri."

CHAPTER 96

"Jack, do you think it is too late to try and convince Pauli you could help him financially and save his business? Give it another try, because he only had the Russians helping him and he is probably blaming them for stealing his money."

"Probably yes. When I didn't answer his phone call, he called someone else he trusted and quickly arranged the funding he needed. The problem is, we don't know any of his friends. We can only hope he stays in France.

I will try to call him once more and see if he can accept my help."

Jack again, clicked on Pauli's number and waited for the phone to ring. On the second ring, he heard this announcement, "This number has been disconnected and is no longer in use."

"Debra, we have lost him. His phone is disconnected, and I would guess, he has moved. It means, we start over again looking for the untraceable man.

I suggest you and I put out emails to our team and to Perry with our suspicions and how we learned about what has now happened. Maybe, if we are lucky, he has relocated to a country where one of our team lives?"

A few hours after the conversation, they sent emails to the team and Interpol providing the bad news and asking them to once again, check their contacts about any news regarding the bomb makers business.

In a separate email to Boris, they asked him to watch the parcel delivery schedules once again for two things. First, does it appear that schedules into France have changed? Secondly, is there an increase in deliveries within any of the watched countries outside of France and Germany?

To Ethan and Anna, they warned that Pauli might have moved from France and could possibly have relocated in the Netherlands or Belgium.

They asked Franz to also be aware of Pauli moving back to Germany.

They advised Perry of the situation and they had notified all their team members. Any further information regarding Pauli's location would be immediately supplied to Interpol.

Now it was Jack's turn to be stressed, and it would be a while before he got over the mistake of not answering the phone call from Pauli.

CHAPTER 97

In a short time, Henri and Pauli were working together as teammates. Pauli quickly discovered Henri was a lot smarter than Fillip was and the results were beginning to show.

Henri had many reliable contacts in a few countries and sales began to increase under his leadership. He avoided anyone who he suspected might be an undercover agent for Interpol or another foreign agency. This included Vladimir because he didn't trust the Russians.

Pauli had told him of Vladimir wanting to do more business in Africa and Henri assured him, it is already well covered by my contacts. He had two contacts who had several sales into the country when they were buying quantities of arms and munitions and he now got them to sell his devices.

It wasn't long before killings in many areas began to increase and Interpol along with the agencies of many countries started investigating how the deadly devices were entering the countries.

Perry as a senior director of Interpol had received negative comments from several countries about the increase in killings. He knew who was suppling the devices but from where they were being manufactured or shipped, he did not have a clue.

He scheduled a meeting with Jack, Debra and Bascal to try and determine how they could slow down or stop the selling of the deadly devices. The meeting was scheduled for the following week and each person should be prepared to offer a newer approach or be able to provide the latest information from their numerous contacts.

Jack and Debra once more emailed their contacts and requested an update of any information they may have regarding the case.

Within a day, Boris sent them data showing material flows had decreased significantly into France but had grown even larger, in the Netherlands. He could not pinpoint the area where materials were going, but he was sure it was in the Netherlands.

Jack provided this information to Ethan and asked him to try and get information from his street contacts.

Two days before their meeting with Perry, Debra received a call from Ethan with the following comments.

I have received what I believe is good information about shipments into the Netherlands and a guess as to where they are going. I trust the person who gave me this information as being very reliable. Here is what I learned from him.

The goods are coming in from an Iranian repacking house and then sent to Germany, France, and Belgium. They are then trucked into Netherlands to the city of Nijmegen close to the German border. Where they end up is not known, but the delivery location city is a real clue.

My contact knows the devices made by Pauli are being produced here in the Netherlands, but the exact location is not known.

One other fact of interest, Pauli has a partner named Henri. Nothing else is known about him.

"Jack, I just learned some interesting information from Ethan. She then told him what Etan had provided to her.

Since the meeting was tomorrow morning, lets just present it at the meeting."

Jack agreed but was happy to know they now had some information that Interpol could investigate. A thought came to mind, and he immediately called Boris.

"Boris, this is urgent. Can you check tonight on delivery companies going to or from Nijmegen in the Netherlands. They will be receiving goods from Germany, France , and Belgium. If you can also find where they frequently go from that city to somewhere else in the Netherlands.

Debra and I will attend an important meeting tomorrow morning at Interpol headquarters and this information will be vital. Call me anytime tonight regardless of the hour if you find anything worth reporting. You can also call me tomorrow morning when we are at the meeting because this news will be welcomed. I hope you can do it tonight. All my best to your family."

"Jack, I was just watching TV and getting bored. I will work on this right after we disconnect and will give you some kind of report for your meeting. My best to Debra."

Debra overheard the call and hoped that Boris could find something of interest to further investigate. It was getting late, and they headed for the bedroom as they both felt, the case would suddenly become interesting again.

It was four am when Boris called. Jack picked up the phone and said "Good morning, Boris."

"There, Jack, here is a wake call. There is one company delivering goods to Nijmegen about twice a week coming from Germany but stopping in France to pick up more packages. This same firm is also delivering things to that city from Belgium, once or twice a week.

Now here is the good part. Within a day after receipt in Nijmegen, the same company picks up goods and delivers them to the city of Uden, about twenty to thirty kilometers from Nijmegen. The same truck is used for each trip.

They have delivered goods twelve times over the past month to the same location. Where it goes from there is unknown, but I would guess it is close by.

I say that because Uden is a small town of about 42,000 people and in a farming area. A good place to hide. An email with details is on its way to you."

"Boris, you just won another bonus."

"I already have Pauli's money." Boris was laughing as he talked.

"You may get to keep it. Go to sleep now. You have done a great job."

"You can also go back to sleep. Talk to you soon."

CHAPTER 98

Jack and Debra arrived at the headquarters just about nine am and were escorted to the conference room where Perry and Bascal were waiting for them. They greeted each other and then sat at the big table.

Perry began to speak but Jack interrupted him.

"Perry, before your opening statement, we have some important information to give to you and Bascal which may alter your statement. Debra will start and then I will continue as there is a lot to digest."

"Okay, Debra your turn."

"Two days before our meeting, I received a call from our contact in the Netherlands and here is what he told me.

The materials for Pauli's operation, are coming in from an Iranian repacking house and then sent to Germany, France, and Belgium. They are then trucked into Netherlands to the city of Nijmegen close to the German border. Where they end up is not known.

My contact knows the devices made by Pauli are being produced in the Netherlands, but again, the location is not known.

I was also told; Pauli has a partner named Henri.

Jack it is your turn."

"What was told to Debra set the stage for another of our contacts to gather information on delivery trucks servicing the city of Nijmegen. At four AM this morning, I was given the following information.

One company delivering goods to Nijmegen about twice a week coming from Germany but stopping in France to pick up more packages. This same firm is also delivering things to that city from Belgium, also once or twice a week.

Within a day after receipt in Nijmegen, the same company picks up goods and delivers them to the city of Uden, about twenty to thirty kilometers from Nijmegen. The same truck is used for each trip.

They have delivered goods twelve times over the past month to the same location. Where it goes from there is unknown, but we would guess it is close by.

Uden is a small town of about 42,000 people and in a farming area. A good place to hide. Here is a copy of the trucking company name and address and the details of each delivery. Interesting is the weight of the packages which I would guess is the typical weight of Pauli's materials."

"You two have had a busy two days. What we just heard is fantastic. Bascal will immediately put three or four agents to investigate further without letting anybody outside of Interpol know. We have tipped our actions to frequently and this one will be different.

Bascal, I want three agents to learn all they can about this delivery company with letting the company become aware of us. I want one agent to find Henri who more than likely is a resident of Netherlands, and he is Pauli's partner.

I want the agents to understand this assignment is top secret. It is not to be discussed with any other agent or person within or outside of Interpol.

We have spent a lot of resources getting to this point and I want to see a conclusion soon."

"Perry, per your instructions, the agents will only report to me, and they are not to discuss their assignment or findings with anyone except me or you."

"Jack and Debra, you have once again proven why your government trusts you to solve problems. I know it is frustrating at times, but the result is always good. Thanks for your help and I promise you daily reports."

"Let's hope the next meeting is a celebration dinner."

"It will be Interpol's treat."

Chapter 95

The day of the meeting, Bascal would meet four capable agents and would give each of them an assignment to cover all aspects of the investigation.

"This case has been difficult from day one and almost a year later and a large number of killings, we may be close to capturing the bomb maker and his partner.

It is vitally important the ever step you take is in secrecy. We have had many opportunities before, and they were lost due to our revealing who we were as an agency. Do not repeat our prior mistakes.

Do not mention names nor ask questions which raises concern to the person who must answer your question.

All of you are to work undercover and you are not to reveal who you work for or any other aspect of your job.

As I go around the table, I will give each of you a new first name. It will be the only name you use when talking about this case. You are now known as Georg, Mary, Mikel, and Petrov and you are to work as a team.

Starting today, the team responsibilities are as follows.

You must investigate Belgium Delivery Services. They are bringing packages of known danger into Nijmegen at least twice weekly from Germany, Belgium, and France. The packages are then transported to Uden and we don't know where they go from that town.

The bomb makers partner's name is Henri. Find out who he is today. It is suspected he was possibly in prison with the bomb makers nephew, Fillip. That's all clues we have currently.

Another assignment is to draw a circle ten kilometers around Uden and see if you can identify a lone farmhouse isolated from its neighbors. Driving around would raise suspicion. Study aerial views and if necessary, we can use drones or aircraft capable of photographing specific areas. I have authority to make those decisions.

Lastly, you are to arrange means of surveillance for each of the assignments I have presented. I suspect you will need special vehicles capable of video observation. I also have that authority.

Once more, I trust each of you to do everything in your power to always maintain secrecy. All of you will report to me every other day until this case is ended.

I have arranged for you to occupy a conference room on the second floor. Besides a large table, it now has four desks with computers and telephones for your use. It is off limits to everyone else.

Good luck and stay safe."

The meeting ended and the four agents left to go to their new office on the second floor. They agreed to gather at the conference table to begin planning their activities.

Mary was the first to speak. "Congratulations, we have been appointed to capture the bad guys. We all know that until now, all Interpol efforts have failed. We now get the chance to set the record straight and bring honor to the agency.

All of us have extensive experience in our careers and so let's use it to successfully end this case. I suggest we start by discussing each of the assignments and how we will approach them.

How do we find a guy named Henri who may have been in prison a long time ago and who may be friends with Fillip Curie, the nephew of the bomb maker.

Quite frankly, we can't ask local contacts without raising suspicions.

Any ideas?"

Georg raised his hand and said "Interpol has an extensive data base of illegal arms dealers in various countries and areas. I have used it before successfully to find people of interest. Typing in just the name Henri will provide a list of all persons known with first or last name plus their known specialty.

Since they are operating in this area, he could be an illegal arms dealer and could be from here or a nearby country."

Petrov also answered. " I have also used that data base and it is well organized. We don't want to go out on the street asking anybody if they know Henri. The data base is your best starting point."

Mikel raised his hand and said, "I think that is a good start, but we have a slightly different problem. I know this area well and there are a lot of isolated farmhouses within ten kilometers of Uden. I will not drive around because it will certainly start people talking about a strange car possibly casing a home.

Do any of you know what success Interpol have had with drones. It might be the safest way of exploring. We should find out."

Mary began to speak again. "It seems we have problem assignments so why don't we select one to start that requires all of us to work on and then our results might show us, what comes next.

Let's also use email to continue to talk to each other about what we learn and when problems occur. This case has not been easy the past few months and I don't see it getting better until the four of us come up with good evidence to lead towards arrests."

Investigating Belgium Delivery Services should be our number one priority. It will require extensive surveillance in at least four countries. Interpol has recent data on delivery movements in the four countries and we should study that closely to see how we can gather additional information.

They all agreed to end the meeting and do some individual thinking about the delivery company and plan on meeting tomorrow morning to formulate a plan.

CHAPTER 99

The same day Interpol was forming its plan to find the bomb maker and his partner, Pauli was busy assembling circuit boards for some of his new designs when Henri returned to the house.

"I just picked up a lot of material for you. You should be busy all week long. There is another order expected later this week and I will pick it up at the same location.

The receiving and shipping company is doing a good job and it does not appear that anyone is looking for us. Hooray let's just make more devices and much more money.

I'm hoping by the end of next year, we can both say goodbye to our business and go somewhere else to relax."

"I hope you are right Henri. This working sixty hours per week is beginning to bother me. But I also like the thought of being one year away from retirement. It eases the stress on me."

"Pauli, if you can train me to do some of the easier work, I am willing to do it. Picking up materials and shipping orders is easy, and I have time to do other stuff. Think about it and don't be bashful about asking."

"Thanks Henri, you are right. Let me think about it tonight and I will let you know tomorrow."

The next morning, as they were eating their breakfast, Pauli had a question for Henri.

"I am happy you want to help me assemble the units. Can you read drawings which show connections between assemblies? Do you know how to solder?"

"My answer to both questions, is no. But I am a quick learner and I will listen carefully if you instruct me on what is needed and how to do it."

"That's reasonable. Come into the lab with me and let's start on something easy."

"Let me show you how to read a technical drawing. For example, the piece I am pointing to is a connector and the piece it is plugged into is a circuit board. What I will train you to do is assemble a cable to that connector and then plug it into the board.

The cable to the connector must be at least twenty centimeters long. This is easy for you to do and I will train you how to do it.

Pauli taught Henri several assembly steps he could perform and reduce Pauli's workload. After three days, Henri was working by himself and Pauli had been relieved of some of his stress.

Henri continued his regular pick-up and shipping duties and everything appeared to be okay. He was positive nobody was paying any attention to their activities.

CHAPTER 100

On the second day after the agents had been selected as a team to investigate several activates of the bomb maker, they again met in the conference room to discuss the Belgium Delivery Service.

Mary spoke first, "Let's pick-up on how we ended last night. Any overnight thoughts?"

Mikel raised his hand and began to speak. "After our meeting ended last night, I stayed around for a while and did some research on the company.

They have been fined twice for failing to report items to customs which violated import laws. In both cases, the items were illegal arms being shipped from Russia to Iran.

The company has been under new ownership for about a year now and apparently continues to bypass customs because we know explosive materials are being sent to the bomb maker. They are not being inspected by customs and are not listed on any known shipping documents.

These findings are not what we are investigating but it can be added charges once we catch them supporting the bomb maker."

Georg jumped into the conversation, "Good job Mikel. We now are certain they run a crooked business. Now let's see how we can catch them."

The team debated about where and when they should begin surveillance of the delivery operation in Nijmegen and then delivery to Uden. They decided to ask Bascal to provide a schedule of shipments from the three mentioned countries and then into Uden.

They could then determine if more than one delivery van is being used from each area and how they would use surveillance at different locations without exposing themselves. They felt they could accomplish this task in two weeks. They would then move to tracing the pickup by the bomb maker in Uden and where it eventually ended up.

"Let's get the schedule and we will divide up to cover the four countries," asked Mary.

Petrov agreed to talk to Bascal today about obtaining the delivery schedules and then the team will meet again to plan whatever actions are necessary.

The team also decided that Mary would look to see if she could find Henri, Mikel would check the usage of drones and Georg would look for additional information about Belgium Delivery Services.

They would again assemble in the morning hopefully with addition data about delivery schedules. The rest of the day would be spent on the individual assignments.

The next morning Petrov presented additional information from Bascal.

"Hence forth, we will receive a daily update on the movement of goods and deliveries to Nijmegen and Uden. We will only be aware of the deliveries but not about materials contained within the delivery."

Two days from now, a van will leave Germany and enter France close to Nancy. It will pick up packages somewhere in the area of Nancy and then travel to Nijmegen. Packages will be consolidated there, to ship to Uden. The drop off point in Uden is undetermined.

Bascal suggests we concentrate our efforts on the van leaving Nijmegen for delivery in Uden. Where they get their packages in Germany or France will be handled by other agents. We are to learn the route between the two cities and where they drop off the goods in Uden.

There are four of us and here is what I suggest. The are two decent routes out of Nijmegen leading to Uden. We find two observation points and wait and see what route is being taken. Then both vehicles take the unchosen route to speed towards Uden and arrive at different observation points to learn what route the van follows in Uden. We must do this without being seen.

Along the way, we notify the other two agents of the route being taken and they will assume surveillance in other preselected spots."

Mikel spoke next and suggested they begin searching for decent surveillance spots using goggle maps. We can find restaurants and places along the routes where we will not be suspicious.

We can also find motels along the routes to spend the night. We should be able to complete our search in an hour or so and then head for our first destination."

The four selected several spots along both routes in and out of Nijmegen

And decided to take individual vehicles. Two of them would station themselves at the two routes heading for Uden and the other two would wait at Uden until notified of the route being taken by the suspected van.

They would then move into preselected surveillance spots.

They all departed early after noon and would meet in Uden for dinner. Two of them would then leave to spend the night near Nijmegen while the other two stayed in Uden.

By six am on the day Interpol expected a van to carry the illicit materials, from the terminal in Nijmegen to Uden, the agents were stationed at two points along the selected highways waiting for the identified van to pass on its way to Uden. They would then confirm the route to their agents in Uden to get into place for further surveillance.

About an hour after they had begun their surveillance, a Belgium Delivery Van passed by and the agent texted the other members that the van was on the N324 to Uden. The van should arrive in thirty to forty minutes on the north side of Uden.

The two agents who had been in the Nijmegen area quickly got onto the A50 to quickly drive to Uden and with communication with the other agents stationed near the N324, they would determine where they would be able to follow the van within Uden.

The use of multiple vehicles would ease the chance of the van driver being suspect of being followed.

One vehicle began following the van as he was still on the N324 and turned off after a mile and about a half mile further, another vehicle followed for about four streets and turned away. Another vehicle had stopped at a restaurant along the van's route and where he had a good view of the road. The van stopped about a block away at what appeared to be a warehouse and within a minute, a shiny black car stopped directly behind the van.

The driver exited the car and walked towards the van. The van driver also exited the van and walked to the rear of the van to open the doors and then gave the man a couple of boxes which the man carried to the car and then returned to the van to retrieve more boxes.

Within five minutes they left and each headed in a different direction. The car with the driver who had picked up the boxes passed right by the agent who had observed the transfer from the restaurant parking lot.

The agent had two of the other agents on his phone while the transfer took place and one of them was close enough to get behind the car as it travelled through town. He stayed behind him for another four blocks before turning on a main street and soon there was different car following the suspect.

They followed the suspect until he left Uden and got onto the A50 south and at that point, they had called Interpol for assistance for possible aircraft assistance but it was not available.

About fifth teen minutes later, the four agents meet again at a restaurant to talk about what they had observed.

Mary began, "we had good day. We learned the drop off point, we got the license number of the pickup car and a picture of the pickup driver. We also know the lab maybe somewhere off the A50, probably within ten to twenty kilometers away."

"I want to add something." Said Mikel. "There is a very good possibility that there is more than one drop off spot. I suggest we do this same exercise at least three times to ensure we are on the right track. It will be easier the next time especially if the van again uses the N324. We will know where to hide and maybe able to accomplish our goal without following the van."

Pavlov interrupted Mikel and told them the car was registered to a Netherlands citizen named Hendrik deVries alias Henri who served time with Fillip.

CHAPTER 101

With the information he had received from the agents, Bascal arranged a meeting for the following day with the four agents and Jack and Debra. Although a lot had been accomplished, a lot more had to be done, Bascal asked Jack to have his computer guy to again try to determine pick-ups and deliveries within the next few days.

Jack and Debra arose early to attend the meeting and information from Boris was waiting for them on his computer. They left their apartment and made their way to the Interpol offices for the meeting.

All attendees were on time and Bascal was the first to speak.

"Mary, Mikel, Pavlov, and Georg, you all did a great job and gathered enough significant information to move us a lot closer to catching the pair of killers. We still have a way to go, but another couple surveillance trips, should allow us to locate the house where they are building their bombs.

I have asked Jack and Debra to join our group, because they have their own contacts who have been feeding us the information, which allowed us to send you on this last trip. We will hear from them in a moment and it should set the stage for us to return to Nijmegen and Uden to learn additional information.

Lets hear from Jack now."

"Thanks, Bascal and thank you people for what you accomplished the last few days. For us who have worked on this case for months, this is the closest we have ever got to the suspects. We hope the data I am about to give you will get us another step forward.

As of this morning I received additional information on the movement of packages from Germany, France, and Belgium. It is disturbing to learn the quantity of items is growing.

There will be another assembly of the packages in Nijmegen in two days and shipment the following day to Uden and our contact states, it appears it will be dropped off and picked up by Henri at a different location. It was only identified as stop two.

I am sure we all wonder if there is also a stop three."

"Thanks Jack. The information we have received from you and Debra recently has moved this case far along the path to conclusion. We are not there yet, but each piece of information, gets us closer.

Here is our plan for the next week. You are each getting new vehicles and then returning to Uden to take up separate residences for the next few days. Jack and Debra will also drive there and will also be available for surveillance wherever you might need them.

After you learn the drop off , pick-up spot, you are to station yourselves at least three kilometers apart on A50. You are not to follow the suspect; just observe the direction he is heading. We will slowly determine the location of interest.

Thank all of you for attending and stay safe and well hidden from the delivery van and the suspect. A single misstep will cost us dearly."

Chapter 102

Henri and Pauli were working in the lab trying to keep up with orders which had increased over the past month.

"Henri, I am starting to run low on explosive materials. When will we receive more deliveries?"

""I will be doing a pick-up in two days for many items. We should not have any problems as deliveries seem to be arriving at the various countries on time and then forwarded to Nijmegen. I'll meet the driver in Uden and they will be here about thirty minutes later."

"Any problems of anybody following you or the van driver?"

"Not yet. The driver has been instructed that if he senses he is being followed, then return to the terminal and we will designate a new delivery route and drop off point. I take notice of cars following me but none seems to stay behind me for more than one or two kilometers."

"Sounds like we are pretty safe for now."

"From my experience, they would have caught me by now but I doubt if they even know I am involved with you."

"Your right. After I talked to you back in France, Vladimir called me to make a deal. I brushed him off and quickly hung up the phone and then I threw it in the trash. Nobody knows where I went or how I got here.

Even the Russians who stole my money, have no idea where I am and I don't accept any orders from them."

"That is good Pauli. We don't anyone nosing around and especially Interpol agents. We probably have another two or three months here and then we will move again for the last time. Based on our order backlog, we may have more than a million Euros in the bank by then and we could say goodbye to this business."

"Henri, I hope you are right because I am getting tired and worrying to much about being caught.

"You can stop worrying as I place close attention to every step we take. I also do not want to get caught and I dream about a nice beach in South America with a lot of good-looking women."

Pauli laughed at that comment. "All right, I will stop worrying and only think of good-looking women."

Henri also laughed and they both went back to doing their work and not worrying about Interpol watching them.

CHAPTER 103

Jack and Debra were driving to Uden in separate cars and would meet at a motel on the A50. They checked into the motel and when they had brought their luggage into the room, Jack opened his computer and using Goggle maps, selected locations for surveillance up to thirty kilometers south of the motel.

Debra felt they could place three agents plus themselves three or four kilometers apart to see how far Henri drives on the A50 before turning off.

At no time are they to follow Henri's car but simply report his car passed their position.

Jack and Debra felt by doing this, it would probably take two or more attempts to identify where he turns off the highway. Once they knew which exit, he takes off the A50, the task of finding the house would be a lot easier.

After Jack identified what he thought were safe vantage points to observe, he and Debra drove one car to carefully look at each stopping point and whether a car would be out of place at the spot if seen by the suspect.

Four of the five selected spots were deemed okay and they were able to select a fifth spot nearby the one they had eliminated.

The communicated with the four agents and agreed to meet at a fancy hotel on the northeast side of Uden or dinner and further planning.

The all got together at the restaurant and quietly discussed their approach of surveillance for tomorrow. Like in their previous attempt, they would station one agent at the N324 and on at the A326 and one of them would notify everyone about the route the van would be taking.

They would then pick surveillance points where they thought the van would enter Uden. The other agents would then try to determine where pick-up spot two was located and try to observe the exchange of packages between the van and Henri's car.

Four of them including Debra and Jack in separate cars would station themselves at the predetermined lookout points along the A50.

Exactly at seven AM, the van once again was on the N324 route and both agents speed towards Uden on the A326 to prepare surveillance spots hoping to find spot two.

About thirty minutes of entering the N324 route, the van was seen entering Uden about two blocks from the previous pick-up point. The van pulled into a large mall parking lot and stopped about three cars opposite from where an agent had parked. Using a mirror, the agent had a good view of the exchange and notified the other agents where Henri's car might enter the A50 route.

Henri and the van driver talked for about five minutes before each left the parking lot and went in different directions. The agents were well prepared to watch as Henri's car entered the A50 a couple blocks from the mall parking lot.

As in his past pick-up, he headed south and without realizing it, he would be seen passing agents every three kilometers who would photograph his passing by their lookout point. He never did pass the fourth agent and had turned off the A50 about ten kilometers from Uden.

Jack's car was closest to where Henri had exited the route. He determined there were two exits Henri could have possibly taken or it could be a ruse to see if he was being followed. Jack did not exit at either off-ramp but noted the names of the location and where they might possibly end.

He notified the other agents that they were done for the day and were to meet at Jack and Debra's motel room around noon time for lunch. He and Debra would plot their next moves.

If at first, you do not succeed, try, try again and Jack and Debra had good experience and success in trying again.

CHAPTER 104

The four agents met again in Jack and Debra's room where they had prepared a lunch of sandwiches and soft drinks. They had gathered to discuss their next move.

"Once again, you guys did a good job and we gathered more evidence. We also learned where Henri had exited the A50 but I am not entirely sure of which direction he went after exiting.

I don't believe it is where he normally exits the A50, because it is only about seven kilometers from Uden. I think he was testing to see if he was being followed.

Both those exits he could have used went to small villages and I don't think their lab is in or near a small village. If it was, people living there for years would question what goes on in the house on the outskirts of the village. They would also wonder, who owns the sleek black car seen driving through the village.

I didn't think we would obtain our goal on the second attempt but maybe on the third or fourth, we may hit the jackpot. Let's now plan our next event, which will happen in two more days.

Two days later, two agents were stationed where they could observe the route the delivery van would use to go to Uden. The first two trips they observed, the van used the N324 but this time, the A326 was selected.

The information was quickly exchanged with the other agents and they began to move to different locations and they knew the van would arrive in about thirty minutes. There were only two exits the van could use to enter Uden which made coverage easier.

Interpol would have five separate cars for surveillance and one would follow the van for two blocks and another car would be close enough to follow for a few more blocks until the van parked. Interpol would call this stop three.

The van stopped in an older part of town where there was little activity. Within minutes, the Black car driven by Henri stopped behind the van to pick-up the packages. The entire transfer took less than five minutes and the black car left and headed in the direction of the A50 route.

This time though instead of heading south where agents had positioned themselves, the black car headed north. Fortunately, one of the agents had planned for a north route and the Black car passed his lookout point about four kilometers from Uden.

It then exited the route and using a round-about, reentered the A50 and headed south. This benefitted the Interpol agents as five other cars were in position to obverse the route heading south.

Jack had taken a position some five kilometers further than where Henri had last exited the route. Jack made a good guess and after the Black car passed him, he waited thirty seconds and then headed south hoping he would see the car from about a kilometer behind it. He held this position until Debra passed him and he got off the route at the next exit.

Debra was behind three other cars and held her speed limit to maintain her position yet being able to keep an eye on the black car ahead. They rode another six kilometers and she watched as the black car exited the route. She continued until the next exit and then returned to the route heading north.

Meanwhile she had provided Jack the exit number and he also exited off the same ramp, a few minutes behind Henri. He slowed down quickly when he realized there was nothing but open land as far as he could see in front of him. He pulled over to the side of the road and decided not to travel any further for his own safety.

Henri had arrived at the house about five kilometers from where he had exited and began unloading the packages. He was sure he had not been followed and had made another easy trip to Uden.

Jack immediately notified all agents to assemble at a restaurant about five kilometers from his current position. From there, they would begin their plan to find the house occupied by Henri and Pauli.

CHAPTER 105

All six agents gathered at the restaurant Jack had selected for the meeting. They were given a large table in a smaller room after Debra had asked the waitress in Dutch if they could use the room for a short sales meeting.

Jack started the conversation. "I exited where Debra had told me Henri had left the A50. Within a minute after I exited, I realized there was nothing there except open land as far as I could see. I am sure if I had driven further, I would find the house occupied by Henri and Pauli. I would not do that alone.

Here is what I propose. I will call Bascal in a few minutes and see if we can get verification of a lonely farmhouse, not far from where I parked. I think they could do this using computerized maps or have an aerial view of the area. I doubt if the farmhouse is more than five kilometers from the exit off the A50.

Let me see if we can get verification within the next hour or so."

Jack then called Bascal and gave him the exact location off the A50 and requested they do a quick map search to determine farmhouses within a five-to-ten-kilometer distance on the exit road. As a last resort, an aerial survey would also work.

Bascal agreed and they would begin immediately. Jack told him, they would remain at the restaurant for another hour.

They ordered their lunches and slowly ate while waiting to here from Bascal. When the waitress came to their table again, Debra, speaking Dutch, asked the girl if this was a big farming area.

"Not really, there are a few farmhouses here and there but it is a lonely place."

When the girl left, one of the agents had an idea. "We rent a truck capable of hauling a small tractor and drive down the road and see if we can locate the house. We continue to drive to the first junction we encounter to exit safely. If we find more than one house, then we will have alternative plans."

"That is a good suggestion, but let's wait to we hear from Bascal."

They had been there less than one hour when Bascal called Jack.

"Jack, we hit the jackpot except there are three houses on that road before it ends at a junction leading back to the A50. So, you now must determine how you scout three houses along a road nine kilometers long. The houses are each separated by two to three kilometers and there is nothing surrounding them on either side of the road. Let me know your plans."

Jack then relayed to the other agents what Bascal had told him.

"Personally, I like the tractor plan and we can drop one agent within one kilometer of each house and they can then use binoculars to try and find the Henri's black car. Once we find it, we pick up each agent and return to Uden where we plan our assault."

Debra had paid the waitress and they each left to reassemble at Jack and Debra's motel to plan for tomorrow.

When they all were comfortable, Jack asked each person to provide a way of capturing Henri and Pauli without anyone getting harmed.

Georg answered first. "I suggest we wait until Henri leaves the house and arrest him somewhere else."

"Mikel, what do you think?"

"We can arrest Henri while he makes a pick-up of materials without endangering anyone. We should also arrest the driver of the van.at that time."

"Mary, your next."

"I believe what Mikel just said regarding Henri. Pauli is another story. Based upon his being bullied when he was young, I don't think he will give up easily. Assaulting his house is dangerous because he may blow it up.

He may also try to kill himself and some of us."

Lastly, Pavlov got to state his approach. "I believe both Mikel and Mary said.

However, Mary is correct about Pauli's being captured because I think he will not surrender and will try to kill us bullies. The tough question is, how to lure him out of the house?"

Debra entered the debate by agreeing with all four of the agents. "All your comments are relevant and we better think long and hard on how we are going to catch Pauli.

We would like to catch him alive and be able to retrieve information about his contacts, which I assume is stored on a computer in the house.

There is also the question as to how he removes the trace elements in the explosives.

There must be a way of getting him out of the house alive without a threat to any of us."

"Debra, I just thought of a way I might be able to do it. It will be tricky but it might work.

We arrest Henri and put him in Isolation for at least three days and do not allow him to contact anybody. We get all the telephone information from Henri's phone and I call Pauli with a story of Henri being arrested in Uden.

I learned this from the delivery company after one of their drivers was also arrested with Henri. I was also using that company for my arms business and the driver who usually picks up my stuff told me to be careful because Interpol has Henri and his phone.

Sometime ago, this same driver was delivering to Henri and he had been given Pauli's number to call if anything bad happened to Henri and he shared it with me today.

I think Pauli trusts me and I can call him and tell him to move immediately or he will be arrested soon. He tells me he cannot do that as he doesn't have a car.

Along comes Vladimir to the rescue. I get directions to the house and show up to help him load his stuff in my car. Then as he walks out of the house with nothing in his hands, we arrest him."

"Dangerous Jack, but it might be workable. If we go about sunset, we can have agents all around the house without being seen," was Debra's suggestion.

All four of the other agents applauded and Jack had a big smile on his face.

CHAPTER 106

After Jack had presented his plan. He called Bascal to review what he and the other agents were planning. Bascal agreed with his plan and told him he would have four more experienced agents in Uden by tomorrow morning.

Bascal told him, he had received information from Boris regarding additional shipments schedule to be delivered to Uden in two days. This would be a good time to arrest Henri and the van driver. He then told Jack , if you need anything else to make this plan a success, call me at any time.

Jack told the agents the news Bascal had given him. They still did not know the house location and it their plan was to be a success, they needed to know where the location of the house.

"We have only one day to determine the exact location of the house. Can we quickly arrange a truck and tractor combination?"

Pavlov spoke up immediately. "There is a rental agency in Uden who has large trucks and rents tractors. I can call them now and find out the availability of each item."

"Do it now for pick up by ten tomorrow morning. If the truck and tractor are available, two of you go tomorrow morning to pick them up and the other two agents will meet you and ride to your destinations. Be sure you bring binoculars and stay hidden from sight.

Debra and I will remain here practicing my call with Pauli. We will also meet with the four new agents and bring them up to date regarding our plans. Stay in touch with us if you need our support.

Remember, if we tip off ourselves to Henri, we will lose a good opportunity to catch them without a fight."

The call by Pavlov was confirmed and the truck and loaded tractor will be waiting for pick-up by ten AM.

Hearing that news, the four agents left and would meet tomorrow after the truck was rented.

The next morning the picked up the truck/tractor combination and entered the A50 for the trip to the exit and road where they would begin the search for the house occupied by Henri and Pauli.

Thirty minutes after leaving Uden, they were on a narrow road where they would determine which house was occupied by the bomb makers. They passed a small house and about a kilometer away from the house, one agent exited the truck and quickly went into the field and would then sneak closer to the house they passed and do surveillance.

Another three kilometers on the road, they spotted a second house and again drove past it about one kilometer to drop off another agent. This procedure was repeated one more time and then the truck continued and found a parking spot just beyond a junction in the road.

About seven minutes after he parked the truck, he received a call from the second agent and he had discovered the house as Henri's black car was parked in the rear of the house. All the agents were notified, the truck would pick them up within minutes.

Two of the agents were back in the truck and as they passed the house in question, Henri was on the porch watching them go by. The truck continued the road and picked up the last agent before returning to Uden.

They hoped Henri had not spotted the agent in the field near his house or when they picked him up.

The agents returned the truck and then went to Jack and Debra's motel to meet the other agents and report on their successful discovery.

CHAPTER 107

After the truck passed, Henri went back into the house and Pauli had also seen the truck and tractor and wondered why it was there.

"Henri, what why do you think that truck was on this road?"

"It's probably coming from the farm about five kilometers from here. Nothing to worry about.

Tomorrow, I have another pickup in Uden, Can I bring you anything?

"No, just bring back the materials so we can finish up the units we have partially completed."

"Pauli, before I forget, I called Vladimir this past week to talk to him about new orders and he told me, he has four or five pending. I told him we could meet in Uden tomorrow if he was available. He told me he was in France but it is a short drive to Uden and we can discuss the orders and about what may happen in the future."

"That is good Henri, because I trust that guy can do good for our business.

Okay, well today I intend to do nothing but assemble connectors to the cables and maybe get some of the soldering completed. Then, I'll be done until we get more of the materials tomorrow."

"Sorry, I meant to tell you, when you are soldering, be sure you are not using excessive solder. Too much and during shipment you may experience solder balls shorting out circuits. This could be a big problem."

"I'll do my best and pay attention."

They both went back to the lab to work on the devices and did not think anything more about the truck and tractor.

CHAPTER 108

While Henri and Pauli were working on new bombs, the agents were planning their moves for tomorrow.

The two agents that had been watching the routes taken by the delivery van would leave for Nijmegen this afternoon and would be in position to verify the route being taken by the van tomorrow.

Six additional agents would be ready to take up various positions dependent on the route being taken and where the van would enter Uden.

They were all prepared to arrest Henri and the van driver as well as confiscating all the packages which were to be picked up by Henri.

To them, it was the beginning of the end of the bomb makers career after killing many unsuspected people.

Debra and Jack would wait at the motel and work on Jacks story he would tell Pauli. After consulting with Perry and Bascal, they felt Jack should call within two hours after the arrest of Henri and push on the urgency of the situation.

They all felt, Pauli had to leave the house immediately or face arrest within hours. He is to be told, Interpol has Henri's phone and car and their being able to find Pauli quickly is very likely.

If Jack can successfully lure him out of the house, they could arrest him immediately. They have enough agents to get this done.

The next morning, all the agents received word that the van was travelling south towards Uden on the N324 and should arrive in Uden within thirty minutes. The agents stacked out their positions to know where the van would enter Uden and then the direction it would take to the pick-up point.

When the van arrived, it headed in the direction of the original drop-off point and the agents knew this area very well. The van stopped in front of the warehouse and within two minutes, Henri's car pulled in behind the van.

Suddenly agents' cars appeared from all directions and the street was blocked by their cars. Very quickly guns were pointed at Henri and the driver who seemed in shock that this was happening to them.

They were handcuffed and put into separate cars which left the scene immediately. Two tow trucks soon arrived and took the van and Henri's car to the local police station for further inspection.

The other agents left and went to Jack and Debra's motel to await the call to Pauli.

CHAPTER 109

Twenty minutes after the arrest of Henri, Jack called Pauli.

"Pauli, it's me Vladimir, I am not sure if you know, I was to meet Henri today. As I drove to the location where we were to meet, the road was blocked by police cars and I watched as two men in handcuffs were being put into police cars. One of them was Henri. I quickly turned my car around and left the area and I just stopped to call you.

You need to leave your location fast because in one hour or so, they will know where you live. Get out now."

"Vladimir, I have no car and I can't leave."

How far are you from downtown Uden?"

"Maybe ten Kilometers."

"Gather whatever you need and I will be there in about twenty minutes or less. Give me the road directions."

"Take exit 27 off the A50 south and drive about five kilometers and our house is the second one on that road."

"I'll find you, but you be out front ready to go because I will not wait much longer and I do not want to be arrested."

"I will be out by the road waiting for you. Vladimir, please hurry.

"I am headed for the A50 south now."

Jack left the motel and began a ride he had waited a long time to do. He was about to capture Pauli.

The other agents would head for the road and come from two directions once they were sure Pauli was in Jack's car.

Jack reached exit 27 within ten minutes and raced down the road to the second house. As he approached the house, he could see Pauli on the road out front of the house. He had very few possessions in his arm and Jack hoped he wasn't carrying a bomb.

He alerted the agents he was about to pick up Pauli and to move in quickly from both directions. He stopped the car in front of where Pauli stood and told him to get into the car quickly. As soon as Pauli was seated, he hit the gas pedal and they were racing on the road towards the Junction which connected to the A50.

One kilometer up the road, a police car was blocking the road and Vladimir slammed on his brakes before hitting the police car. He jumped from the car and began running into the field and was being chased by an agent.

Other agents had surrounded Vladimir's car and Pauli meekly opened the door and stepped onto the road. He was not carrying anything and the agents were happy to see he wasn't about to blow himself up.

He was arrested without incident and while he is being placed into a police vehicle, he saw Vladimir handcuffed and walking with his head down towards another police vehicle. The vehicle with Pauli inside left the area before Jack was placed into the other car.

As soon as the first car was out of sight, they took the cuffs off Jack and they all shook his hand for the good job he had done.

He got back into his car and headed back to the motel to give Debra the good news.

Chapter 110

Debra had already received news from Bascal and she was waiting outside to meet Jack as he drove into the motel parking lot.

"Well honey, you did good. Both guys are now sitting in a cell in Uden and will be transferred soon to an Interpol facility in France. Can I give you a loving hug now?"

Jack was all smiles as he exited the car and took Debra into his arms and gave her a romantic kiss.

"Wow, putting guys in jail certainly arouses your passion. We must do this more often."

"No, we shouldn't. I want to retire and have some romantic nights with you instead of chasing the bad guys."

"That sounds good to me too. Perry wants you to call him, so let's go to our room and get comfortable and you make your calls and I will relax."

Jack smiled and they went to their room for him to call Perry and their close contacts to share the good news.

"Perry, I'm safe and thanks to your help, Bascal and the many agents, we did what for a long time we felt was impossible."

"Jack, it really was a team effort and you and Debra plus your close contacts, all made the almost impossible happen. I am not sure what kind of bonuses you were thinking to give your team, but we can talk about when we meet in a few days.

We easily got into the house and there is a lot of information for us to process over the next few days. We have their computers, cell phones, information about the materials and yes, we even know how to remove tracers from explosives.

Let us do our job for the next three days and we can meet to wrap up any loose ends. You and Debra can now make plans to return to the USA anytime after Monday of next week. I am sure you both are happy to hear you are going home."

"Those are nice words Perry but we must work out the lease cancellation, return your equipment and clean out our apartment. All good things to do before we go home. Again, thanks for all the support and let us know what day will be most convenient to meet with you. See you soon."

"Okay Debra, now I will call Franz and Boris to thank for their help and you can call Anna and Ethan to give them some good news. You might tell them; we will be giving them bonuses for helping us within the next few days."

"I'm calling Franz first. Hello partner, I have some good news for you. With the help of Interpol and our team, we arrested Henri and Pauli earlier today and they now sit in jail. Thanks for your help and maybe you'll come visit us in the USA after we pay you a nice bonus."

"Thanks Jack. I am thrilled you were able to get the job done and happy that we could help you and Debra. We will visit you in the USA probably later this year. Please stay healthy and travel safely. Thanks for the call."

He then clicked on Boris's name and he answered on the second ring.

"Hi Jack. What bank do you want me to drain today as I am running low on funds and my wife wants a new car."

"You are a funny guy. I have good news for you. The bomber case is closed for us. We arrested Henri and Pauli earlier today and a lot of the good information that led to the arrests, came from you. Debra and I are thrilled it is over and we can return home.

We will remain in Paris probably for another week as we tie up some loose ends. We will be providing a bonus to the entire team in the next few days.

How much of Pauli's money do you have put away? We will use it as bonus money and if you don't mind, once we settle on the amounts for each team member, you can distribute it."

"I'll send you a text with the balance and then let me know how to slice it up and I will be happy to do so. Thanks for the good news and it's a good one to post on your resume."

'Stay safe my friend and give regards to your wife and with the bonus buy her that new car."

Boris and Jack were laughing and both knew they had taken a dangerous couple off the streets.

CHAPTER 111

Four days after the arrest of Henri and Pauli, Jack and Debra met with Perry and Bascal to summarize the final phases of the investigation.

Perry again thanked them for their support and the success of bring the case to a successful ending. He left it to Bascal to provide details of what they had learned for the computers, notes, cell phones and other items they were able to seize after the arrests.

"Jack and Debra, it has been my pleasure to meet both of you and to work with you over the past few months. It seems like it has been a long time since we started to investigate this case and much has transpired since then.

We had a few missteps along the way, but with you and your teams help, we made to the finish line. Your professionalism inspired us and we hope we did not get in your way too often.

Since the arrests and our obtaining a lot of data and equipment from the farmhouse, we have uncovered a lot of information about how the bad guys operated.

We learned about their sources of materials and how they successfully evaded customs and laws to carry out their murderous plans. We learned how to remove trace elements and how to avoid normal shipping routes and services.

In summary, we received an education on how to beat Interpol and other lawful agencies. We could write a textbook on to become a successful crook based on the information extracted from Pauli's notes and equipment.

We will summarize all this information and send it to our partners worldwide to give them a better understanding of methods used by today's bad guys.

There are a couple of things we found which will be of interest to your government. Although to our knowledge, they never shipped one of their deadly devices to America. They were in communication with more than one group and I am sure your people know of these groups. We will send a complete report to the FBI in about two weeks after we finish looking at all the information, we have gathered for this case.

Again, thank you Jack and thank you Debra. We wish you a speedy and safe trip home."

Debra spoke first, "Thank you Perry and Bascal for all of your assistance and your support to get all of us safely to the conclusion of this case."

"Debra just said everything I could say. We are glad we could be of assistance to you and we were losing for awhile but we ended up winning the game.

Perry, at one point, we spoke about a bonus for our team. The team has Pauli's funds that we found in a Russian controlled bank and if it is okay with Interpol, it would be a suitable bonus for our team members."

"Jack, we no nothing about those funds that Pauli had taken from his account. If there is enough for a bonus for your team, that is fine. Besides, we save Interpol and the FBI some money. Good luck to you all."

The meeting ended and Jack and Debra would return to their apartment to begin making arrangements and packing for their trip home.

CHAPTER 112

Debra and Jack woke early and after their first cup of coffee, the began planning for their trip home. Jack would make reservations and Debra would arrange cancelling the apartment lease.

They planned on leaving in two days and after being away for a long period, they yearned to be back in the USA and in their home.

They were in the middle of getting organized when Jeff of the FBI called to congratulate them for their fine effort. He looked forward to having a debriefing session with them after they returned and they were to call him when they were ready to meet with him.

After the call Jack and Debra sat down for a few minutes to discuss the bonuses for the team.

"Debbie, Boris has 750,000 Euros taken from Pauli's account and I think we can work out how to divide it up among the four team members. My suggestion is Franz and Anna, 100,000 Euros each. Ethan 200,000 Euros and the balance of 350,000 Euros to Boris. What do you think?"

"I know Ethan provided some key information and over the last month or so, Boris was our source of information which provided the keys for us to unlock the gate.

How about 125,000 each for Franz and Anna, 200,000 for Ethan and 300,000 for Boris?"

"It sounds fair to me and I will send a text to Boris to distribute the funds today."

Jack made travel arrangements and texted Boris the instructions for distributing the bonuses.

Debra had reached agreement with the owner of the apartment and they would vacate it in two days. After completing those arrangements, she began packing all their personnel items, clothes, and weapons.

Two days later, they were bound for Virginia and home. After all the activity and excitement of the case in Europe, it was nice to be home.

A few days after arrival, they attended a debriefing at FBI headquarters and then returned home to relax and be retired once more.

"Jack, do you ever think we will ever retire?"

"It depends whether the wizard of fiction dreams up a new story for us."